# THE
# SUSPECTS

An addictive crime thriller that will keep you guessing

# JODIE LAWRANCE

*Detective Helen Carter Book 3*

JOFFE
BOOKS

Joffe Books, London
www.joffebooks.com

First published in Great Britain in 2021

Cover art by Nebojsa Zorić

ISBN: 978-1-78931-925-5

# PROLOGUE

*1971*

Ping. A shot zipped over his head. Police Constable Loughton ducked and scrambled behind a Bedford van. His heart constricted. Another shot churned up gravel in front of him. Shit. They knew exactly where he was. The siren in the distance was getting louder — that was something. Another shot. His knees buckled and he winced as they connected with the ground. He fumbled for his pocket radio.

'Leonard? Are you all right, Leonard?' Loughton dragged himself forward, desperate for a glimpse of his partner. They'd been split up as soon as they'd climbed out of the Zephyr and shots were fired. There were at least three of them in balaclavas. Another shot, this time to the side. It was close. He was in way above his head, they both were. They shouldn't have investigated; they should have called for backup straight away.

He should have listened to Leonard, but no, he had to get the promotion. Had to impress. Now it was going to be the end of him. Another shot, metal against metal. The noise piercing his eardrums. He could see their squad car now, both doors were open, he'd have to make a run for it. He sucked in a breath. His whole body trembling. The sirens pierced through the haze. Shit, he noticed the tyres were flat and what was left of the windscreen sparkled under the light that spilled out from the warehouse.

*Bang. Bang.*

He squeezed his eyes shut; this would have to be over soon. Everyone within a five-mile radius must be hearing this racket. He bolted towards the car, keeping his arms wrapped around his head. He just made it, diving behind the front bonnet. That's when he noticed him.

Leonard was lying face down on the other side of the car, arms splayed. 'Leonard!' Loughton scuttled forward and dragged Leonard around to shelter. His shirt was a riot of red. Leonard's lips parted and it looked like he was trying to say something. Instead, only a gurgle bubbled from him.

A movement from the side caught the corner of his eye. Loughton twisted around and saw a man with broad shoulders and muscular arms clutching a sawn-off shotgun. He hadn't seen them; the man was creeping towards the van to where Loughton had been. The bastard was going to finish the job. Loughton eased Leonard to the ground and pushed himself up, crouching low to ghost behind the man. He clenched his fists and crept behind him. The frost made smoke of his breath. Just as the guy was turning Loughton lunged but took a punch to the stomach. Winded, he doubled over, but he got a grip of the balaclava and it came away in his hands. A shot tore into Loughton's thigh. He bit down hard as burning pain radiated from the wound.

Loughton fell backwards, the man raised the shotgun and fired. He closed his eyes and pictured the face of his wife. This is how it would end. She would have to identify his body. There wasn't anyone else. He opened his eyes again, looking down the twin barrel. It clicked again. Empty. Then the man swung the weapon and it connected with Loughton's temple. His world faded into darkness.

# CHAPTER 1

*1979, eight years later*

The sun had gone down. Jimmy Osbourne squinted in the darkness as he stood out on the balcony. The only light coming from the fag that trailed smoke to the sky. He took a deep drag and closed his eyes. He listened to the waves crash against the sand underneath them.

Sensing her behind him he opened his eyes and exhaled a sigh. Even in the gloom, he could see the worry on her face.

'I told you I wanted some time alone,' he grumbled and shoved past her into the living area of the top-floor apartment. He groped for the light switch, but she got to it first.

'You're safe here. You don't have to go.'

Osbourne bit the inside of his cheek. 'We've already had this conversation.' He threw himself down onto the sofa, shoving her cassette player aside. He forced a smile. 'You don't mind if I borrow that for the trip, do you?'

Her jaw tightened. She shrugged and moved towards the fireplace.

Osbourne dropped the tape player onto the table and stubbed out his cigarette. 'It's not really my style anyway.'

'As soon as you land, that copper—' She looked like she was going to spit the name. 'That Loughton will be on to you.'

'If there was some other way, I would,' Osbourne muttered. 'We need the money.'

'I saw him in Marbella a few months ago asking questions.'

'I know. There's no extradition treaty.' Osbourne shook his head. 'There's nothing he can do. He never found me anyway.'

Her ice-blue eyes bore into his. 'He won't need an extradition treaty if you land on his doorstep.' She tapped her temple. 'Think about it. You can't keep tenants in your flat in Edinburgh.'

'So?'

'He's the one been chasing them away. He's smoking you out, and you're playing into his hands.' She looked like she was blinking back tears.

'Don't worry about Loughton. I know what I'm doing, and he'll get what's coming to him.'

Her laugh was flat. 'I hope you're right.'

He clambered up from the sofa and brushed a stray strand of blonde hair away from her perfectly made-up face. 'We need that money, and I worked hard for it.'

'I know you did—'

'We also need Loughton out of our lives for good. It's the only way.'

# CHAPTER 2

Acting Detective Sergeant Helen Carter stared out the drizzle-coated front window of the Mini. The radio crackled. The sounds of Boney M died out, replaced with the chimes of the hour's news. Depressing stuff — binman strikes, fireman strikes, and apparently the army and their Green Goddesses were tackling a blaze in the city centre. She made a mental note to avoid heading through town on the way home after the shift.

One headline made her smile, that monster Reggie McKenzie being sentenced to life imprisonment for the murder of three women. It was too late for them, but Helen took comfort in the fact that they had some sort of justice. He wouldn't be able to murder again. It had been a difficult case and one that she wasn't going to forget in a hurry.

She sunk back into the driver's seat. She had planned to take a few weeks' holiday after putting him behind bars, just to get away and process everything that had happened. They had barely finished celebrating in the pub that night when the tip-off came in that suspected cop killer and career criminal Jimmy Osbourne had been spotted in Edinburgh. She had to find out why.

She slipped a sideways glance at Detective Constable Terry McKinley. In his late twenties, he wasn't much younger than her, but he was beginning to look older. The smoking and drinking that came with CID was starting to take its toll. He had his head down, reading a copy of the *Evening News*. The headline declared that smallpox had been eradicated. McKinley's blond hair flopped onto his forehead. He was assigned to the CID office as an 'aide' and Helen couldn't help noticing that he did a lot of the tasks the others in the office didn't enjoy doing, such as collating reports and fact-checking. Many of the older generation preferred to get out on the street — that's what they saw as actual police work.

'You need a haircut,' Helen remarked as she fixed her attention back out the window. He was starting to remind her a bit of Robert Redford.

'It's the fashion, it's supposed to be like this.' He folded the paper and tossed it up on the dash.

'I wouldn't know about that,' Helen scoffed.

'Have you been to Spain?' McKinley asked. 'I've always fancied going on one of those package tours.'

'What's brought that on?'

'Ach, there was a competition in the paper.'

She shook her head. She had been meant to go there on her engagement, but that felt like a lifetime ago now. A lump settled in her throat. 'My last holiday was a Pontins.'

McKinley blew out a sigh. 'Do you still want me to help you sort out your dad's things tomorrow?'

Helen cleared her throat. 'If you don't mind.'

He shook his head. 'No, it's just that we were meant to do it before and . . .'

'No, I need to do this.'

'Are you sure?'

'I want to get it over with. Once and for all.'

McKinley's smile turned to a grimace.

'I'll even make you a bacon roll.' She arched an eyebrow. 'Or two.' A wave of anxiety hit her. Going through her late dad's things was something she had put off as long as she could.

'My mum's told me she's getting married again.'

He angled his body towards her. His knee grazing against hers. 'You never mentioned it before?'

'I just found out. It all seems to be happening really fast.'

'Have you met him yet?'

Helen shook her head.

'I'm going to need a fag soon. I can't concentrate.'

'Wait up,' Helen replied.

A young lad of about fourteen with a shaved head caught her attention, it was the second time he had passed them on his Grifter in twenty minutes. He gave her a broad smile and slowed to get a look into the car as he passed. Her stomach knotted.

'I would have brought something to read if I had known we'd be sitting here this long. That paper's two days old.'

'You live and learn.' She reached over into the passenger-side cubby and retrieved her bottle of tropical juice. That was probably the closest thing she would get to being abroad. She took a glug then swallowed the last aspirin from the bottle in her pocket. The juice had gone tepid from the heat in the car. She grimaced and wiped her mouth with the back of her hand. A headache was brewing, and she wanted to stop it before it had a chance to build.

Shit. The boy rode around the corner again, and Helen stiffened in her seat. The lad hopped off his bike and confidently strode towards the car, motioning for her to wind the window down, which she did.

'What's this then?' McKinley muttered. He had his hand braced on the door handle in case he needed to make a quick exit from the car.

'Awrite, darlin'? Jimmy wanted me to ask you something.'

'And who are you?' Helen asked.

'A pal of Jimmy's.' He had one leg on the road and the other braced on the pedal: he too was ready to make a quick exit. 'Jimmy wanted me to tell you that he's flattered that you think he's important enough to follow around.'

'Is that so?'

'Aye.' He licked his lips.

Now that Helen was talking to him, he looked younger than she first thought. He had a pudgy round face dotted with freckles and a rainbow-striped ski jacket that looked like it once belonged to someone bigger. Helen made a move to wind the window up.

'Wait! Before you go.'

'You're pushing your luck, son,' McKinley scolded.

'Jimmy wants to know if you or your two other colleagues — you know, the ones parked in the Ford Granada.' He bobbed his head in their direction. 'Do you want anything from the chippie? He said it's a cold night out and you've been following him for the past two days.'

'Bugger off,' McKinley growled. 'Unless you want to spend the night down the station.'

'Sorry—' the lad sneered — 'Jimmy said you lot don't get paid very much so he wanted to help out. Charitable service and all that.' He started down the road, humming the *Z-Cars* theme tune as Helen watched him disappear in the wing mirror.

The radio chirruped. 'That will be our colleagues in the Ford Granada,' Helen muttered as she reached for the handset.

The angry voice of the detective inspector crackled into the car. They had lost sight of Jimmy Osbourne and were to head back to the station immediately.

\* \* \*

A smile twitched on Jimmy Osbourne's lips as he watched the Mini pull out into the street, followed closely by a Ford Granada revving its engine. Osbourne pulled open the window and stuck his head out, watching the cars disappear around the corner.

# CHAPTER 3

The briefing was about to start, and Helen Carter was still at her desk, rifling through her folders — her notebook was somewhere among this pile. Detective Constable McKinley waited for her in the doorway, clutching a battered-looking cardboard box in both hands. He blew out a sigh, and shuffled left to right to adjust for the weight.

'I'm coming, I'm coming,' she muttered. *Bingo.* She had left her leather book in the top drawer of her pedestal. She caught sight of the faded photograph of her brother. Her stomach lurched as she shoved it into the back of her police manual. She couldn't start thinking about him right now. It was too painful, and she couldn't afford the distraction.

Most of the officers were piled into the main briefing room. It resembled a small school theatre and went back about ten rows. It was windowless and stiflingly hot when full, but this evening's last-minute meeting would only be for those involved in the Jimmy Osbourne case. A mist of cigarette smoke hung above the officers in the room.

There was a projector and a podium at the bottom of the stage, and a table holding two Manila folders and a canister of tape. McKinley dropped his box next to the podium.

'More tapes,' he explained.

Helen settled into a seat on the third row. Close enough to the front. McKinley slotted in beside her. She noticed Inspector Craven over on the right-hand side. He looked deep in thought and had what looked like briefing notes spread out in front of him.

General chatter rippled through the room. A couple of constables in the row in front were eagerly discussing darts and what they were going to sink in the pub later.

Helen rubbed her eyes with the palm of her hands. When she looked back up, the door opened and an officer with thick brown hair was walking towards the podium. He was wearing a grey tailored jacket and an orange shirt. He looked tall and muscular, but Helen noticed the lack of movement in his left knee — from a prosthetic leg perhaps. He was handsome and reminded her of an actor from the telly, but she couldn't place who.

He stepped up onto the podium and cleared his throat. But it was only when Inspector Craven called for silence that the noise died away in an instant.

'I'm Detective Constable Ian Loughton. I've been asked to get your team up to date on everything I have on Jimmy Osbourne.' He spoke with a slight accent that Helen found hard to trace. It only seemed to come through on certain words, and he sounded bored, like he had already been through this script before.

A couple of grumbles came from the back row.

'So . . .' There was a brief pause as he flicked through his notes. 'Jimmy Osbourne returned to Glasgow Airport from the Costa Del Sol on 21 November.' He clicked to a slide showing Jimmy leaving the airport and heading into a taxi. 'From intelligence gathered we believed he was planning to rob various jewellers in the city and possibly around the rest of—'

'Why come back to Edinburgh though?' DC Randall piped up. 'I mean, between the Costa Del Sol and here, I know where I'd rather be.' He glanced around the room for agreement.

Loughton nodded then carried on. 'He's not the only gangster making his home in sunny climates, it wouldn't take much for him to get on the wrong side of someone.'

Loughton clicked to a new slide. 'But I believe this is the reason. This is McDaid's factory in 1971.' The photograph showed a black-and-white photograph of a factory and a shot-out police vehicle in the centre. 'Jimmy Osbourne, Malcolm Black and Mel Evans. Black and Evans were arrested at the scene. We believe Osbourne escaped with over seventy thousand pounds of unmarked notes and that money has been stashed away in a safe location.'

'Jimmy Osbourne was found not guilty.' Helen furrowed her brow as she spoke to Loughton.

'He was.' Loughton shrugged, giving her a hard stare. 'He had an alibi at the time of the robbery. However, he was arrested six months later for petty theft and boasted to his cellmate about his part in the robbery and the killing of PC . . .' Loughton drew breath as if to steady himself. 'PC Leonard Matthews. This cellmate was able to tell us things about that robbery that were never released to the public.'

Randall raised his hand like a petulant schoolchild. 'What details?'

Loughton looked like he was taken aback by the question. 'Well, for starters, how many times my colleague and I were shot. Now, just over three days ago, there was an attempted robbery at Rothberg's, a jewellery shop. Typically only deals in high-end stuff. The thieves tripped the alarm before they got away with anything. But two days earlier, this photograph was captured by a local photographer.' Loughton clicked the control for the slide, pulling up a picture of what looked to be Jimmy Osbourne leaving the shop with his hands in his pockets. It was grainy and taken from a distance, but Helen would bet money that it was him.

Loughton panned the room, making eye contact with Helen. 'We need to bring him in.'

An officer directly behind Helen spoke up. 'Shouldn't we keep following him? We don't know for certain that he was involved in the attempted robbery.'

Loughton shook his head. 'Now he knows that we're onto him he won't do anything — we need to bring him in.'

Helen narrowed her eyes. 'When?'

'That's something I'll be planning with DCI Murphy.' He slammed his folder shut.

'What if we have to release him again due to lack of evidence?' Randall chimed in.

'Then we try and get as much information as we can out of him before that happens. We can't let him get the money I believe he's back for.'

* * *

Having got back to her desk, it took Helen over an hour to clear through her reports. One was a house robbery and the suspect was caught selling his stolen hoard in a pub. She filed that one away. Opposite her, Randall was typing, two-fingered, on his typewriter. He blew out a frustrated sigh, but she kept her head down, not wanting to engage him in conversation. The sooner these were away, the sooner she could investigate the files on Osbourne. Radio chatter filled the silence and noise from a conversation in the corridor filtered through the partially open door. Someone talking about going fishing at the weekend. Helen's grip on her pen tightened.

Thoughts of her brother creeped in — he used to enjoy fishing with Dad on the rare weekend that he was home. Her stomach twitched. Twenty-two years and ten months since the accident and it never got any easier. The look on her mum's face, she'd never forget that. Closing the last folder, Helen clenched her jaw. Dad was never the same either, and finding out he had a ten-year-old son from another relationship that he had kept a secret from her still shook.

'It was me that got the tip-off about Osbourne,' Randall muttered, pulling Helen from her thoughts. 'Now they have that DC Loughton coming in telling us how to suck eggs.'

Before she could answer, an exhausted-looking Terry McKinley burst through the door. 'I have the files you asked for.'

'Great.' Helen motioned to an empty space on her desk. She wanted to go through everything they had on Jimmy Osbourne. She was surprised that he'd been photographed outside the jewellers — that seemed sloppy — and she wanted to speak to the photographer too.

McKinley arched an eyebrow. 'I saw DC Loughton with the chief inspector and he didn't look pleased.'

Helen frowned. They'd find out soon enough the station was worse than a high school for gossip.

* * *

Silence hung over DCI Murphy's office. Loughton shook his head and drew in a breath. He had suspected this was what the briefing had been leading up to.

Murphy gave him a concerned look. 'This is a promotion,' he eventually said. 'We need someone like you on the team.'

Loughton forced a small smile. 'I like the work I'm doing. I don't want a promotion.'

'You're wasted in Traffic.'

Maybe that was true. Loughton rolled his shoulders — the seat was considerably lower than Murphy's and it was starting to give him neck strain. He wanted to investigate Osbourne on his own time and in his own way, without interference.

'I want you to work with Sergeant Helen Carter,' Murphy carried on.

Loughton glanced at the family photographs on the desk, Murphy's raven-haired wife and daughter smiling broadly. He swallowed hard. It reminded him of what he had lost.

'I'll need to think about it.' Working with someone like Helen Carter would be difficult. He knew of her reputation and she'd no doubt get stuck into the case. He worked better alone.

'There's nothing to think about.'

'For how long?' he asked.

'As long as it takes.'

'And do I have a choice?'

Murphy shook his head.

# CHAPTER 4

That was enough. This had gone too far. Detective Inspector Jack Craven shoved the *Evening News* into the waste bin under his desk and leaned back in his chair. Someone in the department had been feeding information to the press for months. Sighing, he surveyed his office. The photographs of Edinburgh that he had been given were still sat in a cardboard box next to the radiator. He had called it an office, but really it was a glass partition within the CID room, bare apart from the scuffed teal desk and matching chairs that he'd inherited from the old DCI years ago.

A headache brewed behind his eyes and he massaged his temples with his thumbs. He was only halfway through the mounds of paperwork that had accumulated on his desk, but that was going to have to wait for another time. He needed an early night to clear his head.

Giving up, he rose from his chair as the ring of his telephone echoed. The rest of the office had already emptied, leaving him alone for the first time in a while. He looked down at the black handset. Sighing, he snatched up the receiver. 'Inspector Jack Craven.'

He heard someone take a deep breath on the other end of the line. 'Oh, thank goodness, I finally got through to you. I didn't know who else to call.' The voice was female. Shaky. Sounding breathless. Recognition dawned on his face and the hairs on the back of his neck prickled. It was his ex-wife's mother, Laurel. He hadn't seen her for at least five years, maybe more, and she'd be the last person who would want to speak to him. She'd barely said two words to him in the last decade.

'What is it?' His mind raced. She would only call if something bad had happened to the twins. He perched on the corner of his desk, feeling his heart tighten in his chest. If Milton had done something . . .

'It's probably nothing.'

'You wouldn't be calling me if it were nothing.'

'I don't want to bother you,' Laurel replied, keeping her voice low, as if that would hide the worry in it.

'You're not doing a good job of that,' he remarked. 'What is it?'

'It's Liz . . .'

He swallowed hard; his mouth was dry. He'd only recently got back on good terms with his ex-wife. He just wanted to shout down the phone for her to get to the point. 'Has something happened?'

'I don't know.'

He sighed. 'So, what are you worried about? Liz is a grown woman.'

'I haven't been able to get a hold of her for the past couple of days. It's not like her.'

'Maybe she's just been busy?'

'Have you heard from her?'

'No, but we can go weeks without speaking.'

'I'm really close to jumping on the next flight over. There's one I could get this evening . . .'

'Don't do anything rash.' He dragged his palm down his face.

'Has she spoken to you about the twins? Or about Milton?'

'No, we don't . . . I know they've split up.'

He heard her take a breath. 'I speak to her most days.'

He slipped another glance into the main office. DS Helen Carter had returned. He gestured towards his phone, and she gave a small nod in return.

'Listen Laurel, I have to go.'

'No, Jack, I need you to go there and see if she's okay. She's been really depressed lately. I'm worried.'

'Okay.' He sighed. 'I'll head there shortly, then get her to give you a phone.'

'Thank you. Are you going to go there now?'

'Aye.'

'Please be quick, I'm going out of my mind with worry.'

'Aye, I will,' Craven muttered. He looked up as his office door opened to reveal an apologetic-looking DC Randall. Randall gave a small shrug. Craven was in no doubt who sent him here.

'I need to go.' He hung up the phone and glared at Randall.

'Sorry, boss.' Randall stepped into the room. 'The DCI's on the warpath again and he's demanding to speak to you.'

Craven dropped his head to his hands. It would be better to go and speak with him, get it over with. That would give more time to deal with whatever was going on with Liz.

'Sorry, boss,' Randall muttered. 'But I had to come and tell you. You know what he's like.'

Craven knew what the DCI was like all too well.

'Did he say what it is about?'

'No —' Randall raised his eyebrows — 'only that you were to go up to his office straight away.'

Craven sighed. Whatever it was that the DCI wanted could wait.

# CHAPTER 5

Craven's mind raced. It wasn't normal for Liz not to pick up the phone, and as he got further up the path, he noticed all the lights were out in the townhouse. That was surprising for her, especially with it being overcast and gloomy. A knot formed in his stomach when he noticed the front door was ajar by a few inches. His shoulders stiffened as he pushed it open. No sign of a disturbance. No damage to the door. 'Liz?' He strained to hear anything. 'Jack? Annabel?' He peered up the stairs and could see the children's bedroom door was wide open. 'Jack? Annabel?'

Giving up, he patted the wall for the light switch. He always told her to lock the doors, that Edinburgh could be a dangerous place and he had thought she took his advice. The door was always locked when he visited, and she had taken great care to change the locks after she chucked him out. The smell of cigarette smoke grew stronger as he neared the bottom of the hallway, his boots clattering against the tiled floors. 'Liz?' He swallowed hard, then shoved the lounge door open.

Craven's heart constricted when he saw her slumped on the sofa. Lit fag almost at the tip but still burning, ash on her pink dress and the cream carpets she was so fond of.

'Liz.' He kept his voice soft, concealing all annoyance in his voice. 'Liz.' He fumbled for a pulse and released a pent-up sigh upon feeling the beat underneath his fingers. 'Where are the kids, Liz?' She looked pale, her lips a tinge of blue. 'Liz.'

Her mouth parted slightly at the sound of her name. Her eyes rolled in the back of her skull. He brushed a stray strand of blonde hair from her face and knelt, his foot connecting with an empty vodka bottle, sending it skittling under the couch, where he heard it clink with another one. 'Liz.' He took the cigarette from the limp damp hand and stubbed it out in the glass ashtray that was already stacked high with butt ends. 'Liz!' He shook her shoulders. 'You need to wake up. Bloody hell, what are you playing at, eh?'

A sigh whimpered from her. He took a breath to steady himself. 'Where are our children?' The kids must be away with friends, there was no way she would put them in danger. He laid her back down on the sofa and headed into the kitchen.

Craven held his head in his hands as he waited for the kettle to boil on the Aga. Yesterday's dishes were stacked in the sink, and the remnants of last night's dinner sat on a plate on the worktop, some kind of yellow-looking curry. He was never really into any of that, but he knew Milton loved all that foreign food. He scraped it into the bin. He noticed a half bottle of wine beside the kitchen tap and poured that down the sink too.

The window above the sink was ajar and the banana-patterned curtains billowed. He tugged the window shut. This wasn't like Liz at all, she was always so house proud.

He had been so sure that days like this were firmly in the past. Would have bet money on it. Even when their marriage ended, she had kept a lid on it. Well, she'd had Milton to support her then, didn't she? He was her rock through it all and now he was gone.

Maybe he should call an ambulance, get her checked out. No, she would go mad if he did that, and the boys at the station would likely find out. The kettle whistled, pulling him from his thoughts. Tugging open the fridge, he made a tutting sound. Empty, apart from a rotten head of broccoli. He shoved it shut then turned his attention to the cream cabinets on the walls — there must be something in them.

A few minutes later, he returned to the lounge with two mugs of extra strong coffee and a packet of custard creams, so old that he had to brush dust from it.

He thumped the mug down onto the table, spilling some onto the oak. Liz would not like that, and he wasn't using a coaster either.

He got his hands under her armpits and manoeuvred her into a sitting position. 'Right, you need to wake up now.'

'No,' she murmured.

'You're pissed.' He placed the mug in her hands. 'You need to drink this.'

'My head's splitting.'

'I'm not surprised.' He lifted the mug to her lips, and she took a loud sip then grimaced. 'There's no milk in that.'

'You don't have any milk. Where are the kids?'

'At a sleepover.' Liz frowned. 'They're not due back until tonight.'

'That's good.'

'I just got carried away.'

He caught a whiff of vomit on her breath and leaned away. 'I thought you'd put all this stuff behind you.'

'I had. This is just one little slip.'

'You could've set the house on fire.'

'How?'

'You had a lit cigarette in your hand when I found you.'

'Oh . . .'

'"Oh"? Is that it?' He sighed, then handed her the packet of biscuits. 'You need to eat something.'

She fumbled with the packet, tearing a corner off the wrapper. 'I wouldn't call this food.'

'Do you want me to run to the shops?'

She shook her head. 'I'm sure you have better things to do than my shopping.'

'I don't mind.' Craven looked around the living room and noticed that all the family pictures that included Milton were gone. The place would need a good tidy up before the kids got home. 'This is all my fault,' Craven muttered.

Her eyes flicked up at him, then away. 'No, this is Milton's fault.' She crunched down on a custard cream and spoke in between bites. 'I know you were looking out for us.'

'I could have been better about it. Instead, I rush in like a bull in a china shop, accusing him of all sorts.'

'It's too late now.' A sigh heaved from her thin body. 'We were really happy. I should have known it would all go wrong.'

Craven looked away. As much as he had disliked the pompous arsehole, he had thought Milton genuinely loved Liz. 'I think you need a break. I can look after the twins.'

'Seriously?' She arched an eyebrow. 'Do you think you could? It's hard sometimes. They keep asking lots of questions.'

'Aye, we'll be fine. Have a laugh.'

'Ha! Wait until you need to play bad cop all the time.'

'Keep drinking the coffee.' He lifted the mug to her lips.

Dark circles marked her eyes, which looked red and puffy from crying, and her blonde hair hung thinly in clumps.

'You gave me a fright. For a second I thought . . .'

'I didn't think anything could scare Inspector Jack *Craven*.' She gave a smile. 'I'm sorry though.' Her smile fell and she looked like she was about to cry. 'What are you doing here anyway?'

'Your mother called me at the station.'

'Oh, *God*!'

'She's been trying to call you.'

'I unplugged the phone.'

'Why?'

'Milton's been calling me. He wants to sort everything out and give us another chance.'

'Do you want to?'

'Not right now.'

'Do you want me to have a word with him, get him to back off?'

'No, he's not that bad. I just . . . I just can't face it.'

'If you're sure.' Craven sipped his coffee, dreading to think what would have happened if he hadn't come here. He had seen many a house fire in his career caused by a cigarette and drink.

'Right.' He clambered up from the sofa, wincing as his knees creaked. 'I'm going to get us something to eat.'

'Jack, I never would have done this if the children were here.'

He nodded his understanding.

'Don't you need to get back to work?'

'Soon, and you better phone your mother or she'll be on the first flight over.'

Liz groaned.

# CHAPTER 6

Helen lifted the wedding reminder card from the mat — it was marked with a boot print. She placed it back on the shelf. One of the delivery men must have knocked it onto the floor. Cardboard boxes had been stacked the full length of the hall and there were still more to come. She could hear the van's engine idling outside. She manoeuvred past the crates and peered out the lounge window — she counted another five more boxes still to come. It was only the one man bringing them up, the other waiting in the van. He puffed out his cheeks and was wiping sweat away from his brow with his arm. She hadn't thought this through very well.

'The door was open. I'm coming in.' Helen recognised the voice of Terry McKinley — he had offered to help her organise the boxes to see what she wanted to keep and what could be charity-shopped or dumped. It was strange to think that all her father's possessions were now sitting in the hall-way of her little tenement.

'I'm through here,' Helen called back.

McKinley appeared in the doorway, still in the process of shrugging off his jacket to reveal a paint-stained shirt rolled up at the sleeves.

'That's the last of it from my dad's cottage. The tenants move in tomorrow.'

'That was fast.' He threw his jacket onto the sofa.

'They wanted it quickly, and I didn't want to leave it sitting there lying empty.' Helen frowned. 'It was stressing me out, just having it sit there.'

'Fair enough.'

Helen forced a smile. She was grateful to him as she'd been dreading going through the boxes by herself. She picked up an empty box and handed it to him.

'What did you think of that DC Loughton from the briefing?' McKinley asked.

Helen considered this for a moment. 'I know he was badly hurt in the line of duty. I never got a chance to speak with him.'

'Neither did I.'

Helen slung a couple of books into the box. 'Is there something I should know?'

'I saw him leaving DCI Murphy's office, and he looked angry.'

'Interesting. Then again, it's easy for the DCI to get on anyone's nerves.'

'Anyway, what are you going to do with this place?' McKinley glanced around the room.

Helen shook her head.

'It's just you've been here over a year and it doesn't look like you've unpacked either. There's crates of things in every room.'

'I don't know,' Helen said with a smile. 'I might go and see if I can get one of those fancy new flats that were in the papers or one of them up the New Town.'

'Oh, aye, and with one of them nice green bathrooms and a separate shower.'

'Now you're talking.' She smiled again.

The telephone sounded from the living room. Helen exchanged a look with McKinley, and he followed her through to the lounge.

'Helen Carter?' Helen lifted up the handset and plonked herself down onto the sofa next to a box.

'It's Jack here.'

'Inspector?'

'Is McKinley there with you?'

'He is.'

'Well tell him to get back on shift. I need you both down here and back on the Osbourne job.'

* * *

'Ach, how can you eat at a time like this?' Helen shifted awkwardly in the driver's seat and threw a look at McKinley, who was now tearing open a second chocolate bar — and that was after a cheese roll and a couple of bags of crisps. For the best part of an hour, he'd been crunching, munching and slurping. She grimaced — her lower back had been niggling at her since this morning, and being stuck in the car seat wasn't helping.

'I'm still starving.' He scrunched up his crisp packet and shoved it in the side-door cubby.

'I don't know where you put it all.' She took a sideways glance at his slender waist — all she had to do was think about chocolate and she would gain five pounds. She wound her window down a crack and wafted away the cheese smell. 'You must have worms or something,' she muttered.

'I'd eat while you still can. There's no point waiting.' McKinley gave her a sly smile, then blew away a stray strand of blond hair that had flopped onto his forehead. 'It's only going to get worse.'

'Is it?' Three hours in the passenger seat of the Granada and her bum was numb. She stretched her legs into the footwell and flexed her toes. Her boot connected with an empty bottle of Cresta.

'And anyway, I didnae have my breakfast this morning.' He bit the chocolate bar. 'Didnae have lunch either, come to think about it.'

'You had a bacon roll this morning.'

'Oh, I forgot about that, right enough.'

'Still . . .' She shoved the bottle over her seat and slipped a glance at the flat — the lights were still out. 'Do you think he'll show?'

'Aye, give it time. You sure I can't tempt you?'

Helen shook her head.

'You're not still on that grapefruit diet, are you?'

'I had a grapefruit for breakfast . . . once.'

'Rather you than me.'

'Aye, I can see that.'

'Have you tried the Sleeping Beauty diet?' He grinned.

She arched an eyebrow. 'And when would I have time to do that, exactly?'

'Ach, I'm just messing.'

'Here we go.' She bobbed her head towards the flat that was now lit up like the Blackpool Illuminations. Before she could open her door, the radio crackled — DC Randall and his team in the Granada across the road. They were ready to move too. She clicked open the door. 'Come on then. It's showtime.'

McKinley clambered out of the car and shoved his hands in his pockets, breaking out into a jog to keep up with her. She pointed for DCs Bell and Randall to head around the back and they nodded their understanding, Randall grabbing a steel bin and moving it to the fence so he could climb over.

Piss and stale smoke stung her nostrils as she climbed the narrow concrete staircase to the first floor. It was so narrow McKinley had to follow in behind her.

'Where's the DCI?' McKinley whispered. 'He should be here.'

Helen shrugged, then banged on the glass panel of the flat's door. She took a step back. The door was a faded red but with various dents and boot marks and a split frame. Her muscles tensed as a figure loomed towards the glass.

It swung open and Helen stuck her boot in over the threshold so he couldn't close it again. 'Jimmy Osbourne, we need to have a little chat.'

He grunted, pulled the door wide and shouldered past Helen, forcing the air from her body. She tried to grab his shirt collar but missed. Icy pain trailed up her spine. He was nearly six foot and muscular. McKinley got hold of an arm but was easily shoved free and landed against the railing with a thud.

'Stop!' This time she managed to grab some fabric and it tore away in her hand. Jimmy grunted in frustration and shoved her again, but she managed to grab onto the railing to stop herself spilling backwards down the steps.

Jimmy gave the briefest hesitation then ran for the stairwell entranceway and straight into Randall, who levelled a punch to Jimmy's gut. Jimmy crumpled onto his knees.

As Helen scrambled back to her feet Randall looked her up and down, a sneer forming on his face. 'I stopped him for you.'

Helen paused, trying to regain her composure. She headed down the stairs towards Randall. McKinley followed, clutching his stomach. The colour had drained from his face.

'That's why I don't eat,' she said to McKinley.

McKinley groaned in understanding. If he was going to chuck up his lunch, he had better not do it in the car on the way home.

'Jimmy, you're coming to the station with us, and you're going to help us with some enquiries.'

'Am I now?'

'Get him up.'

Randall nodded and lifted Jimmy up to his feet. Jimmy narrowed his eyes and clenched his fists but soon thought better of it when he saw the expression on Randall's face.

'You're hurting my arm.' Jimmy tried to wrestle free. 'Help! Help! Police brutality. Ow, my head!'

'Nobody touched your head.'

'I think I've got a concussion.'

'Shut it,' Randall warned, 'or you really will get one.'

Helen heard the flat door on the floor above click open.

'I think they want to murder me,' Jimmy bellowed for the benefit of the stairwell.

'You shut up,' Randall seethed. Both Randall and Bell kept a tight grip of Jimmy's arm as they dragged him out of the stairwell towards the back of the van.

'You're hurting me, pig!' Jimmy was spitting. 'I haven't done anything wrong.'

'I'll give you something to whinge about if you don't get moving,' Randall snapped back.

'I think you've broken my ribs. I want a medical examination at the hospital.'

'Do you, now?' Randall sounded exasperated. 'Was that before or after you assaulted two officers?'

'I'm not saying nothing to you. I want my solicitor. I know my rights.' A smile twitched at the corner of his lips.

'That'll be sorted soon enough.'

'That was police brutality, that was. You all can't get away with that nowadays.' He flashed Helen a smile, showing a missing front tooth. 'You better get him put back in his box, darling. If you know what's good for him.'

Randall shoved him forward and he stumbled over his feet. Helen grimaced, thinking that Jimmy was going to face plant onto the concrete, but Randall managed to pull him back to his feet. She knew Randall had been a boxer and bodybuilder in his younger days and still looked like he could handle himself.

Helen waited until they had bundled him into the back of the car then headed back inside to look around his flat. Hopefully, that would give them something more to go on. The lights from their cars and the chatter and static from their radios had announced their presence to the street. Curtains around them twitched, and Helen could feel eyes on her as she headed back into the stairwell as though she was an exhibit in the local zoo.

'What a mess,' McKinley muttered, nudging the scuffed lounge door with his boot, not wanting to touch more than was necessary.

The bare floorboards groaned under their weight. Helen cast a glance around the empty room. Judging from the black marks on the floor, even the carpet had been recently torn up. Body odour and damp assailed her nostrils. The warmth from the fire hung in the air. An army-style sleeping bag had been rolled out in front of the lounge fire alongside a couple of crushed lager cans and the remnants of a fish supper in crumpled newspaper. Bay windows coated with condensation faced out onto the street and she could see most of the police presence had gone. A bedsheet was draped over the curtain pole to form a makeshift screen.

Some rooms had light bulbs dangling from the ceiling, others just exposed wiring. There were a couple of packed boxes in the hall. Helen peeled back a flap and rummaged through them: kitchen utensils, plates and old-fashioned patterned cups. It looked like they had been thrown into the box without a second thought and some of them were smashed. She knew that Jimmy had rented the flat out for the past couple of years, but the tenant had left in the few weeks before Jimmy had returned — maybe this was what they had left.

'Helen, you need to see this,' McKinley called out from the kitchen.

Helen's stomach knotted and she braced herself for what McKinley might have found. The kitchen was a doorless galley in between the bathroom and the living room, with oak-coloured units and a beige worktop. McKinley was at the far end of the room, in front of the window. He was holding something that she couldn't quite see. She sighed and approached him slowly.

'What is it?'

He turned to face her and held out a small box of Milk Tray chocolates.

Helen gave him a look. 'That's what you called me through here for?'

'Aye, there's a card with them.' He handed her the white envelope from the top of the box.

Her heart raced, as she peeled open the envelope. Inside was a small card with a sunflower on it. In barely legible writing the card was inscribed: 'For DS Carter, you seem quite fond of these, X.'

'What are you going to do about it?'

Helen frowned and slipped the card into her pocket. She took the box of chocolates and chucked them into the empty bin. 'He's just trying to get under my skin.' Helen swallowed — her throat felt dry.

'How did he know you like them?' McKinley asked.

'We had some in the car a couple of days ago. He's telling me that while we've been watching him, he's been watching me.' Helen shook her head. Her heart was still racing.

She had a quick look around the other rooms, but apart from some peeling wallpaper and rubbish, all of them were empty of furniture and personal items.

'I've got a bad feeling about this,' McKinley carried on.

'You can't think like that. He's guilty, we just need to find the evidence. He's nowhere near as smart as he likes to think he is.' Helen replied. 'He will make a mistake.'

'Why do you think he's come back to Edinburgh?'

'I think he stashed the money from his last robbery, and he's back in Edinburgh to collect it.'

'Doesn't look like it's here.' McKinley snorted. 'If I was him, I wouldn't have come back from Spain. He was in the clear there.'

'He's playing with us.'

## CHAPTER 7

The entrance to the station was teeming with life by the time Helen made her way inside. She had parked in the furthest space from the entrance to give herself a chance to clear her head, but the walk hadn't done any good. She looked up as the second set of double doors slid apart. A worried-looking woman was tearing at a nail sitting under a poster in the waiting area that read "Thieves beware". The stale smells of alcohol and smoke hung thick in the air. She manoeuvred past a group of men that she overheard were waiting for their friend, and they seemed to be getting more impatient with every second that passed. Jimmy was at the bottom of the corridor still being booked in, thrusting his finger in the face of the bored-looking desk sergeant.

'I've done nothing wrong!' he was shouting. 'You're going to regret this — you haven't got anything on me!' He was enjoying being the centre of attention and was waving his arms dramatically, much to the annoyance of DC Randall.

Helen shook her head. Judging by the fact that he was only just being booked in, he had no doubt been examined by the doctor, whereas her ribs ached with each breath and she'd just need to get on with it. Maybe grab a hot bath when her shift was over.

'Are you heading back up to CID?' Helen turned to see DC McKinley, who looked like he had jogged to catch up with her. His hair hung in clumps against his forehead and his cheeks were flushed with pink.

'Yes, I want to check a few things.'

'That didn't go too well, did it? I like the way he's the one that gets examined by a doctor and we're the ones he laid into.' He gave her a smile. 'Bloody typical, isn't it?'

'Could have been worse. I thought you were going to go flying down those stairs.'

'I nearly did. That wouldn't have improved my standing in the department, would it? He caught me in the guts too, you know.' McKinley grimaced and hunched over in an exaggerated movement.

Helen shook her head in disapproval. 'I told you not to eat all that rubbish.'

'I was nervous though, and I eat when . . .' His cheeks flushed with pink again.

They brushed past Jimmy and Randall. McKinley stopped on the staircase and stepped aside to let a uniformed officer pass. He looked like he was considering what to do next. 'I'm going to go down to the canteen,' he muttered.

'Get me a coffee, will you? I'll meet you up in the office in a bit.' Helen gestured towards the female changing room.

'Aye, no bother. I'm going to get some food too, want something?'

'Again?' She paused. 'Aye, get me something, a roll or whatever.'

McKinley nodded.

Helen noticed he was rubbing his shoulder as he headed down the corridor.

Once booked in, she would let Jimmy Osbourne stew a bit, enough for him to think about being more cooperative and give her enough time to gather her senses a bit. She slumped down in the changing room, gingerly feeling her ribs. Bruised, but the bones were still in place. After a full thirteen hours on shift, all she wanted to do was sink into a hot bath and then sleep, lots of it. Fat chance of that though.

When she got back up into the CID room, she spotted a foam cup, a cheese roll and a bar of chocolate on her desk. She sighed, exactly what she needed. The lights were on in DI Craven's office and the blinds were down. It wasn't like him. She sat down at her desk and sipped the coffee. She lifted the top off the roll — too much butter, but it would do.

'Craven's been acting strange,' McKinley said in between mouthfuls of chocolate bar. 'You think it's anything to be worried about?'

Helen glowered. 'I'm sure we'll find out soon enough.'

* * *

Craven's stomach churned as he lifted the paper. The article in question was four pages long, covering the Reggie McKenzie case. An anonymous officer had reported that officers missed opportunities to apprehend McKenzie sooner and that previous attacks were missed over a decade ago because officers didn't take reports from the victims seriously. That might have been true decades ago, but not now, not his team.

Craven grunted, pushed himself up and walked over to Helen's desk, dropping the paper onto it. Helen scowled as she glanced at the headline. He left as she shoved the paper into a drawer, slamming the CID office door behind him.

## CHAPTER 8

'I can't believe you've got one of these.' Dennis lifted the Atari console that was in front of the television then whistled. 'What I wouldn't do for one.'

'It's just *Pong*, it's not that good.'

'You're lucky. I've not even got a telly.' He made sure to put the console down exactly as it was. 'You don't even have to go to the arcade anymore with this.' Dennis swallowed. That mucky old room he called a home barely fit his bed and a ratty old chest of drawers.

'I guess,' Robbie muttered.

Dennis crossed over to the other side of the room. The house was always warm and clean, and had a fridge brimming with food — none of the cheap stuff either. 'When's your dad getting back?' His stomach rumbled — he hadn't eaten all day.

'He's not meant to finish work till after five.'

'Good.' Dennis threw himself back onto the sofa and put his feet on the table. 'Gives us plenty time to have some fun.' He slipped out a packet of fags from his pocket and placed one to his lips. 'You want one?'

Robbie dithered, but took one and placed it behind his ear.

Dennis sparked his up, took a long drag then blew out the smoke in the shape of an 'O'. 'You've got such a nice house. I don't know why you complain about it so much.'

'It's not the house that's the problem.' Robbie was doing a rubbish job of hiding the upset in his voice.

'What's the matter?' Dennis asked, even though he knew what the problem was.

'Want something to eat?' Robbie offered, wanting to change the subject.

'Aye, you got any Wagon Wheels left? And them crisps? And the drinks with the straws?'

Robbie returned a few minutes later with the snacks bundled up in his arms. He chucked them onto Dennis's lap. One of the juice cups bounced onto the carpet.

'Careful you don't spill it,' Robbie reminded him. 'My dad'll go mad.'

Dennis nodded, knowing exactly how 'mad' Robbie's father could go over any little thing these days. Homework not done on time and it would be a black eye or bruised ribs. Or if he was feeling extra generous, a couple of whips with the studded belt. Or the time he washed Robbie's mouth out with a manky old bar of soap for swearing.

All designed to make Robbie a man. Dennis shuddered as Robbie slouched down on the sofa next to him and grabbed a biscuit.

Dennis forced a smile and picked up the packet of Golden Wonder Kung Fuey and held it up for Robbie to see. 'You should learn this.' He pointed to the Bruce Lee figure. 'Then your dad wouldn't be able to hit you.'

Robbie's lip curled upwards. 'Do you really think I'll be able to get away from here?'

'Aye.' Dennis arched an eyebrow. 'Once we have enough money, we'll be able to go anywhere we want. Do anything we want. Anywhere in the world.'

'I wish.'

'I'll be coming into some money too.'

Adrenaline charged through Dennis's body as the living room door thumped open, rattling against the wall. Dennis flinched and the crisps spilled all over the carpet. Dennis swallowed hard and stood up. Robbie slunk back into the sofa.

'What the hell is he doing here?' His dad snarled at Robbie. 'I told you he was banned from this house.'

'I was just leaving.' Dennis stepped forward and William Fields moved to get in his way. He grabbed Dennis by the scruff of the neck. Dennis tried to pull himself free, but it was no good.

'You're not going anywhere—'

'Dad, please. We were only going to play with the Atari.'

A sneer played on William Fields's lips. He released his grip on Dennis then pulled the Atari from the front of the TV and threw it onto Robbie's stomach, who groaned and doubled up in pain.

'This is my house, and you live under my rules.'

'No' for long,' Robbie snapped back. Big mistake.

'Oh really? You're going nowhere, son.'

Dennis was shoved backwards, and he landed with a thud on his bum. Icy pain trailed up his spine.

'What have you been telling him, eh?'

'Nothing,' Dennis muttered.

'Filling his thick head with stupid ideas. You're nothing but a bad influence, and scum like you always get what's coming to them.' He stabbed a finger into Dennis's chest.

William Fields knelt in front of Dennis and gave him a hard stare. 'Get those crisps picked up and God forbid I ever see you in my house again.'

Dennis scrambled to pick them up and shove them in the packet. He exchanged a look with Robbie then fled the house, leaving his friend to face his father alone.

CHAPTER 9

Having stared at report after report Helen needed a break. She wanted to blink away the sight of the graphic and bloody crime scene photos. From the medical reports, she could see that Loughton was lucky to be alive. His twenty-seven-year-old partner hadn't been so fortunate. Helen had a quick skim of her in-tray, still piled high with reports that she'd need to sign off.

Giving up for now, she pushed away from her desk. She was amazed Loughton had managed to keep working for the police — if that had happened to her, she was doubtful that she would do the same. She stood up from her chair and stretched her legs, but it wasn't enough. She decided to head down to the holding cells on the ground floor of the station.

The cells were dimly lit and hidden behind two sets of double doors. She could smell the faint whiff of vomit, which was probably coming from one of the cells.

Detective Constable Randall was waiting outside in the corridor. He was sitting on an uncomfortable-looking plastic chair. He had his arms crossed and looked deep in thought.

'Everything is under control, *Sergeant*.'

Helen ignored the dig. He still hadn't got over the fact that she had been promoted over him. He was mid-forties, with more experience but with an attitude that made him difficult when he was in one of his moods.

She leaned against the cool brick wall. The lights flickered. Helen glanced up at the ceiling.

'They've been doing that a while,' Randall muttered.

'Have you been in there?' Helen asked.

Randall hesitated. 'For a bit. Arnie Bell will stay with him until the end of his shift. I just thought I'd stay here for a while.'

For some reason it was a lot cooler in this part of the station. Maybe because the corridors were wider and the floor tiled. Helen nodded. She looked around the corner to where the cells were. Through the glass panel of the double door, she could see Jimmy Osbourne sat behind cream-coloured bars with his arms by his sides. DC Bell sat on a chair in front of the cell. Bell had his head down. His shoulders looked tense. Jimmy was just staring at him unblinkingly with a manic expression on his face. He looked like he was enjoying the situation and trying to intimidate them, which was probably why Randall was sitting in the corner. She moved away, not wanting Osbourne to see her. She thought about telling Randall about the chocolates but decided against it. It was just another game that Osbourne wanted to play.

* * *

Most of the CID officers were back at their desks finishing things off before the end of their shift. Helen kept her head down after she caught sight of the angry scowl on Jack Craven's face. He stomped into his office and slammed the door. She slipped a glance towards the glass partition. The blinds were partially open. Craven threw a folder onto his desk and snatched up his telephone receiver.

'Here we go again,' Helen said to DC McKinley, who was helping her finish the last of her reports. McKinley huffed in frustration. He must have known that Helen was looking at him because he looked up and gave her a thin smile.

'Still nothing,' he muttered, shoving the folders to one side.

Helen nodded; exhaustion had started to take its toll. Her eyes drooped and she blew out a sigh. There was nothing in her pile either.

DC Randall hung up his telephone and coughed. 'That's Jimmy Osbourne's brief arrived, and he's not best pleased by the sounds of things.'

'That was quick. How does the brief know he's here?' Helen asked.

'That's an interesting question.'

'Maybe one of the neighbours called,' McKinley interjected. 'I saw the one upstairs watching everything.'

'Anyway, his brief is talking with DCI Murphy as we speak. Something about police brutality.'

'Right.' Helen dragged a hand though her hair. 'Could this night get any better?'

'Apparently not,' Randall muttered, rising to his feet.

Helen sighed. 'This means we have to charge him.' She glanced at her watch. They now had a lot less time than she'd hoped.

'Who is his brief?' Helen asked.

'Keith Steele.'

Helen rolled her eyes. Keith Steele was no better than a criminal himself and charged a pretty penny too.

# CHAPTER 10

Jimmy Osbourne was sitting at the interview table, arms crossed and a cocky smile plastered across his thick features. He sat awkwardly. Helen knew that the seat he was in had a bent leg. Randall hadn't wanted any of the suspects to get too comfy, so he had loosened the chair legs a few months back. Osbourne winked at her, and she could see Randall's shoulders tense from the corner of her eye.

'You were quick off the mark.' Helen directed this comment to Keith Steele, an overweight man in his late thirties, with slicked-back black hair and a tan that looked like it came from regular holidays abroad. He knew how to work the system and had an impressive reputation for getting his clients off charges.

'I have to be, don't I?' he snapped back, then softened his tone to ask Jimmy how he was feeling.

Helen rolled her eyes as she sat down opposite. Randall remained standing.

Jimmy sucked through his teeth. 'I don't like to make a fuss, but I'm still in a lot of pain.'

'You were examined by the duty doctor and he couldn't find anything wrong with you,' Helen replied. 'Not a mark on you, apparently.' She motioned towards the doctor's report clipped to the front of her file.

'Medicine can be subjective,' the brief interrupted. 'I'm inclined to ask for a second opinion.'

'If you feel it's necessary, but it's already very late.' Helen shrugged.

Jimmy grinned again. 'You can't keep me here.' He wagged his finger at her. 'I know you've got no evidence. I'm an innocent man.'

Helen flicked open her folder to the right page, making extra effort to take her time. She looked up and smiled. 'Where were you last Tuesday at 2 p.m.?'

'Where was I?' He tore off a piece of his nail and spat it onto the table. 'Don't know. Not sure I can think that far back.' He jabbed a finger towards Randall. 'That copper thumped me on the head, and I think it's affected my memory.'

'Why don't I jog your memory then?' Helen carried on. 'You were seen leaving Rothberg's Jewellers two days before an attempted robbery there.'

'Me?' He made a show of looking aghast. 'Well, I'm afraid it's a case of mistaken identity.'

'Really?'

'Oh aye, I'm not a thief.'

'So, you weren't at Rothberg's Jewellers then?'

He shook his head.

'There were witnesses.'

'Aye?'

'Now why would that be?' Randall asked.

'Because you were there,' Helen continued, 'and you slipped up.'

'You've got it all wrong, darling.' Jimmy Osbourne smirked. 'I just have one of those faces, lots of people look like me. I'm generic, as my old mum likes to say.'

'Generic? I'd say that you're anything but,' Helen remarked.

'Whoever it was that *thinks* they saw me must have been mistaken.'

She slid the photograph towards him. 'Are you going to deny this was you?'

He shrugged and made no move to look at the image.

'I think you'll find that if you interview that person again, they'll have realised the error of their ways.'

'A photograph is hardly compelling evidence,' Steele chided. 'I'm surprised that this is all you could come up with.'

'Should have stayed out of the country,' Randall chimed in, a sneer playing on his lips. 'Where did you bugger off to? Spain, was it?'

'Aye. Sunny, sunny Spain!'

'Why come back?' Helen asked.

'I missed my old mum, and believe it or not I missed cold, grey rain.'

'Oh, that's sweet,' Randall muttered. 'Wee mummy's boy, are you?'

'I am, as a matter of fact. She's getting old, needs looking after.'

'Why not take her off to Spain?'

'She's lived here all her life, and she's not too well these days. You'll probably not know this, but there's also an economic slump.'

'Really?'

'Aye, Spain's not what it was. Sad, really.'

Helen turned to another page in her report. 'I heard you've had an economic slump of your own. I think that's why you're back. You're hoping to pick up where you left off.'

'Is that so?'

'Seventy thousand pounds was never recovered from the factory heist, and I can imagine you're desperate to pick up your share of that.'

'That is a lot of money,' he agreed and exchanged a look with Steele.

'Can you get to the point, Constable, it's getting late and I'm sure we've all got better things to be doing,' Steele muttered.

'Sergeant,' Helen corrected him.

'Apologies, it's Acting Detective Sergeant, isn't it?' Steele smiled.

'I feel sorry for the two cops in that factory job — one died, and one was left a cripple, is that right?' Osbourne shrugged. 'But I was found innocent.'

'But we both know you're anything but.'

'It's like that TV show.' He made a clicking sound and turned to his brief. 'You know the one? What's it called?'

'*Ironside*?'

'Ah *Ironside*, that's it.'

'You're nowhere near as clever as you like to think you are,' Helen replied.

'You seem to think you know it all.' Osbourne sounded bored.

'I know you have that money stashed somewhere in Edinburgh. We're not going to let you get away with it.'

'Is that so?'

'Have you thought of writing fiction?' Steele asked Helen.

Helen pointed at the photograph between them. 'Why don't you tell us who your two friends are in this picture?' Helen prompted. 'Do yourself a favour.'

He slid the photograph away. 'Never seen them before in my life . . .'

'That photograph is incredibly grainy, that could easily be my client, or it could easily be John Wayne. I can't tell.'

'You're going to spend a long time behind bars, why not let us make a deal?'

'Aye, like I've no' heard that line before, darling.'

'Why don't we give it some time, and you can discuss it with your brief.' Helen stood up from the table and exchanged a look with Randall, who nodded.

'You're wasting your time, sweetheart,' Jimmy called after her, then sung the line, '"I ain't saying nothing."'

Randall shook his head as they left the interview room. 'I'll be surprised if he says anything, his kind never do. We don't have enough to charge him with the robbery either, it's all circumstantial. His brief will know that too.'

'Well, we need to find something then,' Helen replied. 'I also want to go and speak to his mum, see if he's telling the truth about her ailing health.'

Randall frowned. 'I wouldn't believe anything that comes out of that bastard's mouth.'

Helen slipped a glance through the glass partition in the door. She could see Jimmy Osbourne laughing with his brief. *He's far too cocky*, Helen thought. 'He'll make a mistake sooner or later.'

Randall didn't look convinced.

She dragged a hand across her forehead. 'I'm going to call it a night. I need some sleep and you look like you do too.'

* * *

Helen unlocked the door to her flat. It was on the top floor of an aging tenement to the west of the city and just a twenty-minute drive to the station. It wasn't in the best area of Edinburgh, but the flat was cheap and she hardly spent any time there apart from sleeping. She tossed her satchel behind the door so that it would be easy to find in the morning.

It had ended up being a full fourteen hours on shift. The balls of her feet throbbed and her head pounded.

Heading through to the kitchen, she glanced up at the clock — she was now due back at the station in less than six hours. Her stomach rumbled and she fancied a glass of wine. She was sure she had a bottle left somewhere, but there wasn't one in any of the cupboards, so she had to make do with a cup of cocoa and the last two digestive biscuits. Setting them down on the coffee table, she rifled through her box of records and placed a Dave Clark Five album on the turntable. She sighed and surveyed her surroundings. Most of her things were still in their original cardboard boxes from when she moved in. She supposed it was because the plan was always to live with Ted in his five-bedroom townhouse up in the New Town. She slumped down on the sofa and closed her heavy eyes. She had driven past it a few weeks ago and saw the 'For Sale' sign had been changed to 'Sold'. She wasn't surprised, it was a lovely house.

* * *

Helen awoke with a start. Her forehead slick with sweat. She rarely needed to bother with an alarm clock these days. The usual nightmare did it for her. The one where she was back in that horrible house being tortured. Maud raining down blows on her. She swallowed, she could still taste the dust and damp and feel the silky cobwebs against her skin. She would never forget her first case in CID.

On the rare occasion when she did get enough sleep to dream, then any slight noise in the tenement would wake her up — a creak from the ancient water pipes or footsteps from upstairs. It was one of the reasons for her wanting to sell the place.

It was still pitch dark outside and light from the lamppost illuminated the cheap thin curtains. She tossed and turned for a while, but it was no good — once she was up, that was it. She rubbed her groggy eyes and wandered through to the kitchen. The flat was chilly, but her body felt clammy and her head glistened with sweat. She looked down at her forearm and ran a finger over the two star-shaped scars that dented her arm. They had faded and healed well but were a constant reminder of what she had gone through.

Her mind was racing. The case . . . the crime scene photos . . . She spooned some Nescafé into a mug, then peeled her damp nightdress away from her stomach as she waited for the kettle to boil. It had been a few weeks since this last happened. She wandered through to the bathroom, her feet stinging on the cold lino. She tried to avoid looking at her reflection, but the quick glance that she did have showed the anxiety in her eyes.

She slid open the cabinet and pulled out the bottle of pills the doctor had given her when she was in hospital. The prescription had 'Take two a day' scribbled on it, but she only took them when she was desperate and they had lasted over a year.

She swallowed them with a mouthful of tap water and wondered what it was that was driving her to reach for them now. Pills downed, she headed back to bed.

## CHAPTER 11

Craven had been one of the first in this morning, which surprised him as Helen was usually in before him with her head down, sifting through the mounds of paperwork that would accumulate on her desk from the nightshift. He hadn't liked her coming into the department — a female psychology graduate and the daughter of a retired DCI — but ultimately it was out of his hands. He had fought hard to remove her from the department when he had been told she was coming in as Robert Keaton's temporary replacement.

He drummed his fingers on his desk and thought about getting himself his third cup of coffee, but he had to try again. He wouldn't be able to relax until he did. He dialled Liz's number for the third time that morning and it rang out again. He dialled it straight back. Same again. He looked down at his watch — maybe she had unplugged the phone again and was sleeping off a hangover. He just needed to give her some time.

Craven dragged the palm of his hand down his face. If she had been drinking again this morning, he couldn't blame her. Despite what she said, he couldn't help feeling responsible. He was the one who had questioned her husband, taken him away and accused him of murder. A part of him had wanted Nairn to be guilty. He had weaselled his way into his family and taken his place and he had let that blind him. Pushing back from his desk, he slipped a glance at the office. Helen Carter was entering the CID suite. He caught her eye and looked away — the last thing he needed was her trying to get involved. He looked down at the telephone.

Giving up, he grabbed his jacket from the stand and headed out the office. He needed some air.

* * *

Helen was in the process of taking off her jacket as Jack Craven stomped out without so much as a 'Good morning'. She was tempted to go and ask him if there was anything that she could do to help, but it was far too early in the morning to have her head bitten off. She turned her attention to the files that had been stacked up on her desk overnight. A list of nursing homes in the Edinburgh area rested on top. Jimmy had refused to disclose what nursing home his mother lived in, if she even did. Helen struggled to believe anything that came out his mouth.

She looked up at the clock above Craven's office. It had just gone past six thirty, giving her a quarter of an hour until shift handover. She glanced around the room. DC Bell's desk had a full mug of milky coffee on it and a half-eaten banana. Cigarette smoke lingered in the air — she could tell he hadn't been out the room long. He would have had a long night, watching Jimmy Osbourne in the cells.

One of the sheets in her in-tray caught her attention. Loughton, the officer who had headed the briefing, would be working on secondment to CID. She picked up the sheet. That would be why he had left DCI Murphy's office in such a huff then. It hadn't come as the biggest surprise to her. They were down on numbers in CID.

She slipped a glance at the unclaimed desk next to hers. It had been used for storage for the past six months and was piled high with boxes and a couple of broken typewriters.

It was going to take a while to go through all that lot, and no doubt it was one of the things she'd be expected to take care of.

* * *

When Craven pulled up the handbrake in front of Liz's house the car engine sounded like a roar in the early-morning silence. He noticed the net curtains move in the neighbour's house — she was a nosey old bat. He couldn't remember her name. He took care to not slam the Granada's door and headed up the path. Two glass bottles of milk had been left on the doormat. All the lights were out. He rattled the letter-box and stepped back not expecting any answer.

'Jack.'

He turned to see the next-door neighbour standing at the gate. Her hair was in rollers and it looked like she had just draped her big grey jacket over her Victorian-looking nightdress.

'She's not here,' the old woman carried on. 'She had a wee bag with her.'

'When was this?'

'Over an hour ago.'

* * *

Helen slammed the phone down in frustration. Jimmy Osbourne was right. One of the witnesses who had come forward to identify him was now claiming that it wasn't Jimmy he had seen outside of Rothberg's Jewellers and now all of them were refusing to come in for the identity parade this afternoon. Two were complaining that they had been coerced into saying they had seen Jimmy by the police in attendance.

She clambered up from her chair and began clearing the desk. Hopefully when Loughton started with the department, he would be able to add more to the investigation. She blew out a sigh as she lifted one of the heavy typewriters onto the floor. She could only imagine how hard it must be to see the man that left you with life-changing injuries get away with murder and more.

The telephone rang, pulling her from her thoughts.

'Helen Carter.' She wiped sweat from her brow with her arm.

The staff sergeant sighed. 'Jimmy Osbourne's not feeling well.'

'He's just chancing it.'

'Aye, well, he's saying he's got chest pains, and he's not looking good. I'm going to get the doctor to examine him again. The last thing we need is for him to die in the cells.'

'No, you're right. Keep me up to date.'

'Of course.'

Helen hung up and looked up at the clock. This was no doubt just another ruse to waste more of their time.

Helen had a lot to do, but first she was going to speak to one of the witnesses. She lifted up the folder. Hilda, fifty-five, who had worked in Rothberg's Jewellers since the age of eighteen.

* * *

Hilda Avron gave Helen a wary look as she approached the counter of the small boutique jewellers. Helen retrieved her warrant card and placed it down on the glass counter above rows of expensive-looking engagement rings.

Hilda shook her head. Her face looked tight with worry. 'I have nothing to say to you.' Her hair hung around her shoulders in loose curls, freshly died in an auburn shade. She looked closer to forty than fifty-five.

'No, I'm sorry. I can't help you.' She peered past Helen, obviously worried who might be looking. 'Now, if you don't mind, I have a lot of work to do. I would like you to leave.'

'Hilda, you positively identified this man as one of the robbers.' Helen opened her folder and showed Hilda the black-and-white photo of Jimmy Osbourne.

'No, I did . . .' She let out a shaky sigh. 'What I mean was . . . I was in shock. I didn't know what I'd seen, and I still don't.'

'You don't need to be afraid, we can keep you safe.'

'All I know is that this wasn't the man I saw.'

'Hilda . . .'

Hilda let out a small sigh and shook her head. 'I can't help you. You say you can keep me safe, but I read the papers.' She nodded towards the photograph. 'And I know what he's capable of.'

Helen turned back to the woman, who now looked to be on the verge of tears. 'If you have a change of heart, you know where to find me.'

\* \* \*

'It took me a while, but I managed to get through to the nursing home where Jimmy's mother lives,' McKinley explained as Helen entered the CID room. He gave her a thin smile when he noticed her expression.

'How did it go?' McKinley asked. 'Or shouldn't I ask?'

She shook her head and flung the folder with Osbourne's photo onto her desk. 'All the witnesses are terrified. They're not going to be any help.' She couldn't blame them, really. Would she do the right thing in the same situation? She couldn't honestly say.

She sat down at her desk. 'What did the nursing home say?'

'She has advanced-stage dementia and has taken a turn for the worse these past few months.'

'How old is she?'

'Eighty-five.'

Helen gave a small shrug. A good age. 'Did they happen to say if Jimmy visited her at all?'

'Yes, he's a very caring son, apparently. Been in most visiting times since he came back from Spain.'

Helen frowned. That didn't sound like Jimmy at all.

'Are you still on for the pub later?' McKinley asked.

Helen pursed her lips as she took the paper with the name of the nursing home from him. 'I'll see how I feel.' She took a long breath as she shoved that paper on top of the others.

'What's next?'

'Where's Craven?' Helen asked.

'He left about an hour ago.'

Helen opened the next file on her desk — prison transcripts from Osbourne's cell mate implicating him in the robbery in 1971. She skim-read. There was no obvious benefit that the cell mate was getting from reporting on Osbourne. He was due to be released anyway, and Helen's gut instinct was to believe what she was reading.

'I forgot.'

'What?' Helen asked, leaning back in her chair.

'Your mum left a message for you. She wants to go over some ideas for the wedding.'

Helen groaned. She'd work up to that later.

## CHAPTER 12

'You'll never guess who I heard was going out with Sally,' McKinley muttered. He took a swig of lager.

Sally was McKinley's on-again, off-again girlfriend, a fledgling actress who never seemed to make up her mind what she wanted — whether it was Terry or a glamourous life in London.

'Who?'

'Neal Atkinson.'

'Who?'

McKinley made a face. 'Tall guy works in Traffic. Always in a mood.'

Helen shook her head.

'Drives that cherry Jaguar.'

'Ginger hair?'

McKinley nodded.

'Did he not just get married recently?' Helen asked.

'Aye, a couple of months ago.'

'Is she not coming back to work at the station?'

'She isn't.' McKinley raised his brows, looking surprised at the question. 'I forgot you knew about that.'

Helen forced a smile. 'I never forget anything, me. Is there no chance you'll work things out?'

'I can't see it.' He dragged on his cigarette, the smoke escaping his mouth as he sighed. 'I know you're not her biggest fan anyway.'

'It's not that.' Helen made a face. 'And I think it's the other way around. She had the problem with me . . . and my lack of style.' Helen tugged at her olive-green polo neck as an example.

McKinley shrugged. 'She's got a part in a play.'

Helen sipped her wine. It tasted a bit sweeter now. 'Really?'

'She's offered me tickets for it too.'

'I used to enjoy a bit of amateur dramatics.'

He shook his head. 'It's not really my cup of tea. It's Shakespeare or something.'

Laughter erupted from around the bar counter — Jack Craven plying them with his charm, no doubt.

'What about Ted?'

'Nothing to tell.' She held up her own barely touched glass of red. 'Cheers.' The pub was rammed with most of the officers from the station. The drink was a bit bitter for her liking, but she would suffer through the glass.

Terry McKinley leaned in over the noise of the packed bar, the alcohol on his hot breath tickling her cheeks. 'You'll just get drunk then tell me anyway.' The air was thick with tobacco smoke and stale lager. His aftershave wafted towards her. His brown shirt was crumpled around the collar and stubble peppered his chin.

'I don't get drunk.' She shuffled to make space between them.

'The night is still young.' He drained the last of his pint and slumped back in his seat. His cheeks looked flushed with pink. His blue eyes looked glassy.

'Young?' Helen chuckled. 'It'll be last orders soon.'

'Will it?' McKinley fumbled with his shirt sleeve to see his watch.

'There's a giant clock above the fireplace.'

'So there is.'

'I've got an early start tomorrow.' Helen looked down at her glass struggling to think of something to say. These end-of-month drinks were always an awkward occasion but a rite of passage at the station.

'Ach, you can't.' He slid his glass to the side.

'You look like you've had enough already. Maybe you should think about getting home too.'

'I just don't tolerate alcohol.' He wiped away some foam from his top lip with the back of his hand. 'I've only had a couple.'

'Why drink it then?'

He glanced around the dilapidated post-war boozer. 'Have you tried sitting in here without a drink in your hand?'

It was a cheap little back-end place encased on both sides by the ruins of derelict buildings — the slum clearance that never quite finished.

Helen shifted in her seat. 'You've not had a good day then?'

'I never have a good day.' A worried crease furrowed his brow.

'That's not true.'

He raised his eyebrows. 'Our new DCI hates me more than our inspector does.'

He motioned towards Inspector Jack Craven, who was leaning against the bar chatting to a bottle blonde in a tight pink dress.

'Jack's just bad-tempered full stop. You might have to just take it on the chin. You remember what it was like when I joined?'

'I know you had it bad.'

'It gets better. It wasn't that long ago, I had them taking bets on how long I would last.'

'I can't seem to do anything right.' McKinley paused for a moment. 'It's getting worse.'

'Don't let it get to you, that's how you make mistakes.' Helen struggled to think of anything useful to say. She had been through it before, and a lot of the time still was. If it wasn't DC Randall leaving out his dirty mags for her to get an eyeful, it would be other officers blanking her or 'forgetting' to give her vital information regarding a case.

He made a face and retrieved a packet of Marlboro from his pocket, which he placed on a scuffed beer-barrel table, then patted the pockets of his Sherpa ski jacket. 'Have you got a lighter?'

'Sorry.'

'Ach, found one.' He draped his jacket over the back of his chair then fumbled with his packet of fags.

'Talk of the devil.' She slipped a glance at DC Randall — he had a gut that spilled out over his suit trousers and thick, brown hair that had started to grey around the ears. He was used to being top in the pecking order —until her arrival, that is. DC Bell, his trusty sidekick, was standing next to him at the dartboard, both nursing pints. Randall looked away as soon as they made eye contact.

McKinley gave her an earnest look. 'Now, I've told you what's bothering me. It's your turn.'

Helen's eyes narrowed. 'Nothing's bothering me . . .'

'Aye right,' he scoffed. 'Tell your face that.'

'I've just got a lot on my mind.'

'Like what?' he asked.

She exchanged a glance across the room with DI Craven, who was placing drinks onto a silver tray.

'Where to start? There's having zero evidence on Jimmy Osbourne, then there's my mum's wedding.' She sniggered.

'How are you feeling about that?'

'I don't want to let her down.' Helen peeled up a beer mat and tore at the corners.

'You'll never let her down,' McKinley replied, and giving her his usual smile, he nudged her shoulder with his elbow.

She considered this. 'I hope not . . . I know she wants me to bring someone to the wedding.'

He ground his cigarette into the ashtray. 'I could go with you.'

McKinley must have sensed her unease because he tried to change the subject. 'We have Constable Loughton starting in CID tomorrow.'

'I know, that was another thing I had to sort.' Helen frowned.

McKinley scrunched his nose. 'DCI Murphy's prodigy.'

'Who told you that?'

'It's just what's been going around the office.'

Helen was always the last to know any of the gossip.

McKinley rubbed his nose. 'Last thing I need is another DCI Murphy copycat.'

'What do you mean?'

'Murphy called me an idiot this morning, in front of the entire office. I say called — screamed, more like.'

'What for?'

His face darkened. 'I was late with some report he wanted. I thought he was going to punch me, he was that angry. It's humiliating.' His pint glass hit the table with a thud. 'It took all my will power to not lamp him one.'

*Aye right*, Helen wanted to say. Instead, she raised her eyebrows. 'I've been on the receiving end of that. I wouldn't worry about it.'

'I know, but it's different. You always seem to take it on the chin.'

'What else can I do?' She stared at him, genuinely searching for an answer. 'It gets to me too. I know that nothing I do will ever be good enough, but I just try to ignore it and do the best that I can.'

Helen didn't know what else to say. In the past few weeks Murphy seemed to be becoming more of a controlling presence within the department and a micro-manager.

McKinley sniffed. 'Our charming DC Randall isn't too happy about the new addition to the team.'

'That doesn't really surprise me.' Randall didn't like anyone that might get in the way of a promotion. She had been there six months, and he could barely bring himself to be civil with her. Although, she did pip him to the post for the sergeant's job, and him now having to report to a woman didn't help matters either. She remembered him thinking it was a joke when she got the post. 'Randall's never really happy about anything.'

A smile twisted his lips. 'Sally's got me thinking though.'

'I knew she would.'

'Not like that. I mean just chasing what you want in life. Going places.'

'What do you mean?' Helen asked.

'I've just always wanted to travel and do stuff and maybe I should. I'm young and there's nothing stopping me.'

'You mean leave the police?'

McKinley gave a slight nod. 'Aye, before I get tied down with a family and that.'

'That's a big change.'

'I'm twenty-seven and I don't feel like I've lived, you know?'

She nodded. His dad had left when Terry was still a boy, and she knew he had felt the need to support the family from a young age. That was why he joined the police at eighteen. Now his younger siblings were adults he was in a better position to do what he wanted.

'You can take holidays though.'

'Aye, but I'd like to just pack a bag and go on a one-way flight.'

Helen's stomach clenched. She'd be gutted to lose her only friend in her department.

'And it's not like there's anything keeping me here, either.'

'What about your family? Your friends?'

'I never see them now, not with the shifts I have here at the station.'

This wasn't the first time he had mentioned leaving. He was different to most in the office, and that was maybe why she wouldn't want him to go.

'I do appreciate what you did for me. Keeping me company, making sure that I wasn't alone.'

A smile fluttered on his lips. 'Spending time with you was hardly a chore.'

'I did appreciate it.' Helen shrugged. 'Promise me something?'

'Depends what it is.'

'Just don't make any rash decisions. I wouldn't want you to leave for you to just regret it.' His indecisiveness was what annoyed her most.

'Well, you're the only one.'

'That's not true.'

\* \* \*

Terry McKinley dragged hard on his cigarette, sensing her disapproval. Helen seemed taken aback by his mention of wanting to leave the police force. She was looking down at her half-empty glass, frowning. It was not the first time he had told her he was thinking about leaving, but maybe this was the first time she thought he was serious. She looked up still frowning, her lips pursed. She was the opposite of Sally in nearly every way but just as beautiful. She wore a light dusting of makeup and kept her haircut neat around the nape of her neck. A few stray strands of brown hair hung against her forehead and she blew them away. *Plain Jane*, that's how Sally had often referred to her. He and Helen had become close in the few months after she was hurt and recovering. Eating meals together, he had started to enjoy cooking for her and even just watching the telly. Then she had come back to work and distanced herself. He drained the last dregs of his glass then pushed back from the table. 'You want another one?'

She shook her head. 'Jack's getting this one in. If he can drag himself away from the bar.'

He twisted to see where she was looking. Their inspector was in his late-forties, slick-back hair and chiselled features. Tall, dark and handsome, Sally used to say. He was still chatting up that lassie at the bar.

'He's going to be there all night.' He sighed, stubbing out his cigarette into the overfull tin ashtray.

'You know what he's like.'

'I should have finished with Sally a long time ago.'

Helen's shoulders gave a slight lift. She seemed unsure what to say.

'We were meant to get married, you know, as soon as I got moved into Traffic. That was four years ago.'

'Why didn't you?'

'She was too busy trying to further her career. We had the venue booked and everything. She cancelled the lot. I'm a slow learner.' He rubbed his eyes.

'You can't change the past, Terry, only learn from it.' Helen rose to her feet just as Jack Craven slid the tray onto the table, making her nearly drop her wine glass.

'Right, that's me away,' Helen muttered. 'I'll see you bright and early first thing tomorrow.'

'Ach, I dinnae want to think about tomorrow,' Craven remarked as he took a sip of whisky. 'And you haven't even finished your drink yet.'

'I'm not thirsty,' Helen replied, grabbing her jacket. 'Good night.'

\* \* \*

Outside the pub Helen breathed a sigh of relief and turned her collar up to protect herself from the bitter evening wind. She stopped at the edge of the pavement as a bus sloshed past. The shelter was just ahead, and the bus hissed to a stop. It went her way, but she fancied the walk. She didn't know why she agreed to these nights at the pub. She never enjoyed them. She supposed it was a way to try and fit in. She pushed her hands deep in her pockets for warmth. That was never going to happen, and it was about time that she stopped trying.

## CHAPTER 13

It was 7.24 a.m. when the first sounds of banging leaked through her bedroom window. Two minutes later the sounds of the lorries backing up on the street forced her from her bed. She gasped as she tiptoed across the icy lino and whipped her curtains back. Her feet nipped. She peered out the window. The tenement block opposite had been worked on for the past week after being gutted by fire — it looked like this morning they were stripping back the gaping hole in the roof.

She pulled on her dressing gown and headed through to the kitchen, the sounds of their hammering thankfully less audible through there, as the noise was doing nothing for the headache that had started to brew between her eyes. Coffee would fix that, she thought, as she lifted the jar of instant from the cupboard, shovelled a couple of teaspoons' worth into a mug and flicked on the kettle.

Ted had given her a Teasmade for her birthday, but it still sat unopened in a box on the shelf. She never could be bothered with all the fancy gadgets he was so reliant on. A pang of guilt twitched her stomach. She should have given it back to him. Her eyes fell to the bottom drawer — his camera was in there too among all the matches, candles and wooden spoons. It wasn't likely that he would take them back anyway. He hadn't taken his engagement ring back lightly, but it was the right thing to do for both of them. It took her too long to realise that he was never going to accept her career. She nabbed a digestive from the half-empty packet next to the stove then flicked on the radio, leaving it on a crackly classical tune. Better than listening to a load of the depressing news bulletins that seemed to dominate lately.

A few minutes later, she cradled a hot cup of coffee in her hands at her cramped kitchen table, barely big enough for two battered-looking oak-stained chairs. The whole kitchen needed a refurb. Scratch that, the whole flat needed it, with its mould-speckled wooden panelling in most rooms and threadbare pink carpets throughout. White curtains hung against the kitchen window and billowed from the morning wind despite the window being firmly shut. She supposed the good thing about not sharing a flat anymore was that the carpet in the bathroom was no longer damp and squishy every morning after Ted had his shower. She glanced at the condensation trailing down a kitchen window that was probably fitted before the war.

She took a glug of coffee and winced as it burned the back of her throat. All her dad's stuff had been piled up in the second bedroom. She still had most of that to go through, and there were probably things that she could use to improve the place. The groaning water pipes above her head pulled her from her thoughts.

She stood up and stretched her arms above her head and tilted her head back, releasing her aching shoulder muscles. That old spring mattress would be another thing to go. Now, as she had another couple of hours before she needed to be on shift, she may as well make the most of it.

She groaned — the phone started ringing as soon as she stepped into the shower. She thought about ignoring it, just closing her eyes and letting the hot water warm her icy body, but they'd just carry on until she answered. She turned and angled her head so that her face caught most of the spray, that would have to do. She reached out from the shower curtain and patted along the rail until she felt her towel. 'I'll be there in a minute,' she muttered, wrapping the towel around herself.

She snatched up the phone. 'Helen Carter.'

'It's Dispatch here. A body has been found at the Quicky Save supermarket on Granton Road. Gunshot wound.'

Helen had never been in it but she knew where it was. 'I'm on my way.'

* * *

Detective Sergeant Helen Carter parked up at the crime scene. Her chest felt tight as she drew in a deep breath to steady herself. She caught sight of DC Randall, who was helping to cordon off the crime scene. His face looked red from the bitter wind and he was wearing a thin-looking tweed jacket that appeared too tight to button. She pulled the keys from the ignition and slipped them into her pocket. Her satchel was on the passenger seat and she shoved it under the chair, not wanting to take it into a crime scene. Randall gave her a small nod when he noticed her. He held up the cordon enough for her to duck under as she approached.

'He's down at the bottom of the close.'

Helen spoke to the first officer on the scene, PC Daryl Reid. He spoke in a low voice. 'An anonymous report came in about an hour ago. We were asked to investigate.'

'Right.'

'DI Craven is on his way.'

Helen nodded.

As soon as she stepped past the cordon she spotted the victim at the bottom of the alley. There was no sign of a jacket on him or in the immediate vicinity. After another icy November night in Edinburgh, he wouldn't have lasted long without one, never mind the crimson stain that blotted his abdomen. A sigh heaved from her body — what a waste. She stepped forward, bracing herself for the smell of the rotting bin bags that were piled high around them. Thanks to the binmen strikes most of the city was like this, but at least the cold was keeping the worst of the smell at bay.

Forensics photographers were busy snapping photographs and uniformed officers were cordoning off the scene. A poor officer she didn't recognise had the disgusting job of ransacking through the contents of the decomposing bags for any sign of the murder weapon or items that might have belonged to the victim.

'Have you found anything?' she asked the officer.

'So far, we've found nothing out of the ordinary in the bins.' He spoke with a thick Glaswegian accent and held his hands out away from his body. 'No sign of a murder weapon or anything apart fae rubbish.' He wiped his nose with his arm. His boots were covered in bin juice and what looked to be mud. His unruly mop of hair fluttered in his eyes and across his forehead. He scowled and tried to tame it with his arm. 'As you can see, there's still a lot to go through.'

Helen nodded her understanding and walked towards the victim. The reporting officer was standing next to the body, his head down, busy writing in his notebook. 'Right, so what do we have here then?' she muttered, rubbing her hands together. Male. Youngish — maybe teens, early twenties at most. He had thick chestnut hair that lay flat against his face, wet from the earlier rain. She moved around the body, feeling the eyes of the reporting officer on her. She pulled on a pair of disposable gloves.

The victim's nails were neatly filed. She lifted his clammy, blue hand. It didn't look like there was any useful debris under the fingernails. She placed his hand back at his side. He had lost a lot of blood and it pooled in a chocolate-coloured puddle under his torso.

'Is the pathologist on his way?' she asked.

'Aye, he's due any minute.'

She turned her attention back to the victim. His eyes were screwed shut and his face looked twisted in pain. He had a faded silver scar that cut through his right eyebrow — from a knuckle duster, perhaps. She shook her head. Who had he pissed off to be left to die dumped among the overflowing bin bags and piles of rotting rubbish behind the Quicky Save?

Helen glanced up and down the alleyway. A shiver trailed the length of her spine. This far down the close was fairly secluded from the street and would offer a good amount of privacy from passers-by. She knelt beside his head and frowned. The man lay star-fished on the damp concrete, his blue lips slightly parted, defensive wounds on his hands from where he likely tried to fight off his attacker. The smell of piss stung, intermixed with the metallic odour of blood and garbage, stung her nostrils.

'Do we have a name for this man?' Helen enquired.

The officer shook his head.

'Any identification on him at all?' Helen shivered as a fat blob of rain landed on the top of her head.

'Nothing,' the PC muttered.

Helen noticed the left wrist had two small nicks that looked like they were from the catch of a watch. Robbery gone wrong, perhaps.

Squeaks erupted from the mountain of bin bags behind her and she looked around as a fat black rat popped up from a bag. Helen grimaced and bit down on her lip, fighting every instinct in her body that told her to get up and run. Rats had become an ongoing problem in Edinburgh — the heatwave last summer hadn't helped matters either. She shuddered and forced herself to focus on what was important. The victim's lower abdomen was swollen and stained red. There was a hole in his shirt that looked charred around the edges, and open flesh peeked out from underneath.

'Whoever did this probably left with the weapon,' the officer, Daryl something, said as he walked towards her.

'We need to be sure of that though.'

'Fantastic,' the officer muttered. 'I was just about to finish my shift as well.'

Helen gave a half-smile. *Not anymore.*

'Who found the body?'

'The shop manager. I took a statement from them already.'

'I'd like to speak with them.'

'Of course.' The officer smirked.

Helen sighed. Raindrops pelted her head and cheeks.

A groan rumbled from the corpse. She looked down at him and his lip quivered. *Fuck's sake.* She moved her face inches from his and felt him draw a breath. She pressed on his neck for a pulse and felt a faint beat.

'He's not dead.'

'What?'

'He's not dead! Call an ambulance. Now! Call a fucking ambulance.'

'You're joking.'

Helen fixed her gaze on him. 'Do I look like a comedian? Call an ambulance.'

'But I checked him.'

'Well, I'm telling you he's not dead.'

'Are you sure?'

'I know how to check a fucking pulse, or do you want to come and double check that too?'

The officer stared back at her open-mouthed, then fumbled for his radio.

Helen slipped off her jacket and placed it over the wound to try and stop further blood loss and to protect the man from the rain. She tilted his head back. His airway looked clear, and she held her ear against his mouth and listened to him suck in another raspy breath.

*Come on. Come on.* She placed her hands firmly on the wound, warm blood squelched and bubbled around her fingers. This did not look good. She screwed her eyes shut and kept on the pressure.

'Ambulance is on its way,' the officer mumbled meekly.

'Let's hope they're quick,' Helen replied.

'I don't understand. I felt for a pulse. It was the first thing I did.'

Helen pressed down hard on the wound with more force, hoping it would clot. She didn't look up. 'We can talk about it later.'

He knelt beside her peering over her shoulder. She guessed it would be at least another ten minutes' wait for an ambulance. The Royal Infirmary was on Lauriston Place, the other side of the city. A sigh escaped her — hopefully, it wouldn't take too long with the morning rush and school drop-offs. She wasn't going to hold her breath. 'How long has he been here, since you found him?'

The officer thought about this. 'About twenty minutes. No —' he glanced at his watch — 'it's probably about half an hour now.' He stomped on the spot to get some warmth back into his body.

Icy rain battered Helen's face and her cheeks prickled from the frost. Her arms ached from the force she was placing on the man, but she didn't dare move them. 'Keep breathing.' *Come on. Come on.* The onslaught of rain thickened with what felt like every minute, and her white blouse stuck to her shoulders and back. Relief lightened her chest when she heard a siren in the distance gradually gain volume. She kept pressure on the wound until the ambulance arrived what felt like hours later.

Detective Constable Randall appeared over Helen's shoulder, with his hands stuffed in his pockets and looking bored.

'Where have you been?' Helen asked.

'Just having a look further down the alley. There's some blood.' He bobbed his head. 'I think he might have been shot over there, then staggered and fell here.'

'There's no trail marks,' Helen responded.

'Rain must've washed them away. DC Bell is on his way too — he's our ballistics expert.'

'I'm covered in blood, so I'll go to the hospital with the victim.'

'I'll manage the door-to-door enquires. There's a few shops and houses nearby,' Randall replied.

'Can you interview the shop manager and see what she says?'

\* \* \*

Helen struggled to get her breath back as she watched two ambulance technicians stretcher the victim into the vehicle. She picked up her leather jacket from the ground. It was scuffed and wet with blood, and her shirt and hands were the same. At least she had purchased it in the sales, as there was no saving it now. She peeled off her gloves as she stepped into the back of the ambulance. It groaned under her weight and she grabbed onto the handrail for support. One of the technicians manoeuvred the victim into place then draped a blanket over him. The victim groaned again. He'd lost a lot of blood and would have pneumonia from the Edinburgh cold. He probably wouldn't make the trip to the Royal Infirmary.

Helen slumped down in the hard plastic seat, grateful for the warmth. The engine purred to life and the siren wailed. The ambulance shot forward. 'Bloody hell.' Not only did Helen nearly slip from her seat, so did the victim on the gurney.

'Your driver's not taking any prisoners, is he?'

'Never does,' the technician replied. 'He used to be a racing car driver.'

'Handy,' Helen muttered, as the force of a bump pushed her backwards. She squeezed her eyes shut, the smell bringing her back to the last time she was in an ambulance. She was the patient then, with a concussion, broken ribs and a fractured arm. Could have been worse though — at least, that's what she kept telling herself. They jolted over a bump and the pain that shot through her abdomen told her that her ribs still hadn't fully healed, and Osbourne giving her a dig in them hadn't helped. She allowed herself a half-smile when they pulled up at the hospital and he was still breathing.

The technician was looking at her with a smile on the corner of his lips. 'We all made it in one piece. I tell you, if

I'm ever in an accident, that's the man I want driving me to hospital.' The doors opened, blasting her with icy air. Another clunk and the technician pushed the stretcher down the ramp.

She watched them rush the stretcher through the double doors of the Accident and Emergency department. Helen shakily sighed and walked into the waiting room, feeling the eyes of the people sitting on the chairs on her, a look of disgust forming on the thin features of an old woman.

*You don't need to worry*, Helen wanted to say, *it's not mine.* Instead, she thought better of it and followed the signs for the toilet down the corridor.

'What a mess,' she murmured as she looked at herself in the mirror above the sink. Blood stained her forehead and shirt sleeves and stomach. She turned on the tap and washed her hands in soap until the water ran from pink to clear, enjoying the warmth from the water. She unbuttoned her cuffs and rolled up her sleeves. That looked better. She splashed water over her face and the back of her neck. She wanted a shower badly, but this would have to do. She looked up at her reflection again and dragged a damp hand through her brown hair to flatten it down. She'd had her hair styled into a wedge when she first started in CID, a style that she had kept since. Purple bags pooled under her eyes. Her morning coat of concealer was now long gone, leaving only a thin smudge of mascara. She sighed, rubbing it away with her thumb. Her mother always did say, 'Don't scrimp on the makeup.'

She managed to blot away most of the bloodstains with some tissue and soap, leaving patches of green behind on her crisp white blouse. That wouldn't come out either, no doubt, but it would do for now.

Back in the corridor, she felt in her pockets for change for the vending machine. The lights were out in this part of the building, the only illumination now coming from what leaked through the double doors at the end. She took a few steps and shoogled her jacket, pulling out an empty wrapper and a spare button. Her stomach grumbled — she'd kill for a bar of chocolate and a cup of coffee. *Damn*. Nothing. She had left her bag in the car. She caught movement behind her from the corner of her eye and her heart constricted. Before she could turn around a hand grabbed her shoulder.

She whipped around and came face to face with Detective Inspector Jack Craven.

'You gave me a heart attack.'

'Bloody hell!' He smirked as he looked her up and down. 'You look a right state.'

'Don't, it's been a hell of a morning.'

'Aye, I know. I just missed you in the ambulance. Then saw you go into the toilets.'

He slipped off his tweed jacket. 'I can see right through that top of yours. Even in this light, you cannae go out like that.'

'Thanks.' She gave a smile. 'I think I was a bit liberal with the water in there.' She took the jacket from him, it felt heavy across her shoulders, but she was grateful for the warmth.

Craven was wearing a crumpled mustard shirt with a brown tie that had been pulled loose, and his brown hair looked ruffled from the wind. He brushed past her, and the musky aroma of his Old Spice lingered.

'Please say you have money for the vending machine. My bag is in the car.'

'Aye.' He retrieved some coins from his cords. 'Will this do?'

'You're a life saver.' Helen smiled at Craven.

* * *

DC Randall stared at the puddle of blood on the ground as he puffed on his fag. The lamppost light above him clicked off. He blew out a long cloud of smoke and stubbed his cigarette against the wall. He walked around to the car park at the front of the shop. It was maybe big enough for ten cars.

A pale-blue Austin Morris was parked in the furthest space from the shop.

'Who does that belong to?' Randall asked one of the uniformed officers who was checking a bin by the entrance. The officer shook his head in response.

Randall gritted his teeth. 'You didn't think to check? For all we know this might belong to the attacker or the bloody victim.'

'Sorry, sir.' He scratched his wispy ginger chin with his forearm. 'Been too busy going through all this.'

Idiot. Randall stepped forward and let out a slow sigh. Bad enough reporting to that woman, but nowadays they'll hire constables that can't even tie their own bloody shoelaces. 'Well bloody find out.'

'Aye, sir.'

'And get a shave and a haircut,' Randall spat. 'You look like a bloody hippy.'

\* \* \*

Helen leaned against the wall as she gulped from the foam cup. It tasted more like tepid, soil-flavoured water than coffee, but after the last horrible few hours, it went well with a Curly Wurly. She chewed on the chocolate as she followed Craven out to the foyer. He lit a cigarette and took a look drag, exhaling the smoke slowly. Helen breathed in some of the smoke. It felt soothing, steadying her nerves.

'Hopefully, the doctors will give us an update soon. I don't want to spend the day hanging about these corridors.'

'Hopefully.' He took another long drag on his cigarette and looked her up and down. 'Uniform are still out combing the area for a weapon and doing the door-to-doors.'

'Any idea who he is yet?'

'Still none the wiser.'

'I can't believe I didn't notice he was alive sooner.' She took another glug of coffee and this time it didn't taste that bad. The metallic smell of blood still hung on her and her blouse felt sticky against her skin. She grimaced — as soon as she got back to the station she would dive into a long, hot shower and throw these clothes in the bin.

'You can't blame yourself.'

'I don't, I just—'

'Everyone there thought he was dead. He must have a lot of fight in him.'

She shook her head. 'He'd been there for a long time and he's lost a lot of blood.'

'He's lucky,' Craven muttered.

'He's probably not going to make it.' Helen shook her head. 'How is that lucky?'

Craven looked like he was thinking about what to say, then eventually replied, 'Well, he's in the best place, no matter what happens. I don't think a few minutes would make much of a difference either way.'

'Probably not.'

'Dinnae worry about it then.' He flicked the cigarette onto the ground then put it out with his boot. 'We'll have someone in to help us with the investigation later today anyway.'

'I heard about that. I tried to sort his desk out.'

'He'll make all the difference — according to the DCI anyway.'

'You don't feel the same way?'

'He wouldn't be my first choice.'

'I wasn't your first choice either.'

He gave her a look. 'Aye, that's true. I didn't see you lasting either.'

'This guy might surprise you.'

'Officers.' A middle-aged man in a medical overall stood behind them. 'We have the patient stable and heading into surgery now, but he's lost a lot of blood.'

'Do you think he'll make it?' Craven asked.

The doctor shrugged his shoulders. 'We need to take it one step at a time at this stage, but he's very lucky to be alive now.'

Helen nodded and instinctively looked at the blood on her own clothes. Even if he did survive, he'd be left with lasting damage, surely.

'Can you tell us anything more about his injuries?'

The doctor nodded. 'Gunshot wounds can be tricky. He was shot in the sternum and it ricocheted. From X-rays, we can see the bullet ended up in his abdomen. He's being looked after just now and we're doing everything that we can.'

'What about the size of the entrance wound — do you know how big it is?' Helen knew from her own experience that the wound would vary in size depending on how close the muzzle was to the body.

'I can't say for certain.'

'Were there any burns on the skin?'

'Sadly, I can't tell you much.'

'What can you tell us?' Craven chimed in.

'The wound is a small neat hole and the bullet is intact.'

'That's very helpful, thank you.'

'Keep us updated,' Craven added.

'Of course.' The doctor dragged a hand through his thinning hair and offered a weary smile as Helen handed him her business card.

'Were there any other injuries on him?'

'A few minor cuts and bruises, consistent with collapsing. What I can tell you from the entry wound is that your victim was facing whoever shot him.'

'That's really useful,' Craven replied.

'When do you think it will be worth us coming back?' Helen asked.

'In the afternoon. I doubt I'll have much before then, and we might not be able to remove the bullet.'

They waited until the doctor had left before speaking again. Helen placed her coffee on the window ledge. 'Maybe our victim was being chased, and that's how he ended up in the alley.'

'It looks likely, it's not a professional hit and it must have been loud enough that someone would have heard something.'

'Let's hope so.'

'We'll find more back at the crime scene, I reckon.'

Helen drew a breath. 'Someone out there will know who our victim is. We just need to find them.'

\* \* \*

Stepping into the shower, Helen screwed her eyes shut and turned the knob of the shower all the way round to hot, which was more lukewarm, but it didn't really matter. The jet of water felt good on her skin and shoulders. She tilted her face upwards and doused her face in water.

Her bloody clothes had been stuffed in a carrier bag ready for the bin. She lifted her arms, washing away the last traces of the victim. She tried to push from her mind the images of his face and the rasps of his breath as he had tried to grasp onto life. That was the thing she struggled with the most — living with the horrible things she had to see. She had hoped it would get easier over time, that she would be able to compartmentalise, but so far that hadn't been the case.

She turned around. It was going to be a long day. Once she was cleaned, she'd catch up with Uniform, who were out combing the crime scene for any evidence, and look through the files of missing persons and criminals to see if they could get an ID that way. The water that ran down the plughole was clear, but she could still smell the blood — taste it, even — but after a while it intermixed with the smell of cleaning fluid and mildew. The water finally ran hot now.

Steam frosted the glass enclosure around her and her thoughts turned to the earlier conversation with Terry McKinley. She traced a line in the steam with her finger. She hoped he wasn't serious about wanting to leave the police, but on days like this she could understand. The heavy door to the locker room creaked open, pulling her from her thoughts. Voices filled the space, laughter and chatter about the end of the shift and weekend plans and dates with boyfriends. That was the worst thing about this place. You could never be truly alone for five minutes. At least they sounded like they were going to be quick.

She waited to be alone again before reaching for her towel and venturing out of the alcove. She caught sight of herself in the full-length mirror. Her hair had clumped to her cheeks in straggles, and her body and face were pink. She glanced away, feeling more aware of her thicker thighs. Not being able to go out for her nightly jog had started to take its toll.

* * *

The CID room was buzzing with life. DC Bell was fumbling about in one of the filing cabinets, while Randall made a go at typing up one of his statements. Cooper was on the telephone to someone and was hastily scribbling down a note. Helen spotted Terry McKinley in the DI's office, and it looked like he was explaining something to Craven. He came out of the office looking downtrodden.

The station was only a couple of years old but had lost much of the new-building feeling already. Some of the carpet tiles had been stained from the coffee and the white paint-work coloured from tobacco. She was the only one on the team who did not regularly partake, but the rest of them seemed to chain-smoke.

McKinley was flicking through some folders at his desk. He didn't look up. His blond hair looked recently trimmed by a few inches. The top two buttons of his shirt were undone, and she could see sweat pooled under his armpits. It was his job to sort out statements and retrieve folders which often meant a jog down four flights of stairs and carting up heavy folders every time one of the more senior officers needed something. He would often joke that at least it kept him fit.

She sat down at her desk and began to leaf through the missing persons reports that DC McKinley had left for her. This would have a record of everyone who had been reported missing — she wanted to see if there was anyone matching the victim. It was unlikely but always worth a try.

'Didn't see you come in,' McKinley explained as he shifted in his seat.

Helen looked up from the files. She had only leafed through a couple of the cards but so far no one fitted their victim's description.

'I didn't want to disturb you, you looked busy.' She smiled.

'Aye.' He rubbed the day-old stubble that peppered his chin. 'The jewellery robberies — we have a possible ID on a vehicle. And it was muggins here that had to empty that desk and find a chair that wasn't broken.'

'I made a start, I just didn't get far,' she replied.

McKinley nodded towards the desk. 'Wonder what he's going to be like?'

Helen gave a small shrug.

'I've also gone through the list of known criminals.' He went back to his desk and retrieved a few cards. 'Could these be your victim?'

Helen studied the photographs. 'No, these aren't our man.'

'I'll keep searching,' McKinley commented.

'Thanks.' She looked back down at the files and flicked to the next page. 'I'm expecting the crime scene photographs.'

McKinley nodded.

'We're looking for a handgun?' Helen dragged her hand through her hair. 'So, check house burglaries — see if any guns have been reported stolen.'

'I'm on it already and I'm going through firearms certificates too.'

* * *

*Nothing.* Helen skimmed through the last of the cards. It had been over two hours since she started going through them. Her eyes stung from tiredness and a headache had started to collect behind them. She rotated her shoulders until they made a satisfying crunch. The back of her chair had snapped a few months back, so she couldn't lean back into it for support and most of the time she sat slouched at her desk.

It was now nearly lunch time and she wanted to get back to the crime scene and speak to the locals. She looked up at the clock then headed over to the tea tray for a caffeine hit. She stole a glance at the desk. Craven wasn't happy about their new recruit. He hadn't been pleased when she started with the department either. On her first day he'd had a poll running on how long she would last, with a tin on his desk for the officers to place their bets. She had already lasted a lot longer than the week they had given her. The department saw a high turnover of staff. Drinking problems were rife, and when it got too much it wasn't uncommon for them to be bumped back down to Uniform. It had happened to her predecessor and was the only reason she'd been given the opportunity in CID, even if she didn't like to admit it.

# CHAPTER 14

What the hell was he doing here anyway? Having lost his appetite Loughton sat at the bar, nursing the dregs of a pint in a sticky glass with an untouched packet of ready salted in front of him. Evidently, this was a waste of time. It was unusually quiet — probably the day before payday had something to do with it. A few regulars played darts behind him, lamenting as usual about their wives. One of them explained that 'she' had started an Open University course and was now spending less time cooking and cleaning. She was even wanting to get a job. Loughton glanced discreetly at the overweight man in faded decorator's overalls. The man merely shrugged and threw another dart.

Loughton sipped his warm pint, then wiped his mouth with the back of his hand, savouring the thick smell of old fag smoke that lingered in the air. A chalkboard in front of him boasted that the bar did food (prawn cocktail or egg mayonnaise starters), but he kept getting the odd waft from the piss-soaked toilets every time the bathroom door was opened, and with that he wasn't going to sample the menu anytime soon. Sliding his glass away, Ian made a move to stand up. He'd get a carry-out from a chippy on the way home. His thigh was aching from perching on the bar stool.

'Sorry I'm late.' A female voice spoke behind him. Her sweet perfume trailed up his nostrils.

He turned and smiled. 'I was about to give up on you.'

'Well, I'm glad you didn't.' She slipped onto a stool next to him, her thigh brushing his. She twirled a strand of her long blonde hair. 'Are you not going to get me a drink then? I'm gasping.'

'Aye, sorry.' Ian waved at the barman, who was busy wiping some glasses.

'Gin,' she asserted. 'It's been a long day.'

The barman gave a half-smile and poured the drink. Ian waited until they were left alone to speak again.

'You're better-looking than your photograph, Paula.'

'Thanks, I guess,' she muttered.

'Well, I don't mean anything by it.'

'It's fine.' She smiled while smoothing out a crease in her yellow-and-green dress. She had on the same knee-high leather boots that she had worn in her photograph. She turned her head and looked around at the rest of the bar. Although she was good looking, he noticed a line of smudged foundation across her jaw and her eyes were caked with blue eyeshadow and mascara. On closer inspection, her jaw area had a purple tinge which was hard to notice at first under the hazy light.

She must've noticed him looking at it because she covered it with her hand and her cheeks tinged with pink.

'Sorry,' he said.

'It's fine.'

'What happened?'

'I'm just clumsy. I can't really remember. I don't want to talk about it.'

The redness that warmed her cheeks had now started to trail down her neck.

'Sorry,' he repeated more loudly.

She glugged her gin. 'It was probably too many of these. We can go somewhere else if you want. After I've finished this.'

'Aye.' *Nice.* Inevitably, his gaze fell to her shapely thigh. *Very nice indeed.* 'So, you've had a busy day?' *Smooth, Ian.*

'Yes, really want to let my hair down tonight. I've never been on a blind date before, but Tina said you were a good man.'

'That's right.' He loosened his tie. What did Tina know? He would occasionally go for a drink with her husband, but that was it.

'That must be interesting being in the police.'

'Not really. Pays the bills.'

'Have you got a uniform?'

He shook his head. 'I'm a detective. We dinnae wear uniforms.'

'Pity.' She traced the rim of her glass with her finger. Her ice-blue eyes fixed on his.

'Once I've warmed up a bit, we can go someplace better.' She smiled. 'It's bloody freezing out there, and this place is a bit—'

'Aye.' Loughton rubbed his mouth with the back of his hand. 'I don't know the area that well. I don't really go out.'

'Really?'

'It's a long story. You don't sound so local yourself,' he countered.

'I don't know. I've been about.' She leaned forward and pursed her lips. 'Tell me more about being a police officer. I bet you know a lot of shady characters.'

'It's no' really that interesting.'

It had started to drizzle as they left the pub and the Forth sea wind whipped through his cheap, thin shirt. He buttoned his tweed jacket and shoved his hands in his pockets.

She slipped her arm around his and rested her head against his shoulder. 'I'm freezing.' She grimaced. 'Have you ever been to France? They do these cheap flights now.'

'Are you asking me on holiday?'

'That came out wrong,' she teased. 'But play your cards right.'

'My flat's just around the corner,' he replied, retrieving his keys from his pocket. Home was on the top floor of a purpose-built, council tower block, the middle of an identical block of three in the Sighthill area of Edinburgh. He'd moved in a few months ago, fancying the change from Glasgow. The building was around five years old but it was already starting to look dated, and the facade was showing signs of wear and tear. The rusted car propped up on blocks next to the entrance didn't help either. He could see her looking at it as they walked past.

Hopefully the graffiti-stained lift was still working — climbing ten flights of stairs might be a bit of a passion killer. The sound of her boots clacking off the tiles brought him back to the present. He smiled as he pressed the button and the door puttered then shakily opened. He placed his hand on the small of her back and guided her forward. The smell of coconut shampoo from her hair filled the small lift.

Unlocking the front door, he flicked on the light and slipped off his jacket.

'Nice place you have,' she commented, doing the same.

'Aye, it's new. I'm not sure about living in a tower block though.'

'Really?'

'It gets a bit draughty and rattly when it's windy.'

'You'll have some nice views though.' She brushed passed him and her hand lingered on his. 'I'm going to go check them out.'

He motioned to the mahogany-coloured door at the end of the hall. 'Living room and kitchen are through there.'

He could smell the rain on his shirt, so he made a left into the bathroom and spritzed some Old Spice onto his neck and splashed his face with cold water. His jaw line stung from his earlier shave and — *Damn*, he thought, analysing himself in the mirror — it had started to mottle. He rubbed it with the palm of his hand and sighed. Music filtered through but it was too quiet to make out the tune. It felt strange to have company in the flat. He had got used to being alone.

Paula was sitting on the sofa, crossed-legged with a glass of red in her hand. She motioned to another glass on the table. A David Soul record spun on the turntable and she had the TV guide on her lap.

'Where did you get the wine from?' he asked.

'From my handbag.' She smiled. 'I really like your flat. You'll need to give me a full tour.'

'With pleasure.' He picked up a glass and downed the contents, trying not to grimace at the putrid aftertaste.

She must've noticed because a smile curled her glossy lip. 'It's just a cheap bottle of plonk. You get used to it.' She decanted the last of the bottle into his glass.

Ian sunk back into the sofa next to her and took another sip. This time it didn't taste that bad. She traced his neck with her finger. His head swirled.

'I'm not really sure about those though.' She pointed a perfectly manicured finger at the photographs on the wall. 'Didn't take you for the religious type.'

'I'm not. I mean . . . I was.' He could feel the blood rushing to his cheeks as he looked up at the Jesus mosaic and a small oil painting of the Last Supper. 'They're more family . . .'

'Heirlooms?' she offered.

'I suppose.'

'You are a strange one.'

They looked at each other. Why did he think this was a good idea? She had to be at least ten years younger than him. What would someone like her see in him? *Bloody idiot.* He gulped the rest of his glass and closed his eyes. 'They were my wife's. Alice.'

He noticed her arch an eyebrow. Why the hell did he have to drag Alice into this? His head began to swirl and he swallowed hard. A beautiful, young woman wouldn't want to hear him feeling sorry for himself.

'It must have been horrible her falling down the stairs like that.'

'How do you know about that?'

'You told me.'

'I don't remember telling you. It was a long time ago.' The front of his skull pounded. He should've eaten something earlier. 'I dinnae want to talk about it. Let's not ruin the evening.'

'Sorry, it's none of my business.'

'It's not that.'

'More wine?'

'Nah.' He drained his glass. 'I'm more of a lager man,' he countered. 'I've got a few tins in the fridge, you want one?'

She shook her head and held up her full glass. 'I wouldn't want to get drunk now, would I?'

Ian headed into the kitchen, rubbing his eyes. They were getting blurry. *Bloody typical*, he thought. He grabbed some paracetamol from the worktop and cracked open a can of lager. He reached out for the biscuit tin, crashed forward, and his ribs collided with the counter. He tried to grip onto it for support but slipped and hit the laminate as the tin followed him with a thud. The can in his hand leaked and soaked his side and back with cold lager. Pain shot through his spine and chest as he struggled to get a good breath in his body. His heart pounded in his ears.

'You all right there? You need to get another drink down you.' She smiled, reaching for the paracetamol in his hand.

She opened the bottle and dropped two tablets in his hand. 'Here.'

'What are you, a nurse?' He smirked.

'Something like that.'

He downed them with the rest of his lager. The room moved around him — he could normally hold his drink, but she was drinking him under the table.

He staggered through to the lounge and slumped on the sofa. He felt her next to him.

'Maybe we should just call it a night. I've to be in the station early in the morning.'

'Must be interesting being a copper, I bet you've made loads of enemies along the way.'

He laughed. 'That's what it's like, darling.' His eyes were heavy, he fought to keep them open, but gave in and let sleep take his body. He sensed her moving around but he was too far gone to care.

## CHAPTER 15

The next morning Helen awoke with a start. She must have fallen asleep in front of the telly again; this was starting to become a bad habit. She stretched her arms behind her head until her shoulders gave a satisfying click. Morning light beamed through the gaps in the curtains, illuminating a stream of dust. She clambered her way to her feet, stifling a yawn. The sound of a car backfiring filled the silence, or at least that's what it sounded like. She crossed to the window and pulled open the drapes. The road was now empty. She peered at the building work across the road. It looked mostly complete with new roof and tiles. Hopefully the past few weeks were the last of the noise. Condensation mottled the window; she ran a finger through it. If she wasn't going to leave here, these rotting old frames would need to be replaced.

Despite sleeping on the sofa, she felt surprisingly well rested, and for the first time in a while there was no dull ache in her ribs. She could get used to that. Snowy static illuminated the television. She clicked off the set and did another test stretch — still all good. Her stomach growled as she headed through to the kitchen to put the last slice of bread under the grill.

Half an hour later, leaving the flat, she lifted the collar of her jacket to try and keep the bitter wind at bay. Dark clouds loomed above, threatening rain. She made a quick jog to the car, hoping to avoid the imminent downpour. Brilliant. The engine purred into life as a gust of rain blasted the windscreen. She flicked on the radio and headed towards the station.

\* \* \*

As Helen approached the CID office, she noticed the door was ajar and the lights were off. This didn't look right. She had her hand braced to push the door wide, but she caught the orange glow of a cigarette end from the corner of her eye. The smoke hung heavy in the corridor. Whoever was inside muttered something under their breath that she couldn't quite catch, then the sound of metal on metal filled the silence. Helen looked down the mahogany-panelled corridor. No one else around yet, she could head downstairs. *No.* She shuffled forward, parting the battered door just enough to get a better view but not enough for the hinges to creak and announce her presence.

A male with big, broad shoulders hunched over one of the metal filing cabinets. She had expected to be alone this early in the morning. The hairs on the back of her neck prickled as she watched the dark figure leaf through one of the filing cabinets next to the partition to Jack Craven's office. Ongoing cases. Helen's mind raced. How would he have got past the front desk? And up the three flights of stairs without someone noticing him. *Impossible.*

But then Robert Keaton hadn't been at the front desk when she had come through — he would normally keep an eye on everyone who came in. Her shoulders stiffened and pushed the door open wide.

'Can I help you?' Helen asked, feeling her heart pounding — it was probably loud enough for him to hear.

He carried on skimming. 'Don't think so, love.'

Helen crossed the threshold into the room.

He motioned to Craven's coffee mug on the top of the cabinet. 'I already sorted myself out.'

She scanned her surroundings, nothing else looked out of place and the mound of reports on her desk looked untouched.

'I take it the empty one's mine?'

She blew out a breath, hearing the twang in his accent. Glaswegian almost, intermixed with a slight twang of southern American drawl. He had done well to hide it.

'The desk,' he murmured, shoving the filing cabinet closed. 'That's mine, aye?'

'And you are our new detective, DC Loughton.'

'Guilty as charged.'

He turned to face her — he was wearing an expensive, fitted, tweed jacket and a terracotta tie. He was in his mid-thirties, tall — her neck hurt looking up at him. He had to be at least six foot two, maybe more, with thick black hair that looked neatly combed back. He gave her a small smile, taking care not to drop the cigarette that was dangling precariously from his mouth. His grey eyes were staring into hers. They looked tired. Helen couldn't be certain in the dim light, but it looked like they had a tinge of yellow to them.

'Nice to meet you, Sergeant. We didn't get a chance to speak after the briefing.' He held out his hand. 'But I prefer just to be called Ian.'

She shook his hand, feeling him look her up and down.

'I've heard a lot about you.' He took a drag on his cigarette and exhaled the smoke through his nostrils.

She was tempted to ask what it was he had heard, but seeing as it probably wasn't all good, there was no need to know.

He released her hand and made a show of looking around the office, changing track. 'This is smaller than I imagined.' It was a cramped office containing ten desks, when eight would fit comfortably. Every spare bit of wall was taken up with boards, maps and shelves. Most of the left-hand side of the room was lined with filing cabinets.

'Were you looking for something?'

'Huh?'

'In the filing cabinet? It looked like you were looking for something in particular.'

'No, I was just being nosey.' He gave her a small smile. 'Like to know what I'm getting myself into.'

'You won't find much to help you in there,' Helen replied.

'And how's that?'

'You won't be working on those cases.'

He arched an eyebrow. 'I was looking for your files on known criminals. I don't know Edinburgh very well yet.'

'I can ask DC McKinley to take you through them.'

'Thank you.'

'You're early.' She slid her jacket off and draped it on the back of her chair and looked up at the big clock above McKinley's desk. Over two hours early to be exact.

'I like to get an early start.'

'And that's Jack's mug.'

'Then I better put it back before he gets in.' He took a long swig and crossed over to his new desk. Helen noticed he wasn't putting as much weight on his left leg as he was on his right.

'I'm a bit stiff in the morning,' he commented.

He'd nearly lost that leg, according to the reports Helen had read. 'The office isn't normally this quiet,' Helen commented, struggling to make conversation. She had come in early to get these reports done before his arrival. She noticed a half-eaten bacon roll on Randall's desk, so he was in the office somewhere. No doubt with DC Bell.

'All dealing with Jimmy Osbourne and these jewellery shop robberies?'

'Among others.' She swallowed hard — her mouth felt dry. She would need to get some coffee soon. 'We had a shooting yesterday morning.'

'Seriously?'

'A young lad of about eighteen.'

'Is he—?'

She shook her head. 'Still in hospital, but I don't fancy his chances.' She motioned to the crime scene photographs on her desk.

'I'm sorry to hear that.'

'We haven't been able to identify him either.'

Loughton crossed over to her desk and lifted up a couple of photos for inspection. He arched an eyebrow. 'I don't fancy his chances either.' He flicked them back onto the desk and bobbed his head towards the partition and the end of the office that normally housed their inspector. 'Is he due in?'

'Any minute now.'

He shook off his jacket. 'Do you mind if I—' he asked, motioning to a window that was ajar.

Helen shook her head. 'It's broken.'

He sat down in his chair, slid it back and forth then pulled on the armrests.

'It's not booby-trapped,' Helen remarked. At least she hoped it wasn't. The sound of the chair groaning under his weight filled the silence. She lost her place in the paragraph she was reading and peered at him.

He smiled. 'I've got a bad back. I like a good chair, but this one will do.' He brushed ash off his battered old desk. 'Aye, this will do.' He looked like he was considering what to say. 'I don't plan on being here long. Once Osbourne is behind bars, I'll be gone.'

'I admire your optimism.' Helen got back to her reading. She had a lot to get through this morning. She had barely got to the bottom of the first page before DC Randall and Bell appeared in the doorway.

Loughton stood up, taking better care to hide his injury than he had done with Helen. He held out his hand. 'Pleasure to meet you,' he said to Randall, who sighed before taking his hand. Randall looked more interested in getting back to his breakfast roll.

Helen gave up on getting through the reports before the briefing and made for the door. 'I'm going to go get a coffee, let me give you the grand tour.'

* * *

Loughton tried to compose himself as he followed her to the door. The last thing he needed was for her to think he wasn't up to the job. He tried to blink that night away, but Leonard filled his mind, and the iron stench of his blood stung his nostrils. The hairs on the back of his neck stood on end. *Bang.* Loughton jumped and turned to the noise — Randall was shoving a filing cabinet shut and gave him a look like he was an alien.

'Are you all right?' Helen asked.

'Fine. I'm just fine.' He forced himself to smile. He could tell from her face that she wasn't believing it. 'I could do with that coffee though,' he added.

* * *

'I needed a change,' Loughton replied, stirring milk into his coffee. 'Thanks for getting this. I must have left my wallet at home. I'll square you up tomorrow.'

'Don't worry about it. You were telling me about leaving Strathclyde?'

'Aye, I was sick of staring at the same faces every day.' He plonked himself down on one of the canteen chairs.

Helen took the seat opposite. Her stomach grumbled and she instantly regretting not getting a biscuit or something to go along with her drink. 'Plenty of new faces here.'

'Aye, I'm looking forward to getting out there.' He took a loud sip of coffee. 'Doing some work. You'll need to fill me in on who to watch out for.'

Under the harsh light, Helen could see that he hadn't slept. Bags hung heavy under his grey eyes, which looked bloodshot and worn. 'I'm sure you'll get your wish soon enough,' Helen remarked. She also got the faint whiff of alcohol on his breath.

'Good.' He narrowed his eyes. 'I'm old-school, I like to make an impression on the scum out there.'

'Well, I'm sure you'll get your chance to soon enough.'

'You're . . . intriguing though.'

Helen stiffened in her seat and gave him a look. 'Me?'

'You're not your typical CID,' he commented.

Her heart constricted. *Here we go again.* Usually, this sentence was followed up with comments about how her late father, the DCI, had made it easier for her and that she didn't have to work her way up like the rest.

He shrugged. 'You're a woman, a college graduate, and yet from what I've heard you have the full trust of the DCI.'

She smirked. 'I like to think so.'

'Impressive.'

'You want to know my secret?'

'Aye.'

'There isn't one, I just do my job.'

\* \* \*

As they got back up to the corridor, Helen could see that most of the officers were heading down towards the briefing room. She looked at her watch — she had lost track of time. DC Bell was at the front of the pack clutching a brown evidence bag.

She heard Loughton sighing as they entered the cramped room with its circular table in the middle.

'This is DC Loughton.' Helen gestured towards him.

'Nice to formally meet you.' Terry McKinley stood up and offered his hand across the table. 'I tried to speak with you after the briefing—'

Loughton looked away. 'Sorry, I was preoccupied that evening.'

DC Bell gave a small nod. Helen noticed he had a folder and plastic evidence bag in front of him and he was looking pleased with himself.

'What do you have?' Helen asked, as she sat down at the top of the table. Loughton took a free space next to Terry McKinley.

'The hospital managed to remove the bullet from the lad. I went up to there with Randall early this morning.' So that explained why the CID room had been deserted.

'How is he?' Helen asked.

Bell shook his head. 'Still on the critical list.'

'Great.' Loughton looked bored, like he wanted to be anywhere else but here.

'I've been fifteen hours on shift,' Bell explained to him.

Helen resisted the urge to roll her eyes. He'd never pass up the opportunity to let anyone know how hard he worked, when it was well known he would only do the bare minimum to get by and was often first away in the evening. Randall crashed through the door with a box in his hands and a cigarette dangling from his lips. He dropped the box in front of Helen, dust bursting from it. She gritted her teeth. 'What's this?' Helen asked Randall, locking eyes with him.

Randall motioned to Bell. 'He'll tell you.'

Helen swallowed hard, feeling the acid churn up her stomach.

'It took me a while,' Bell explained to the group, 'but when I got the bullet from the hospital, I noticed there were some grooves or nicks in it.' He slid a photograph across the table. It showed a faded, brass-coloured, warped cartridge.

'Could it have come from the operation to remove it?' Helen leaned forward to get a better look.

Bell shook his head. 'I checked that with the doctor.'

'What does that mean?' Helen queried.

'I think we're potentially looking at an adapted or home-made weapon.'

'Is that hard to do?' Loughton shifted in his seat, a look of concern furrowing his brow.

'Well,' Bell said and grimaced. 'It's not *that* hard to do.'

'How?' Helen exchanged a look with Loughton.

'Maybe a dummy revolver that's been converted. It's even possible to convert some starting pistols,' explained Bell.

'Are we looking at someone with specialist skills?' Helen replied.

Bell considered this. 'Not really, you just need a little bit of know-how. There are some modified guns in the box, so you can see what I mean. Certain types of gun will only need a few small changes, and you might only need to bore through the solid barrel.'

'Great.' Helen shuddered at the thought. 'I think we need to get together a list of camping and hunting shops in the city and see if they've sold anything like this recently.'

'What about rifle clubs?' Loughton asked.

Bell nodded as he tapped his folder. 'I've already put together a list of places to try. DC Randall and I are going to head there now.'

'Good.' Helen nodded.

'I'm also going through any cases where modified guns have been used,' McKinley chimed in.

\* \* \*

After the briefing, Loughton slipped out while Helen was on the phone and headed down the dank corridor to the cells. The lights flickered and a blast of cool air hit him in the face. He glanced over his shoulder to make sure he was still alone. Osbourne sat on the bed in his cell, arms folded and head resting against the brick wall. He looked like he didn't have a care in the world. Loughton clenched his fists. The familiar smell of Leonard's blood stung his nostrils. He took another step forward, and the sharp pain in his thigh flared. The only way to get any kind of relief would be to make sure Osbourne paid. An arm grabbed his shoulder, and he whipped around and came face to face with a uniformed officer with wispy ginger hair who looked taken aback by Loughton's reaction.

'Can I help you?' the officer asked.

Loughton forced a smile. 'No, I was just having a look.'

'And you are . . . ?'

'Loughton retrieved his warrant card from his breast pocket. 'I'm on secondment to CID.' He stepped aside to let the officer past. 'I better be on my way.

* * *

Helen sighed as she hung up the phone on the last number from the list of pawn shops. She had the box of converted guns on her desk. 'Any luck?' Helen asked McKinley, who shook his head. She rummaged through the guns. They were collected from cases over the years, some of them just toy guns that had been sprayed black to look like the real thing. Her telephone rang and Helen braced herself, hoping that it wasn't the hospital calling with bad news.

'Helen Carter.'

'It's me.'

Helen sat up straighter in her seat. Her mum never called the station. 'Is everything alright?'

'I'm just checking you haven't forgotten about this evening?'

'This evening?' Helen dragged a hand through her hair. 'I'll be there.'

'Do you mean that?' Her mum didn't sound convinced, and she couldn't blame her. It wouldn't be the first family event that she had missed.

'I will. I'll even be early.' Helen looked up as she met eyes with McKinley. 'I need to go now, but I'll be there. I'm looking forward to it.'

* * *

'I've got something for you and you're not going to be happy,' McKinley explained to Helen when she returned to her desk with coffee in hand. He motioned to a slip of paper on his desk.

'What is it?'

'Someone did call to report a shooting.'

'What?' Helen felt her stomach tighten as she read it. 'How could this have happened?'

McKinley shrugged. 'The voice was garbled, and dispatch couldn't understand most of what was said. I can't even tell you if it was male or female. Officers did investigate and found nothing. It was put down to being a prank.'

'How far is the phone box from where Dennis was found?'

'Not far . . . about a street away.'

'It doesn't rule out a robbery, but whoever did shoot him didn't want him dead.' Helen dropped the paper back onto the pile.

# CHAPTER 16

A couple of hours later, Helen caught up with Loughton in the corridor. He held the door to CID open for her. Helen took off her jacket and draped it over her chair. The air wasn't as thick with smoke as usual, which meant Randall and Bell had been out for a while. Both of their desks were piled high with folders.

'Any progress?' Loughton asked, pulling her from her thoughts.

She shook her head.

'Well, I've been busy while you've been off gallivanting,' McKinley said with a smile. He had a fag in one hand and a pencil poised in the other.

'This is bound to be good then.' Helen smiled, slumping down into her seat. 'Right, let's hear it.'

'Were you aware of a potential robbery last week where the shopkeeper was threatened with a gun?' McKinley asked.

'No, I wasn't.' Helen crossed over to McKinley's desk.

'I'm not surprised, it didn't even make the newspapers.'

Loughton was at the drinks table but turned around with his coffee mug, his interest piqued.

'Last Monday,' McKinley carried on, 'just before the shop was about to close, a male entered the premises, looked around some of the items in the shop then proceeded to threaten the shopkeeper with a gun.' McKinley manoeuvred around his desk and handed Helen the slip of carbon paper.

'Interesting,' Helen muttered, skim-reading the sheet. 'There isn't much detail about the robber: male, five foot six or so, dark, cropped hair. Why so little information?'

'I don't think the reporting officers took it seriously.'

'Why not?'

McKinley gave a slow sigh. 'Nothing was taken, and the shopkeeper was vague about the gun. Wasn't entirely clear on what happened . . .'

'He could have been in shock.'

McKinley gave another shrug.

Loughton, who had returned to spooning coffee into the mugs, turned to face them. 'We should go talk to him. Now that the dust has settled, he may be able to give us more information.'

'Definitely . . . if we leave soon, we might be able to speak with him before he shuts up shop.' It was on the other side of town, maybe a thirty-minute drive after rush hour. But less than a ten-minute walk from where their victim was shot in the alley.

Loughton handed her a mug. 'Sounds like a plan . . .'

Helen took a sip of her coffee and gasped in satisfaction. She could feel Loughton's grey eyes on her. She looked up to see a smile twist the corners of his mouth.

'What?'

'I was just thinking.' He leaned forward and Helen caught the whiff of instant coffee on his breath.

'That could be dangerous.' Helen put the mug down. It was too weak for her liking anyway.

'Once we've visited this shopkeeper, do you fancy going for a drink? I could do with something better than this.' He made a face. 'I think the milk is off.'

She caught McKinley shifting in his seat. 'I can't.' She flicked to another page in her report.

'No worries.' He stepped backwards.

'I have plans straight after work.' She gave a thin smile. 'And there is just so much going on here.'

'Another time then?'

'Aye, maybe.'

'Well, I can check out this shopkeeper, if you want to get away early. Happy to help any way I can. I'm not feeling very useful yet.'

'Nah.' She pushed away from the table. 'I'm not in that much of a rush, and this could be the lead that we're looking for.'

'Aye, no bother.'

She took one last glug of her coffee — it was still better than nothing. 'Right, you coming then? Let's see what this shopkeeper has to say for himself.'

## CHAPTER 17

The last of the rush hour traffic was dying away by the time they pulled out of the station. Squinting, Helen flipped down her sun visor — the late afternoon sun was catching her in the eyes. Loughton was fiddling with the radio, tuning into a station providing some low background music. They drove most of the way in silence, and it wasn't until they were passing the Northern General Hospital that Loughton spoke.

'Where's good to eat in this city?'

'Depends what you fancy.' Helen drummed on the steering wheel as they slowed behind a school bus.

'Don't know, really.'

'Plenty of places up Princes Street are worth looking at, and there's some nice food in the posh hotels.' Helen flicked on the indicator and pulled around the bus.

'Aye? You're in a rush, you're going to give me whiplash.'

'I just want to make sure we get there before the shop shuts.'

'Fine.' He held up his hands in mock surrender as Helen pressed down on the accelerator.

Less than ten minutes later, Helen wrenched up the handbrake behind a Morris Minor. The shop was in Leith, just a few miles from the station, nestled in between a launderette and a bookie, both of which looked to be doing a roaring trade. Jars of hard-boiled sweets were stacked against the window underneath cigarette posters. She could do with some Opal Fruits. The Dolly Mixture looked good too.

Loughton dragged a hand through his hair and sighed. Helen slipped him a glance.

'Are you feeling all right?' she asked.

'I just have a headache. I'll be all right in the minute.' He retrieved a packet of Player's from his jacket pocket and offered her one.

She shook her head.

'That's smart, it's a bad habit to get into.' He placed one to his lips, then paused before lighting it. 'You don't mind, do you?'

'What do you think?'

'It's just . . .' He looked like he was considering his words. 'Guns bring back a lot of memories, you know.'

'I can understand that,' Helen replied, tugging open the door to the shop. A bell chimed and an almost skeletal, balding man in his late sixties looked up from the counter, eyeing them suspiciously. He was wearing a brown overall jacket.

The shop was wider than it looked to be on the outside, with rows of magazines, sweets, crisps and biscuits.

Helen slipped out her warrant card. 'I'm DS Carter and this is DC Loughton,' Helen explained.

'Oh, aye.' The man went back to scooping mint humbugs into a jar. 'What can I do for you?'

Bleach and polish lingered thinly in the air, getting stronger as she walked to the counter.

'We wanted to ask you about the attempted robbery on your premises last week,' Helen prompted.

The old man raised a bushy eyebrow. 'That's surprising. When I reported it, the last two officers treated me like I was a senile old git.' A smile crinkled his features. 'I mean, I am old, but I'm no' going to imagine someone pointing a gun at me.'

'No, of course not. Can you take me through it?'

He nodded slowly. 'I think so.'

'The shop was about to close?' Helen prompted.

'Aye. I normally get a rush of trade towards the end of the day, but that night it was quiet. Well, until this man came in.'

'Then what happened?'

'I didn't think much of it at first. He had a look around the shop. He was wearing a black woolly hat, so I couldn't really see his face. He grabbed a few things off the shelves. Came up to the counter and demanded that I empty the till and give him a load of fags. I'm barely keeping this place afloat as it is.' He paused, as though he was reliving the moment. 'The lad didn't put up much of a fight.' A broad grin extended across his thin face, revealing a row of broken, crooked, brown teeth. 'Anyway, I'm surprised you lot are interested.'

'Before he ran away,' Helen said. 'Can you tell me about that?'

'I told him no, and that's when . . .'

'When he threatened you with a gun?'

'What exactly happened?' Loughton asked, his voice cold and level.

It surprised Helen, considering the old man wasn't a suspect. She took over the questioning. 'I know you've already been through this before, but it would help us to know what happened step by step.'

The old man was nodding. 'I could tell from the way he was waving the gun around, he didn't know what he was doing. He was asking me to empty the till, not that I've got much in it. It wouldn't have been enough to make him happy, that's for sure.'

'When did you realise he had a gun?'

'When he pulled it out of his jacket pocket and stuck it right in my face. He asked me to empty the till again. There was no way I'd give that waster any of my hard-earned money. I just scrape by as it is, sweetheart. He had it pointed like this.' He made a gun with his hands and raised it to Helen for emphasis. Clearly enjoying the moment.

'That was dangerous.'

The shopkeeper shrugged. 'I didn't think. I just knew I had to do something. I had a bottle of vodka under the counter. I grabbed that and swung at his head — missed and caught him on the shoulder, but it was enough to knock him off balance and he dropped the gun. He staggered backwards, and by the time I got around the counter, he'd grabbed the gun and ran for the door. Aye, stupid I know, love, but this is my livelihood. I fought in the war.'

'Still,' Helen muttered.

'It's no' the first time someone's pointed a gun at me, that's for sure.'

'Can you tell us anything about the gun?'

'Not really . . . I'm no expert on guns.'

'What did it look like?'

'It was that close to my face. I didn't get a good look at it. It looked like a smallish pistol. I thought it was old — an antique or a model. I wasn't sure it would actually fire.' He gave her a smile. 'That's why I started with the John Wayne impersonation.'

'Can you describe him?'

'I'm no' sure. He was just normal looking.'

'Was he young, old, tall, fat?' Loughton interjected. Helen could see he was losing patience.

'Everyone looks young when you get to my age. I think he was in his twenties. He looked well built, big shoulders. The hat came quite far down on his face, so it was hard to get a really good look and he kept his head down when he was talking to me. I think that's how I managed to whack him with the bottle — he didn't see it coming.'

'Did he sound local?'

'Aye.' He paused. 'He was Scottish,' he replied giving Loughton a look. 'But I don't think I've seen him around here before.'

'What was he wearing?'

'Ach, I cannae mind. It was dark . . . a dark jumper and a jacket, maybe a green camouflage one. Do you know the kind that you see all the youngsters wearing? It was that one.'

'Thank you for all your help.' Helen took a card from her pocket. 'If you remember anything else, you can get me on that telephone number. We have an identification book in the station. Would it be possible for you to come down in the next day or two and see if you recognise anyone?'

The shopkeeper nodded.

Outside Loughton sighed heavily. 'He's the type of guy that says a lot but doesn't really say anything.'

'I don't know.' She cast a glance around the street, most of the buildings had shops on the ground floor with flats above. 'I don't think whoever attempted to rob this shop was local. Otherwise, the shopkeeper would've recognised him.'

'Aye, or he's an idiot,' Loughton countered.

Helen stared at him a moment, trying to work out what he was thinking.

'We don't even know if the old man is telling the truth.' He frowned. 'I think he'd struggle to open a bag of crisps, never mind take down a robber.'

'We have no reason to not believe him,' Helen countered.

'It's possible our victim was robbed by the same person.' Loughton shoved his hands in his pockets for warmth as they walked towards the car. 'The supermarket isn't far away.'

'The gun also fits the description of the one that DC Bell said was used in the shooting.' Helen dragged a hand through her hair. It seemed as though Loughton had already made up his mind, but Helen knew it was dangerous to discount any information in a case.

\* \* \*

*No surprises there*, Helen thought when she found the note on her desk informing her Osbourne had been released from custody.

She looked up at Loughton. He looked livid. 'He's still under surveillance, and if he does anything—' she snapped her fingers — 'we'll have him in like that.'

'There was enough to have him charged already.'

Helen shook her head. 'Circumstantial.'

'That's the story of his life,' Loughton scoffed. 'He gets away with everything.'

'Not this time.'

Loughton grabbed his jacket from the back of his chair. 'Can't you see he already has? And as long as he's out there on the streets, he's free to get his money. Free to do whatever—'

'We have eyes on him.'

'Do you think that will stop him?'

Loughton's lips twisted into a sneer. 'I'll see you tomorrow.'

'Osbourne's got one of the best solicitors in Edinburgh. We have to play this by the book, or we'll lose him,' Helen called after him as he disappeared.

\* \* \*

Loughton's stomach churned. He tracked Osbourne down to a corner back-end boozer not far from his flat. He could see him through the misted windows, holding up a pint and smiling at a blonde tart. Loughton's grip on the steering wheel tightened. He spotted one obvious-looking surveillance car up ahead with a clearly bored officer who barely looked out of his teens. If they weren't going to get Osbourne back in custody then he would have to do something himself.

## CHAPTER 18

Helen's chest burned as she ran up the path towards the church, not noticing the puddle just by the steps. *Damn!* Muddy rainwater splashed up her flesh-coloured tights, missing her dress, thankfully. Organ music spilled out from the main room as she entered and she recognised the tune: 'Air' from Handel's *Water Music*. There was still time. Bloody brilliant.

She bolted down the corridor and was met with the warm air from the central heating. Her fringe stuck to her forehead and cheeks. Not an attractive look. She paused behind the glass double doors to gather her senses and to make sure she wasn't going to burst in during the bridal march.

The rehearsal was in full swing. The bride-to-be was at the front in a red tea dress, explaining something to the vicar. Helen waited until her back was turned to slip in and grab a seat in the back row. It groaned under her weight, but no one noticed. She blew out a sigh as she rummaged through her handbag for a handkerchief — a balled-up tissue, anything — she could wipe her brow with, but all she had was a crumpled bus ticket and a red lipstick from the last event she had been invited to. She pulled the lipstick apart and aimed it at her bottom lip.

'You've been rumbled.'

Helen jerked and she felt the lipstick smear onto her cheek. Brilliant. 'Thanks for that,' Helen muttered.

The man sat down in the pew in front and angled his head towards her. His hair was dark, cropped short, but still long enough to be styled. His jaw was sharp, clean shaven. He was wearing a tailored, navy-blue jacket.

Helen felt her heart beat faster. 'Who are you?' she asked, wiping her cheek with her thumb

'There's still some there.' He smiled gleefully.

'Yes, I know, thanks.'

'Anyway, I'm a cousin of the groom.' He kept his voice low. 'Much younger cousin of the groom, obviously.'

'Obviously.'

He motioned to his own cheek. 'You've got a little bit of something . . .'

'Yes, I know, thank you.'

'And who are you?'

'Daughter of the bride.'

He extended a hand. 'I'm Scott, by the way.'

She shook his hand briefly. 'Looks like they're getting started.' She nodded to the front from where her mum was now frowning at her.

He nodded and turned, and she rubbed at her cheek with more vigour. This couldn't be over fast enough.

\* \* \*

The ceremony was followed by a rehearsal dinner in a hotel on Princes Street. Helen splashed herself with some water in the bathroom and smoothed the frizz on top of her head. As no one was around, she gave a twirl in the mirror. It was a sleeveless pink number, a little tight on the hips, perhaps, but not too bad.

Her mum, Ruth, was waiting for her outside when she opened the door, her arms crossed and eyebrows arched. 'I noticed you sneak in late, and you're missing the plus one.'

'Sorry, I couldn't get away from work.'

Ruth stiffened. 'You work too much. It's not good for you.'

'I know, and I told you before there was no plus one.'

Her mum's face fell. 'I can live in hope though, can't I?'

'Yes.' Helen sighed. 'I guess you can.'

'What about Ted? Couldn't he have been persuaded?'

'Mum, no. That finished six months ago.'

'Sorry.'

'It's fine.'

'What about that man from your work, Gerry?'

'Terry? No. I want to keep my work and personal life separate.'

'I think he's a nice man.'

'He is.'

'Invite him then.'

'I'll think about it.'

Ruth arched an eyebrow. 'I suppose that's something.'

'I don't want to rush anything. Not like . . .'

'Things move quickly when you're older.'

'You're not that old.'

'I'm happy.'

Her mum stepped forward and made a face. 'The dress looks good.' She squinted and looked down at Helen's feet. 'Those heels are caked in mud.'

Helen shifted awkwardly on the spot. 'You look lovely, Mum.' It was good to see her mum happy again after all these years. The marriage had come as a shock though, and it all seemed to be moving too fast.

Ruth smiled. 'Just promise me you won't be late for the actual wedding next week.'

'I'll be early.'

Her mum didn't look convinced. 'I just worry about you.'

'I know you do.'

'I need to get back.' Ruth squeezed her arm.

Helen spotted her name plate on the furthest table, where a couple of blonde women were sitting laughing about something. She took a seat opposite them. They gave her a look but carried on talking. Candles flickered on the tables. Helen was tempted by the bread basket. She grabbed a chunk of bread then threw it back in — she would wait for the real food.

'I think all the chronically single people have been stuck together.' Scott slipped into the seat next to hers.

'Seems so.' Helen poured herself some water then offered him the bottle. He shook his head.

'I'm saving myself for the champagne,' he explained.

'Good plan.' Helen sipped her water. 'What is it you do for a living?'

'I'm a lecturer.' He shrugged. 'History.'

'Sounds interesting.'

'It can be. I've recently got back from teaching in America, and I was in France before that.'

Helen's stomach rumbled as the prawn cocktail starters arrived.

'I travelled back for the wedding.'

'You must be close to the groom then?' Helen stabbed a prawn with her fork.

He paused for a beat. 'I'm moving to Edinburgh and taking up a role at the university, so it's a good opportunity to suss things out and get everything sorted.'

'Like what?'

'A place to stay, the best restaurants to eat in — you know, little things like that.' He smiled and placed his knife and fork back on the table. 'What is it that you do?'

Helen grimaced. 'I'm a police officer.'

He swivelled in his chair. 'That's great!'

'It is?'

'Yes! You'll know all the safe neighbourhoods and the ones to avoid.'

'That's something I can help with.' Helen felt herself relaxing. She cast a glance over her shoulder and caught sight of her mum sipping from a champagne flute. She lifted her glass when she noticed Helen and Helen did the same.

'I don't often get out, so I was really looking forward to this wedding,' Scott continued. 'When I'm working on a big project it can be all-consuming.'

Helen nodded — she knew the feeling.

'And it's nice to see Stephen happy again, even if it did take me by surprise.'

'How come?' Helen asked.

'He's been a bachelor all his life and now at seventy he's tying the knot.'

Helen took a sip of her champagne and looked over at the happy couple. She wasn't the only one that was taken off guard by this wedding then.

'Do you know your cousin well?'

He considered this for a moment. 'Depends on what you mean by "well". He's always kept himself to himself, if you know what I mean.'

Helen let out a long sigh and glanced over at Stephen. What had changed for him now?

* * *

Wedding rehearsal over, Helen parked up in front of the supermarket on the way home. She'd grab a few bits and pieces. Maybe some bread and something sweet. She wrenched up the handbrake and clambered out of the car. The balls of her feet throbbed from her high heels. She switched them for her wellies in the boot, hitched up her dress and plodded into the store. Helen stopped in her tracks when she noticed the newspaper rack. One headline caught her attention: 'Police Brutality? Innocent Osbourne arrested, released without charge.'

She gasped but it stuck in her throat. She snatched a paper from the rack and read the article. *Fuck.* She read further. *Fuck, fuck, fuck.* The article also stated that Osbourne was treated for injuries sustained in his arrest. She took the newspaper to the counter having lost her appetite for dessert.

## CHAPTER 19

It was after ten when he got back to his flat. Loughton shook off his jacket and hung it on the corner of the front-room door. The smell of stale alcohol still lingered along with the remnants of last night's food and drink. He picked up a couple of empty cans of lager; he couldn't even remember drinking them.

Not that he wanted to think about his date, it was nothing to write home about and he had no plans to see her again. He ran a mug underneath the tap. Christ, how much had he put away last night? He'd had a stinking hangover and a thumping headache since he woke up this morning. He glugged the water, then swallowed hard — his mouth was drier than the Sahara and there was no more booze in the flat. He hadn't even seen her leave that morning, she was long gone by the time he rose. He was getting too old for all this rubbish, and it was a distraction that he didn't have time for.

He rubbed his forehead and wandered through to the kitchen. Bottles lined the worktop and he swiped them into the bin. He thought of Helen Carter and wondered what her evening plans were — probably a lot more interesting than his, whoever she was spending them with. He lifted the window and closed his eyes, enjoying the evening breeze on his face. The cries of a baby filled the silence, but he couldn't tell from which flat. That would have been him, in another life — a family to come home to, a life to nurture and to take to football on Saturdays. To love.

Pain stung his eyes. He pulled the window shut and he was alone once more. He turned to face the mess. It could wait for another day. Maybe he could do a lot worse than give that bird another call — they'd had a laugh last night. She was a bit thick, not much stimulating conversation from that one, but good for a laugh and passed the time. A chippie, a great big greasy one, that was the cure for all. He patted his back pocket and remembered he'd not had his wallet at work that day. It must be in his jacket. Which one had he been wearing yesterday?

He emptied his jacket pocket and his stomach tightened. He threw the empty jacket onto the sofa. He must have been wearing something else last night. The tweed jacket. It would be on the bedroom floor anyway. He pushed open the bedroom door and rummaged through the pile of dirty laundry. His hand connected with something hard, his leather wallet was at the bottom. *Thank fuck!* Electricity bubbled in his stomach and he weighed it up in his hands — it felt light. If that bitch . . . He ripped it open. Empty. No cards and no cash. There had been at least fifty quid in there at the beginning of the night.

He sighed and slumped against the bed. There wasn't much of last night he remembered. She'd been good at plying him with drink. How could he have been so stupid? He clambered up to his bedside table. She had even taken the passport picture of his wife. What the hell would she even want that for?

He staggered out into the hall, nausea rising in his stomach. He wasn't going to let her get away with this, he would find her and get his stuff back. No one made a fool of him like this. He kept some more money in a tin on the kitchen windowsill. He lifted a couple of pound notes from that and shoved them into his pocket.

He marched in a rage to the pub.

Loughton was pissed, and to make matters worse the pub was rammed with drinkers. He had to nudge, elbow and shove his way to the bar. A man not much younger than Loughton gave him a sideways glance, a sneer tightening his mouth.

'Want something?' Loughton asked, clenching his fists.

The man shook his head and looked back down at his drink, obviously understanding the gesture.

Pity, as Loughton was in the right kind of mood to blow off some steam. The lad skulked away with his head down. Loughton scanned the room while he waited to get the attention of the barman. He studied the punters — damn, she wasn't here. A Rod Stewart record blasted out from the jukebox, and the fire at the other side of the room burned brightly.

'Here,' Loughton called out reaching across the bar. There was no point wasting any more time.

'Can I help you?' The barman eyed him suspiciously. He was wearing a sweat-stained denim shirt and had a filthy rag draped over his shoulder.

'Do you remember me, aye?' Loughton asked, the bar feeling sticky under his fingers. 'I was in here last night.'

The barman looked him up and down, recognition flickering in his grey eyes. 'You stayed for a few drinks. I'm good with faces.'

'That's helpful.'

'What can I get you?' the barman asked.

Loughton steadied himself. 'Do you remember the woman I was with last night?'

'Vaguely . . . blonde bit, right?'

'Aye.'

The barman's eyes narrowed.

'Has she been back in this evening?' Loughton carried on.

'Nah.'

'You sure?'

'Aye. She's not one of the regulars. Sorry, pal.'

He retrieved a business card from his pocket. 'Have you seen her in here before?'

'Listen pal, I am not wanting any bother like that in here. If the lassie dumped you—'

'Ach, it's nothing like that. I'm just wanting to have a little chat with her.'

'Like I say, she's not a regular.'

Damn, he didn't think she would be. It had been his idea to meet her here anyway. It was cheap and close to his flat.

'If she comes back can you call me on that number?'

The barman raised his eyebrows and slipped the card underneath the counter. 'I'll try.'

'I can make it worth your while.'

Loughton gave another look around the warm, smoky pub. There was a group hunched around the dartboard supping pints, no one from the night before. 'While I'm here, give me a double whisky.'

The barman gave a slight nod.

The whisky warmed his throat and Loughton screwed his eyes shut. His stomach warmed. She had a local accent. What did she say she did for a living? He took another sip and grimaced. A nurse maybe, something like that. He drained the last of his glass then ordered a second. He downed his glass in one and headed for the door.

Two teenage girls were sat at the bus stop sharing a bottle of wine. The blonde one took a swig just as he passed. At this time of night, they'd be waiting a long time for a bus. The alcohol warmed his stomach and the icy Forth wind made his head woozy. They giggled as he passed. His stomach burned and fists tightened, but he carried on down the street. He could have let the money go, but not the picture of his wife.

# CHAPTER 20

Helen awoke with a start. She furrowed her brow and listened to the sounds in the flat, unsure of what had woken her. Silence. She clambered up into a seated position. The short days and icy nights were never comfortable in this flat, although this morning sunlight leaked through a gap in the curtain.

She strained to read the time on her alarm, but her eyes were too blurry.

She couldn't remember the last time that she had slept through the night. That was a good sign. She groped the chair, grabbing her dressing gown from the back of it. Maybe things were getting better after all. She draped the gown over her shoulders and wandered through to the kitchen, the chill from the lino floors causing her to shiver. A drill thudded from outside — the building work across the street was showing no signs of ending. She wandered through to the kitchen, stomach rumbling, and placed two slices of bread under the grill, sighing as she rummaged through the fridge for the butter. She was spreading her toast as her phone rang. *Typical.* She wiped her hands on the tea towel and headed through to the lounge to pick it up. She sensed movement in the flat above.

'Helen, it's me.'

She recognised the voice of Inspector Jack Craven.

'Do you have any idea what time it is?' she asked

'Aye, but I knew you'd be up anyway. Are you going into the office?'

She looked up at the clock. 'Aye, in a couple of hours. I was just going to have some breakfast.'

'Right . . .'

'Do you need me there earlier? I can head in now . . .' As far as she was aware, he wasn't in until the late shift but there was something in the tone of his voice.

'What's going on?' she prompted, twisting the phone cord around her finger.

'I need your help.'

'Sounds ominous.'

She heard him breathing deeply. 'I have no one else to ask.'

Nice to know she was his last choice. 'Where do you want to meet?'

'I need you to come to my flat.'

Static from the line filled the silence.

'I wouldn't ask if it wasn't important.'

'Fine,' she eventually responded, 'I'll be there. Just give me half an hour or so.'

'Have you got my address?'

'Yes. I'll see you soon.'

Helen hung up. Apart from waiting outside in the car while he picked up something from his flat, she had not actually been inside before. For all his bluff and bluster, he was always very private.

* * *

Loughton hadn't slept, but had settled on the sofa around five. He kept going over the conversations that he'd had with Paula. He was so angry with himself for being so stupid. He sat up and rubbed sleep from his eyes. The old wounds in his shoulder and thigh throbbed. He thought about Leonard — eight years he had been gone now. It would have been better if he had died that night, but he wasn't that lucky.

Just under an hour later he was in the office, his jaw still stinging from the aftershave. But he needed to look smart. He had dressed himself in his favourite tan-coloured shirt, which paired off nicely with his cords and tweed jacket. He hadn't given the best impression yesterday. He saw the way Carter had looked at him. He had tried to keep his distance, hoping that she wouldn't smell the alcohol that oozed from his skin. Never again. He dragged his fingers through his mop of brown hair, still damp from the station shower. He didn't have one at the flat and couldn't be bothered with the pain of getting one installed. He rubbed his hand on his trousers and took a deep breath, preparing himself for the CID room.

DC Randall was at his desk with his feet up, flicking through a Manila folder, a cigarette dangling from his lips. Whatever he was reading must have been incredibly interesting because he didn't bother to look up. Loughton closed the door and felt eyes on him. He turned to see good old DC Terry McKinley rifling through a filing cabinet. McKinley gave a nod, and he returned the gesture with a smile. He could tell McKinley hadn't taken to him, but he needed to get him onside.

'All right, fella.' Loughton took off his jacket. 'Ready for another day, eh?'

'Aye, guess so,' McKinley muttered, keeping his attention on the filing cabinet.

'I wouldn't mind having a look at your list of known criminals.'

'Why?' McKinley still didn't bother to look up.

'I like to get stuck in and know what I am dealing with an' all that.'

'I've got a lot to go through.'

'Why don't I help?' Loughton offered. 'I like to be busy.'

'No, it's quicker I go through this.'

'What are you looking for, if you don't mind me asking?'

'It doesn't matter.' McKinley shoved the cabinet shut, then started to sift through piles of paper on this desk.

'Is it about Osbourne?' Loughton asked, taking a step towards him. 'If it is—'

'What?'

This guy was really starting to irritate him. 'If it *is*, I'd like to know.'

McKinley looked like he was considering this, then his top lip curled. 'You might be here for one reason only, but that doesn't mean we all are.'

'You know he's a cop killer and he's out there wandering the streets?'

McKinley gave Loughton a cold stare and left the room with a slip of paper in his hand.

## CHAPTER 21

Helen grimaced as she massaged her left shoulder — she must have slept on it the wrong way because she was getting a sharp pain every time she turned her head, and this morning's drive through rush hour traffic hadn't helped much either. She sighed and leaned her head back on the head rest. Craven's flat was on the way to the station. She had managed to park out front without a problem and she could see the lights were on in the ground-floor flat. Nets were draped across the two front windows and she could see movement behind them.

There was a cramped paved garden out front with weeds sprouting out the gaps between the grimy stones.

Craven must have seen her coming up the path because he held his front door open for her and motioned her in without a word. Salt-and-pepper stubble covered his chin and his shirt looked coffee stained and crumpled, the top two buttons undone. Burnt toast intermixed with coffee hung in the air. Helen unbuttoned her damp jacket and hung it up in the hall. The sound of the television drifted towards them — children's programs, it sounded like. Craven ushered her into the kitchen and closed the door behind them. The worktops were adrift with dirty plates, cups and burnt pots.

'What did you want to talk to me about?' Helen asked.

Craven pulled two bits of charred toast from the grill and dropped them on a plate.

'I hope that's not for me.' Helen smiled. 'I've already had my breakfast.'

He pointed to a jar of marmalade on the shelf. 'Pass that.'

She obliged and watched him spread it thickly.

The kettle on the hob squealed, billowing steam into the air. 'Get that, will you?'

Helen brushed past him and retrieved the kettle. She found a jar of coffee in one of the cupboards and spooned some into two cups. She clutched her shoulder — the pain was still nagging her. She pulled open the fridge, but it was empty and didn't look like it was working.

Helen glanced around the antiquated kitchen. It was barely big enough for the two of them, not the kind of place she imagined him in. She always pictured something more luxurious, considering his reputation for womanising. As far as Helen was aware, his ex-wife had been wealthy, but it didn't look like Craven had benefited much in the divorce.

'It's not normally like this,' Craven muttered, knowing what she must have been thinking.

She noticed an old family photograph on the kitchen window frame and smiled sadly. She hadn't seen him look like that before — happy.

Craven cleared his throat. 'The toast is for the twins.'

'The twins?'

'I've had them here overnight.'

That explained all the mess then, Helen thought. As far as she had been aware, Liz had blocked him from seeing them at every turn since she had remarried.

'Why did you want me here?'

'I need your help.'

Helen took the plate from his hands. 'I can see that. Is there any more bread left?'

He nodded, looking relieved.

'No offence, but I'm going to remake this.' She looked him up and down. 'Why don't you go and take a shower?'

'Thanks.' He took one of the coffees.

'Is it just last night you had them?' Helen asked, as she slid the toast into the bin.

His face clouded as though he was considering what to tell her. Craven swallowed. 'Liz has been struggling and I wanted to give her a break.'

'It must have been hard for Liz seeing her husband taken to the station to be questioned about a murder.'

'Liz and Milton have split up. I can't help feeling guilty about it.'

'You shouldn't. It was Milton's actions that caused this, not yours.'

Craven shrugged.

'I'll sort this out, you go and sort yourself out. What time do they go to school?'

He glanced at his watch. 'In about an hour.'

Helen headed towards the door then turned back to face him. 'Don't tell me you asked me to come here to make toast.'

He gave her a look. 'No, this is something more . . . delicate.'

'You've got me intrigued now.'

'I'll explain once I've had my shower.'

* * *

Ten minutes later, Helen sat at the dining table with a mug of coffee. Craven sat opposite, looking pensive.

'This delicate matter?' Helen prompted, carefully sipping her piping hot coffee.

Craven's eyes darkened. 'Someone within the department has been giving out information to the press.'

Helen let out a wobbly laugh. 'You don't think it's me?'

'No.'

'Good.'

'I want you to find out who is.'

'Why me?'

Craven looked like he was considering the question. 'You work harder than anyone else in the department. You're there before everyone else and still there after they've gone. I know this job is your life and you wouldn't do anything to risk it. Well, not for a few quid anyway.'

Helen forced a thin smile. 'I think that's the nicest thing you've ever said to me.'

Craven nodded. He pushed himself up from the table and lifted a folder from the worktop. He placed it in front of her.

She flicked it open. It was full of newspaper clippings from the cases the department had worked on.

The hairs on the back of her neck stood on end as she read the first article. It was from the first case she had worked on in CID, the Picture House Murder.

He stabbed the picture with his finger. 'Someone told the press about the markings on the wall and about the business card we found on the body.'

Helen nodded and flicked to another article. She had seen enough of that cinema to last a lifetime.

This article was about the recent arrest of serial killer Reggie McKenzie. She skim-read: the journalist knew about the blood in his flat and the fact that the police had visited his property previously due to domestic violence, and also that one of his victims was missing a necklace. None of which had been released to the public. The headline read: 'Could Police Have Arrested Mallet Murderer Quicker?'

Helen felt the blood drain from her face as her eyes met with Craven's. 'I'll do my best.'

'There's a list of suspects in the back of the folder. I want to you to feed false information to each one and we will see what makes the headlines.'

Helen blew out a sigh. Could this day get any worse?

# CHAPTER 22

'I hate hospitals.' McKinley sighed as they climbed the steps towards the entrance of the Royal Infirmary. Helen glanced up at the clock tower of the seventeenth-century building.

'I don't exactly love them myself either.'

'No, of course, sorry.'

'Don't be.' Helen forced a smile.

'How was your evening?'

Helen arched an eyebrow. 'It was all right . . .'

'I just heard you say you had plans.'

'I did.' Helen frowned. 'I had my mother's dress rehearsal.' Sometimes it was easier saying she had plans than the truth, and she certainly was not going to become the talk of the washhouse for a chancer like Ian Loughton.

'How did it go?'

Helen hesitated, then shrugged.

'That bad?'

'I was late.'

He grimaced, and she gave him a nudge with her elbow. 'Would you want to go to the wedding?' That slipped out before she had a chance to think.

'What?'

'Not as a date . . .'

'No?'

'It would make my mum happy. If she thought . . .'

'Fine. You've twisted my arm.'

Helen pulled open the double doors and motioned for McKinley to go through first.

'What do you think of our new constable?' McKinley asked, as though he knew what she was thinking.

'Seems capable . . . nice enough.'

'He seemed a bit . . . off to me.'

'In what way?'

'I don't know if I should say.' He looked away from her. 'I'm probably wrong.'

'What?'

'Just this morning, he was going through the files. It was like he was looking for something. He seemed flustered when I walked in on him.'

'Do you know what files he was looking at?'

He shook his head.

'What cabinet was he looking in?'

'The filing cabinet next to the door, you know, the one we keep old case information in?'

'Did you ask him what he was looking for?'

'He wouldn't say. Slammed it shut as soon as I walked in the door.'

The familiar sting of hospital cleaning fluid filled her nostrils as their boots clacked off the marble tiles. Helen looked around the ornate entrance way. It looked like a museum, with thick mahogany railings trailing the staircase and grey stone busts lining the walls. A flight of stairs led to a more modern-looking block. A large plaque on the wall caught her attention. In gold lettering it listed names of people who had donated to building this wing. McKinley tugged open the door to the intensive care ward on the left-hand side, which opened onto a big room lined with beds and a nurse's station in the middle.

121

The nurse in charge gave them a sympathetic smile from behind a teak-coloured desk. Her raven hair was scraped tightly into a topknot and her face was free from makeup.

'How is he?' Helen asked.

'Stable.' The nurse moved around the desk and motioned to a bed with a red curtain partially around it. 'It was touch and go for a while.'

McKinley nodded. 'Has he woken up or said anything?'

'No, but you're welcome to go and have a look.'

'Thanks,' Helen added.

'Before you do though —' the nurse spoke with a thick Glaswegian twang — 'this was found on his person.'

Helen and McKinley exchanged a look as the nurse retrieved an envelope from a wired rack. She handed the package to Helen.

'I put it in the envelope, but it was lying loose in his back trouser pocket.'

'Thank you.' Helen weighed it up in her hand. It felt light but with something heavy at the bottom. Helen peeled open the lip and emptied the contents into the palm of her hand. A small golden butterfly brooch with a small ruby and emerald on each wing. It looked expensive and had survived the victim's attack unmarked.

'We should check if that's from one of the jeweller robberies.'

McKinley nodded. 'I don't recognise it from the inventory I was given but I'll look again.'

A young trainee nurse who looked no more than seventeen was dispensing tea to the other patients from a metal urn. The trolley squealed with every turn of the wheel. The noise reminded Helen of nails on a chalk board and she winced.

McKinley pulled back the curtain for her to go through first. She moved around the side of the bed. The patient was propped up next to a fluid bag dangling from a pole, the cable connected into some plastic tubing in his swollen hand.

He was covered up to his chest in a white blanket which was tucked in tightly. The board above his head was scribbled with the words 'Unknown' and 'Dr MacIntosh'. Helen could see now that the patient looked younger than she had first thought thanks to the bright hospital lights that illuminated his face. At least he didn't look in any pain.

McKinley pulled out one of the two chairs and sat down. 'What do you expect to get from here?' He crossed his legs and swore when his knee connected with the bed rail.

Helen glowered at him.

'Sorry,' he muttered as his cheeks reddened.

Helen stepped forward to get a closer look at the victim's face. He had more colour to his cheeks now than when she had found him in the alley, and his lips were now pink, slightly parted and showing a row of perfectly white teeth. His brown hair stood on ends and his hands were like balloons. It was doubtful he would be of use to them anytime soon.

She brushed a stray strand of hair from her face. 'Fancy a coffee?'

'You talking to me or him?'

'Well, what do you think?' Helen rolled her eyes and headed for the door.

The canteen was right around the other side of the hospital in the bottom of the building. Helen's stomach rumbled as they waited at the counter. She ordered a couple of coffees and two edible-looking cheese rolls.

McKinley blew out a sigh — he stood behind her in the queue and she felt the breath on the back of her neck. Helen frowned; there was an elderly couple in front counting out coppers for their tea and biscuits.

'Here.' Helen retrieved a pound note from her purse. 'Have this.'

'Are you sure, hen?' The old lady furrowed her brow.

'I'm buying his too.' Helen smiled motioning to McKinley. 'It's no bother really.'

'Aye, you're flush now.' McKinley gave her a wry smile as they sat down at the table in the corner.

'I wouldn't say that.'

'The house you inherited from your dad must be worth a few bob.'

Helen shook her head. 'I'm still waiting on the first rent payment to come through.'

Helen took a sip of her tea. Nice and strong, just the way she liked it.

'I tell you, I would love to live in a house like that.' He spoke in between mouthfuls of roll. 'Beats living in a poxy flat.'

Helen looked away, a couple at the far side of the canteen caught her attention. They looked deep in conversation. They had a small brown teddy on the table that the woman was squeezing. Helen wondered who they were visiting. Apart from her recent injury and when her dad was unwell, she had mostly been able to avoid hospitals.

'It's sad, that.'

'It is,' Helen agreed.

'I always think when you go into these places, you never get out of them.'

Helen raised an eyebrow. 'I got out all right.'

'Well . . .'

'When we've finished this, I want to go back upstairs and ask the nurse a few questions.'

McKinley nodded and followed her out when they were done. As Helen approached the empty nurse's station, she slipped a glance at the ward. The curtain was ajar, and Helen caught the shape of a figure sitting down beside their victim. Helen's heart constricted.

'Is that someone with him?' McKinley asked.

'It looks like it.' She tapped him on the arm. 'Come on.'

A woman in her early twenties, with shoulder-length brown hair and a red cardigan looked up as they approached. She made a move to stand up, but Helen put up a hand.

'Who are you?' The woman furrowed her brow. Tears had made track marks down her foundation. 'What do you want?'

Helen retrieved her warrant card. 'We're police officers. I'm DS Carter, and this is DC McKinley.'

She stared at them wide-eyed.

'Who are you?' McKinley asked.

She sighed. 'My name . . . my name is Barbara Levitt.'

'Do you know this man?'

'Yes, I do.' She swallowed hard.

'Who is he?'

She nodded and looked down at him. 'He's my brother. He's been missing for the past few days.' She paused, as though she was searching for the right words.

'How did you know he was here?' Helen asked.

'I phoned all the police stations and hospitals and they mentioned bringing someone in that fitted his description. I just knew it was him.'

'Do you know what happened?'

She shook her head.

'Was he in any kind of trouble?'

She shook her head again.

'What's his name?'

'Dennis, Dennis Levitt.' She blinked back more tears. 'The doctors don't know if he's going to be okay.'

'I'm very sorry,' Helen replied.

'I don't know what I'll do without him.' She sniffed and wiped away a tear with the back of her hand.

'Did he say where he was going on the day he went missing?' Helen asked.

'No.' Her voice came out raspy.

'Did you see him that morning?'

'I think he was going to meet a friend. I hadn't seen him for a few days.'

'Do you have the name of his friend?'

'Do you know what happened?' She let go of his hand and wiped away tears from her eyes.

'We're still investigating.'

'He'd just got paid, so he would've had money on him.'

'How much?' McKinley asked, exchanging a look with Helen.

'About thirty quid.'

'That's a lot of money for a young man,' Helen remarked.

'Where was he working?' McKinley carried on.

'I don't know.'

Helen arched an eyebrow. 'You don't have any idea how he was earning his money?'

'No. Does it matter?' she snapped back.

'It might do. At this stage every piece of information could be vital.'

She shrugged. 'Just odd jobs here and there.' She pushed herself to her feet. 'I'm sorry, I need to go. I need to get some air. This is too much.'

'One more thing, please, before you go?' McKinley spoke softly. 'He was found with a broach in his back pocket. Do you know anything about that?'

She nodded and mopped up a tear from her cheek. 'It belonged to his . . . our mum. It was his good-luck charm. He took it everywhere.'

'Does Dennis know anyone with access to a gun?' Helen asked.

'No.' Her ice-blue eyes flared. 'He was the one who was shot, remember?'

'Do you have any idea why Dennis might have been at the Quicky Save supermarket?'

'I . . . no.'

'We're going to need to take some contact details for yourself,' Helen reminded her.

'I . . . I gave them to the nurse already.'

'Are you able to provide us names and addresses for his friends?'

'Yes . . .' She sniffed. 'I'll do anything that I can.'

* * *

'Do you think it was a robbery gone wrong?' McKinley asked as they walked back to the car.

'I'm not sure.' Helen searched through her pockets for her keys. 'I think if it was a robbery, someone would have taken the broach. It looks valuable.'

'Unless they were scared off,' McKinley muttered.

'Suppose. He did have a clasp mark on his wrist that looked like he could have had a watch on.'

'Barbara was hiding something though. I'm sure of that.'

'What do you want to do?'

'Speak to these friends, then we'll question her again.' She pulled the car door open. 'It'll give her a chance to settle down.'

# CHAPTER 23

'At least it feels like we're making progress,' McKinley muttered as Helen slotted the key into the ignition and pulled out into traffic. Barbara Levitt had supplied them with an address in the Corstorphine area of the city.

Helen nodded as she stifled a yawn.

'Still not sleeping?' McKinley tore at a nail as he wound his window down a crack. The big problem with the pool cars was the thick smell of smoke that hung within them, and this one seemed to stink of pipe smoke, even though she didn't know anyone in the department who smoked one.

She drew a careful breath, not wanting to admit to him that the nightmares that she had since the end of their last case hadn't really stopped. 'It's just been a long night,' she replied, feeling his eyes on her.

He angled his body towards Helen, his knee connecting with her thigh. 'It's just, when I was last at your place—'

'What?' Helen kept her eyes on the road. She knew where this conversation was going. 'Just come out with it.'

'I noticed a bottle of pills in your bathroom.'

'There were pills in my medicine cabinet,' Helen bristled. 'What where doing going in there?'

'It's none of my business.'

'That's right.'

'It's just I know they can affect sleep.'

Helen shot him a look. 'I'm not taking them.'

McKinley looked even more worried.

They drove the rest of the way in silence, broken up with noise and static from the radio. It was about a twenty-minute drive through rush hour. The car jutted to a stop behind some roadworks on Corstorphine Road. Helen slipped a glance up at the zoo — it was on her list of places to visit if she ever had some free time. She found that she only knew Edinburgh based on crimes that had been committed. She had grown up in Glasgow and spent a lot of her childhood in the outskirts of Manchester when her father was posted there.

She took a right turn and the car revved up Clermiston Hill.

'Bugger,' Helen muttered as they slowed yet again for more roadworks.

McKinley wound his window up as they waited behind an old taxi that was pumping out diesel fumes. Helen watched the black smog dissipate into the air. She sighed when the lights changed to green and they started to snake around the corner. A few minutes later, they came to a stop in front of a whitewashed detached bungalow with a maroon Vauxhall Viva parked in the drive.

As she opened the driver's side door, a teenager in greasy blue overalls looked up from the motorbike engine he was disassembling with a wrench on the garden path. Helen noticed his shoulders tense, but he looked back down at his project as they approached the gate.

'Robbie Fields?' Helen asked.

'Who wants to know?' He scratched his acne-puckered chin, smearing oil up his cheek. He dropped the wrench onto the ground with a thud.

Helen retrieved her warrant card from her pocket. 'I do. This is DC McKinley, and I am DS Helen Carter.'

He gave a small nod. 'Why do you want to speak to me?'

'Do you mind if I . . . ?' Helen motioned to the gate.

Robbie shook his head.

As Helen stepped closer she saw that his top lip was swollen, and he had an angry-looking gash on the bottom one. 'What happened to your face?'

He blotted his lip with the back of his sleeve. 'I . . . I hurt it trying to get my engine from my bike.'

'Looks sore,' Helen remarked.

Robbie shook his head.

She looked down at his hands, they looked grease-stained and chapped from the cold, but there were no marks on his knuckles that would show he had been in a fight.

'Can I help you?' A middle-aged man appeared in the doorway of the house. He had grey, thinning hair and was wearing an expensive-looking pinstripe suit and aviator glasses. He dragged on a cigarette.

Robbie's shoulders sagged as the man walked towards them.

'I hope so.' Helen gave a small smile. 'We're—'

'This is private property — we're not interested in whatever it is you're selling.' He waved his hand dismissively.

Helen held up her warrant card, so the man could see it. 'We're not trying to sell anything.'

'Female police officer. How modern.' He blew the smoke out his nostrils and slowly looked her up and down. 'Fine. You'll need to make this quick. I have somewhere else I need to be.'

'Thank you.' Helen slipped her card back into her pocket. 'As I was trying to explain to Robbie, we're investigating a serious incident that happened a couple of days ago.'

'What incident?' the man questioned.

'Are you Robbie's father?' Helen asked. 'Would it be okay if we came inside to talk about it?'

'Just ask your questions here,' he grumbled.

'Okay,' Helen relented as she reached for her pocketbook.

She directed her question to Robbie. 'Do you know Dennis Levitt? I believe you went to school together?'

'Aye, we're pals. Is everything all right?' His voice came out in a whisper.

'Why do you want to speak to Robbie about Dennis? He hasn't done anything.' He stepped forward and gave Robbie a squeeze on the shoulder. 'Isn't that right, son?'

'Yes, Dad.'

'No, but we're hoping he can help us with our enquiries. We're not accusing him of anything.'

'Oh, that old chestnut,' Robbie's father snorted. 'Robbie, go inside.'

Robbie made a move to stand then looked like he thought better of it. 'What do you want me to help with?'

'Dennis was found with severe injuries. He's in hospital—'

'Is he going to be okay?'

'We don't know yet,' Helen answered.

'When was the last time you saw Dennis?' McKinley asked.

Robbie shrugged and exchanged a look with his father. 'A couple of days ago. Maybe three. I'm not that good with dates.' Robbie looked like he was blinking back tears.

'How did he seem? Did he have plans to go anywhere?' Helen questioned.

Robbie sighed. 'No. He was just his usual self.'

'What time of day was it?' Helen persisted.

'Evening. We didn't speak for long. He gave me some advice about my motorbike.'

'Can you think of anyone who would want to hurt Dennis?'

'No, no one.' He slipped another glance at his dad. 'I can't help with that.'

McKinley handed him a card. 'If there is anything you can think of, no matter how small.'

Robbie's dad interjected. 'I think he's told you everything he knows.'

Helen nodded but continued with her questioning. 'Where were you between 6 and 8 a.m. two days ago?'

'I hope you're not insinuating something.' Robbie's dad jabbed his cigarette towards her.

'Not at all.' Helen took a step back.

'He was here.'

'Can anyone verify that?'

'He was here with me.' The father frowned at her. 'I can't believe you're even asking us this.'

'These are just routine questions that we need to go through. Did you see anyone else?'

'Is that relevant?' he snapped back.

'We're just trying to piece together what happened to Dennis.'

'He's been seriously hurt,' McKinley interjected.

'I'm sorry to hear that, but we can't help. We were watching television and cooking breakfast.'

'What were you watching?' McKinley asked.

'I don't like where this is going. Does it matter what we were watching?' He pulled Robbie up by the arm of his overalls. His eyes darted between the pair of them. 'Do I need to get my solicitor?'

'No, this is just routine.' Helen smiled.

'Good. Now, we have things to do.'

'I understand.' Helen slipped her notebook back into her pocket. 'Thank you for your time.'

'My son is a good lad, does well at school.'

'Are you implying that Dennis doesn't?'

'Well, Dennis doesn't do well at anything.'

'What do you mean by that?'

A sneer crept across his face. 'Both of his parents are out of the picture. What does that tell you, eh?'

'Do you know anyone who would want to hurt him?' Helen asked.

The father considered this for a moment. 'I couldn't say. Robbie, what did I tell you about messing around with him, eh? I told you this would happen.'

'You thought Dennis would be shot?' Helen asked.

He dragged a hand across his forehead. 'No, sweetheart. I meant it's no surprise he's in trouble now, is it? He was hardly heading to university.'

'Dad,' Robbie wailed, 'he's not what you think.'

'We have no reason to believe at this point in time that Dennis was involved in any criminality,' Helen responded. 'When he was found he was possibly missing some personal possessions. It was a cold night, and he wasn't wearing a jacket. It's possible he was the victim of a robbery.'

'He normally wears a leather jacket,' Robbie added. 'It's old and scuffed — belonged to his dad.'

'He was found at the Quicky Save supermarket in Granton. Do you know it?' Helen asked Robbie.

'No, he doesn't.' His dad answered for him.

'If you can think of anything else that might help us—'

'No, we can't.' Robbie's father shook his head.

'We'll be on our way.'

He nodded, furrowing his brow like he was half expecting Robbie to be frogmarched to the station for questioning.

She offered Robbie a smile. 'Thank you for your time, Robbie. One last question. We're still trying to trace Dennis's family. Do you know if he has any nearby?'

'No, I don't think he does.' Robbie frowned. 'He's never mentioned any.'

Helen nodded. 'Thanks.'

'I know his parents died in a crash. I'm not sure exactly what happened, it was a long time ago.'

'What about his sister Barbara?'

Robbie gave her a confused look. 'Who?'

'Has Dennis never mentioned having a sister?' McKinley interjected.

'No.' Robbie gripped the handlebars of his motorbike.

'How long have you known Dennis?' Helen asked.

Robbie shrugged. 'It must be at least six years. I mean, he didn't always tell the truth about things.'

'What do you mean?' Helen asked.

'He didn't have a good childhood, and I think sometimes he invents a better one.'

'Right, Robbie, in you go now,' his father commanded and began to lead his son inside.

As they headed out of the garden, Helen slipped a glance over her shoulder and could see Robbie and his dad both watching from the front window. The father was holding his son's shoulder protectively.

'What did you think of that?' Helen asked once they were safely out of earshot.

'The dad was a bit funny, wasn't he?'

'Maybe he just doesn't like coppers.' The police standing in the public had dropped in recent years with corruption scandals hitting the headlines every other week. 'I mean that's hardly uncommon, is it?'

'Maybe.' Helen shook her head. 'From what little I could see of the house, it looked expensive, nice area. Robbie and Dennis seem like chalk and cheese.' She blew out a sigh. 'It's a bit worrying that he seemed confused about Dennis having a sister.'

'Maybe Robbie and Dennis aren't as a close as he's making out?'

'Let's see what we can find out.'

* * *

His father levelled a punch to the back of his head as soon the officers' car was gone. Robbie felt tears burning the back of his eyes. He fell forward, landing on his hands and knees.

'You're a bloody idiot. Even if you haven't done anything the police will blame you.'

Robbie rubbed a knot that was forming on his head. 'They weren't trying to blame anyone.'

Another blow knocked the wind out of him.

'Don't you dare talk back to me. I know what they're like.'

'They're trying to find out who hurt Dennis. There's a difference.' Nausea filled Robbie's stomach, and he struggled to get a good breath into his body. He closed his eyes and gave into the wooziness.

* * *

Jimmy Osbourne was grinning with his hands in his pockets as he crossed the road towards his flat. His lips thinned as soon as he noticed Loughton standing in the doorway, and he stopped in his tracks.

'This could be construed as harassment.' Osbourne looked over both shoulders then frowned.

'If you're looking for the police car that's meant to be watching us, they've been called away on another matter.' Loughton had paid a local lad a pound to lure the officers away. They wouldn't be gone long.

'Is that so?' Osbourne looked down at Loughton's knee. 'It's not very smart, you here all alone, is it?'

Loughton arched an eyebrow and stepped forward. 'I don't know.'

'This obsession. It could get you hurt.'

'Is that a threat?'

'I don't do threats.'

Osbourne was now so close to him that he could smell the whisky on his breath and see the hate in his eyes. Now was his chance, the cop car was pulling back into the street. Loughton levelled a punch at Osbourne's gut. He jerked forward and Osbourne's fist connected with Loughton's jaw. Loughton winced and shoved his body forward. The force must have taken Osbourne by surprise because let out a shout as they both landed in a crumpled heap on the floor. Footsteps slapped against the concrete as the officers ran towards them. Icy pain trailed Loughton's hip and knee. He tried to scramble free. One of the officers pulled him up by his arm.

'Are you all right sir?'

'Where were you?'

'Sorry sir, a young lad reported a robbery, but we couldn't see anything.'

Loughton nodded and braced himself, then tested to see if he could put some weight on his leg. He could.

Osbourne looked up, blood trailing down his chin. 'You're going to pay for this.'

'And you're under arrest for assaulting a police officer.' Loughton grinned.

## CHAPTER 24

Her eyes feeling heavy, Helen looked up from a pile of papers she was sifting through as a cup of coffee was placed down next to her. 'Thank you.'

'I'm still going through my pile,' McKinley grunted as he slumped down in the seat next to her, knocking her elbow and nearly sending her coffee flying onto her lap. She scowled at him.

'Sorry,' he muttered.

'It's fine . . . I'm just . . . frustrated.' She took a sip and grimaced, it was stone cold.

'How are you getting on?' he asked.

'Dennis was given up for adoption at six weeks old.'

McKinley angled his head so he could see the paper.

'He was put into a children's home a few years later. His adoptive mother couldn't cope.' Helen tapped the page.

'Sad.'

Helen nodded.

'Do you know why?' McKinley asked.

'No.' Helen took another sip of her coffee, it wasn't strong enough to combat the exhaustion that made her head feel heavy. She hadn't got enough sleep these last few days.

'So, we're no further forward.'

'I don't know.' Helen dragged her hand through her hair.

'Does it say why he was given up for adoption?'

'No.' She looked back down at the report. 'Only that the parents couldn't cope. They were teenagers, unmarried, and there's no father on his birth certificate.'

'What about his sister?' Helen questioned.

'Can't find anything about her yet.' McKinley pushed away from the table. 'I'll go through car crashes and see if I can find anything that references the mother's name.'

'It's late, you should get home and sleep.'

'I could say the same to you.' McKinley smirked.

'I appreciate you going through all this.' Helen gave him a tired smile.

'I was going to call the school in the morning too and see if they could give us a better picture of what Dennis is like and maybe even give us some more friends.'

'Good idea. We also need to try and find out what Dennis was doing for money.'

McKinley stifled a yawn. 'I have his address here too. It's in a boarding house on Ferry Road.'

'It's not that far from the supermarket where he was found.' Helen blinked hard and stood up. 'I think we should go home and get some sleep. Start on this again in the morning.'

McKinley hesitated. 'Are you definitely going to go home?'

'Aye, why wouldn't I?' She grabbed her jacket from the back of her chair.

'It's just . . .'

'What?'

'It doesn't matter.' He shook his head. 'I just worry about you sometimes.'

'I'm going straight home to a warm bath then bed.' Helen forced a smile.

'Unless you fancy getting something to eat?'

'Another time,' Helen replied, putting on her jacket.

\* \* \*

Loughton closed his eyes as the whisky slipped down his throat. He followed it up with another swig, then another, until the light-headedness started. He wanted the thoughts to stop. *Osbourne's smirking face. Leonard bleeding out next to the police car.* Needed them to stop. He placed the glass on the table and eased back onto the sofa. It was the only thing that dulled the pain, but now it wasn't just a couple of glasses that he needed to get through a long day of work, it was three or four.

A car horn sounded outside, pulling him back from sleep. He groaned and sat back up and put his head in his hands. The trill ring of the phone echoed in the silence. He breathed deeply then lifted the receiver.

'Loughton.'

Static crackled on the line.

'Hello?' Loughton pulled the telephone closer. 'Hello . . . Is someone there?'

He heard a murmur, like someone had taken a breath. Giving up, he hung up the phone. His stomach twitched as he stood up and his eyes met with the picture of Stella smiling on the mantelpiece. Just over three years since she'd died.

Sleep now out of the question, he headed through to the second bedroom. It was stacked with boxes from his previous life. All of the dresses, books and records that Stella had collected over the years. He brushed a coat of dust from one of them, then plonked himself down at his makeshift desk where he kept all of his case files on Jimmy Osbourne. Stella had begged him to forget about him, so they could move on with their lives, but he had made a promise to Leonard on his death bed and he was going to keep his word. All of the shooters would pay.

## CHAPTER 25

Helen paused in the doorway of the CID room the following morning. Loughton had his head down and was raking through index cards in a rolodex. The aroma of stale coffee and fag smoke drifted out into the corridor, despite the window being open and rainwater collecting on the window ledge. Randall was at his desk doing his usual two-fingered typing. Helen took off her coat and hung it on the rickety coat hanger, next to an expensive-looking suit jacket that Helen assumed must belong to Loughton.

He looked up at the disturbance and offered a thin smile.

'I've just been going through everything there is on Jimmy.'

'Have you found anything useful?'

He shook his head. 'The man is untouchable.'

Helen settled in her hard chair and gave her shoulders a stretch. 'No one is untouchable. He'll have slipped up somewhere, we just need to find it.'

'Believe me, I'd like nothing better.' He scratched his jaw and let out a laugh dripping in sarcasm. 'And I wish I could believe that but . . .'

'He's back in custody,' Helen reminded him.

'That's never stopped him before.' He pushed away from his desk.

'What time is the briefing?'

'In thirty minutes.'

Great, that would give her enough time to get everything prepared and grab herself a proper cup of coffee.

Loughton was obviously thinking the same thing.

\* \* \*

Helen was left with a niggling headache after the briefing. It had been a colossal waste of time — exactly as she had expected. The clock was now ticking on Jimmy Osbourne again. DC Randall had interviewed him a few times, but he had kept quiet. They would need to find something to make him talk. She rubbed her aching eyes and sighed. She was sitting in the darkened incident room adjacent to the office, enjoying the quiet. Mumbled conversation trickled in from CID, but she couldn't make out the words. Sighing, she flicked open a file. She had to complete the rest of the arrest reports for Jimmy, aware that all the information they had on him was circumstantial. Rain battered the windows and for a moment Helen thought the lights flickered, but she couldn't be sure. A rattle on the door startled her.

'Come in.'

Loughton bobbed his head around the door. He looked hesitant. 'I hope you don't mind me bothering you. Terry said you wanted some quiet.'

'I do, but it's fine.'

'In that case —' he held up a water-stained cardboard box — 'is now a good time for us to go through these? It is why I'm here, after all.' He closed the door with a soft click.

'What are those from?' Helen asked.

'My own personal investigation into Jimmy Osbourne.'

'Why not?' Helen shrugged. 'Come in, take a pew.'

Loughton dropped his gaze to the floor. He looked stiff to Helen, like he was favouring his left leg but trying to hide it. He dropped the box on the middle of the teal desk, a plume of dust exploding from it. Helen stifled a sneeze as

Loughton sat down opposite. The chair wobbled under his weight and he took a moment to adjust it.

'You've been busy,' Helen remarked, taking a sip of her tea. She couldn't blame him. She would be doing the same if she were in his position.

Nodding, he began rummaging through the box.

'Jimmy took a big risk coming back to Edinburgh. I didn't think I would see him in Scotland again.'

'I thought the same,' Helen agreed and shuffled forward to look in the box.

'Whatever he's here for must be worth the risk.' He angled it away from her and pulled out another slip of paper. 'We just need to figure it out.'

Helen nodded. 'I take it you have some ideas?'

'I've followed Jimmy for a long time, even been out to Spain a few times, but I've never been able to make it stick,' Loughton replied. 'He's clever. He never surrounds himself with a lot of people and masterminds the dirty work.' Loughton blew out a sigh.

'I've also been looking into the recent robbery.' Helen tapped the folder.

'Is that so?'

'There's been a couple of things that haven't sat right with me.'

'Such as?' Loughton probed.

'Two men tripped the alarm, right?' Helen opened her folder and flicked to the right page.

'That's correct.' Loughton narrowed his eyes.

'The staff in the shop gave physical descriptions before retracting them.' She angled the book towards him, showing some pencil sketches she did of the balaclava-clad men. 'One was described as being skinny, with a shaving-type rash on his neck.' She turned the page. 'The other one was described as being six feet tall.'

'So?'

'Jimmy Osbourne is stocky, five foot six in his boots.'

'Well, like you say, Jimmy Osbourne was behind it.' Loughton shrugged.

'Then there's the photograph of Osbourne outside the jewellers, but I haven't been able to track down the photographer.'

'Osbourne probably scared him away. He has a track record of it.'

Helen drew in a sharp breath. 'I want to find him anyway.'

'I think that's a waste of time.' Loughton bristled.

Helen shut the folder. 'Why don't you tell me what you think is not a waste of time?'

'I didn't mean any offence.'

'If you have other ideas, I want to hear them.'

He closed his eyes and took a deep breath. 'I just want Osbourne to face justice.'

'He will.'

'Jimmy comes from a big family, six brothers, and a dozen other previous convictions.'

Helen was nodding.

Loughton's mouth twisted into a sneer. 'Impoverished family, father died in a traffic collision in 1952. Estranged from his siblings, although most of them are now dead.'

'Have you tracked down the ones that are still alive?'

He shook his head. 'His youngest sister, Gina, dropped off the face of the earth in the late sixties.'

'What else have you got?' Helen asked, as she noted the name in her book.

'Not much else.' Loughton clenched his jaw and looked like he was thinking of what to say. 'It's all my fault, that's why I can't forget.'

She had read in detail what had happened, and she knew his guilt wouldn't go away no matter what she said or what he did.

'I was the one that pulled into the factory. We could have waited for backup, but I was desperate for the next promotion.'

'You weren't to know what you were going into.'

Loughton scowled. 'It was just a routine patrol. We were asked to check out an alarm that had gone off in a factory. We didn't think much of it — I mean, we could see no sign of a disturbance.' He took a haggard breath, then patted down his pockets for his cigarettes. 'Hope you don't mind,' he added, retrieving one from the packet and putting it to his lips.

Helen shook her head. She noticed his hand tremble as he took a drag.

'You don't need to tell me this,' Helen reminded him.

'We got out the car to investigate. I remember the sound of glass smashing, then we were peppered with bullets.' He slipped out a photograph from his wallet and handed it to Helen. If she hadn't known better, she could have mistaken the picture for Bonnie and Clyde's car after they had their last shoot-out with the police.

Helen turned the photograph over.

'What happened to Leonard was . . .'

'I'm sorry.' Helen shook her head.

'He was left in a coma. Brain-dead.' Loughton frowned. 'I ended up getting shot in the thigh and the shoulder, but I lived.'

*Survivors' guilt*, thought Helen. 'Could Osbourne be back to see Gina? We know his mother is dying, but she wouldn't even know Osbourne, she's too far gone with dementia.'

'I don't think so. The last bit of information I have about Gina was that she was pregnant and left with an unknown man. That was from one of their neighbours.'

'Unmarried?' Helen asked.

Loughton nodded. 'There's no trace of her after that.'

'She might have been sent away or hidden to avoid embarrassment?'

'That's what I suspected. Apparently, at one point the Osbournes were a religious family.'

The door opened and McKinley poked his head around the door and smiled thinly.

'What is it?' Helen asked.

'A Lisa-Marie Malone is downstairs demanding to speak to whoever has got Jimmy in custody.'

Helen exchanged a look with Loughton. 'That's Jimmy's ex-wife.'

'Oh, really? This will be interesting.'

'Just to warn you, she's really not happy about being kept waiting. She's kicking up a fuss downstairs.'

Helen rose from her chair. 'I'll go speak to her now.'

## CHAPTER 26

When Helen got downstairs a woman with shoulder-length, permed hair was jabbing a finger at the desk sergeant. 'How long do you expect to keep him here?' She was shouting. She looked to be in her late forties, wearing lemon-yellow flares and a red turtleneck top.

'As I said, enquiries are still ongoing. Now, why don't you take a seat?' The desk sergeant motioned to the row of plastic chairs behind them.

'I've been sitting there for the past half hour.'

'Miss Malone?' Helen interrupted.

The woman spun around, arched an eyebrow and looked Helen up and down. 'What do you want?'

'I'm DS Carter. My colleague told me you want to speak to someone about Jimmy's situation.'

'Situation,' she scoffed. 'That's rich. You have him caged like an animal and he's done nothing wrong. No, I don't want to speak to you, I want to speak to a proper copper.' She jabbed a manicured finger towards the desk sergeant. 'Like him.'

'I am a police officer and I know about the case, so why don't you follow me?' Helen smiled. 'And we can talk.' She noticed the sergeant shifting on the spot, trying to stifle the smile that was spreading across his face. 'If that's not good enough, take a seat and wait for one of my colleagues, but that may take a while.'

She looked like she was considering this. 'How long would I have to wait?'

'I don't know, a couple of hours, maybe more.'

'Fine.' The woman relented. 'I'll be speaking to our solicitor about this.'

Helen took her to one of the interview rooms on the ground floor. It was called an interview room, but it was more like a broom cupboard with no windows and barely wide enough for the small table and two chairs. Helen pulled out one of the chairs for Miss Malone and motioned for her to sit.

'Do you want a cup of tea?' Helen enquired.

The woman looked taken aback by her offer. She shook her head and slumped down in the seat. Helen noticed her fingers were painted the same shade as her trousers and she had a tan as though she had been on holiday recently.

Helen took a seat opposite and retrieved her notebook from her pocket.

'I want to know when Jimmy's getting out.'

'I can't answer that at the moment.'

'Why not?'

'He's still being questioned, and I don't know the outcome of that yet.'

'How long is that going to take?'

'I'm not sure yet.'

'This is really helpful.'

'Are you in a rush to go somewhere?'

'I just want out of this place.'

'Don't we all?' Helen remarked, flicking to a blank page in her book.

'This is to do with the robbery last week, isn't it? He didn't do it.'

'How do you know that?'

'He was with me the whole evening.'

'Where?'

'At my flat. We're thinking about giving our marriage another go.'

'Another go? I thought you divorced.'

'We did. But we're going to get married again.'

'Interesting.'

'We had a lot to talk about, as I am sure you'll understand.'

'I'm going to need your address. Were there any witnesses to verify this?'

'Witnesses? I am the witness, and I am telling you he was with me.'

'Are you sure?'

'Of course I am.'

'Just so we're both clear, you do realise that giving any false information would make you an accessory.'

'You calling me a liar?'

'Not at all. I just wanted to make sure you're aware — before you commit to anything.'

'Aye, well, you lot have always had it out for him.'

'Miss Malone, your on-again soon-to-be husband has a list of offences, violent offences, as long as your arm.'

'People change. That was a long time in the past, and it doesn't mean that he's done anything now.'

'Do you work, Miss Malone?'

'What?' She pursed her lips, surprised by the change of topic. 'I . . . I get by.'

'That's not what I asked.'

'I'm in between jobs at the moment. I needed a break.'

'You've been on holiday recently?'

'Why would that matter?'

'I just wondered if you ever visited Jimmy in Spain.'

'No, I . . . he didn't want me to.'

'Okay, Jimmy was photographed outside Rothberg's Jewellers two days before an attempted robbery. Can you explain that?'

'It's just coincidence.'

'Really?' Helen chuckled. 'You're going to have to do better than that.'

'No problem.' Lisa-Marie smirked and lifted her handbag onto the desk. There was a long silence as she rummaged through it.

'This proof enough for ya?' She slapped a green card onto the table.

'What's this?' Helen asked, reaching for it.

'A receipt. For one big diamond ring.'

Helen opened the card, inside was a typed receipt for two hundred pounds from Rothberg's Jewellers dated the same day that Osbourne had been photographed leaving the jewellers.

Lisa-Marie flashed her a toothy smile. 'My man is good to me.'

'This doesn't prove anything.'

'Eh?'

'It doesn't mean he wasn't involved in the robbery. Actually, it could be that he's trying to give himself a reason to check out the place he wanted to rob.'

'He wasn't. We only went there because I got a card offering a discount through the door. Even though they wouldn't accept it.'

'What card?'

Lisa-Marie made a clicking sound and glanced down at her bag. 'It's in here somewhere.'

'And this discount card didn't work?'

'Aye, they said that they'd never seen it before, but Osbourne agreed to buy me the ring because I really wanted it.'

Helen's watched in anticipation as Lisa-Marie pulled out the card. 'Here you go.'

Helen took the piece of card with gold lettering. It offered twenty per cent off all jewellery. 'And it was just put through your door like this?'

Lisa-Marie nodded.

'I'll need to keep these.' Helen turned the card over.

'Do what you like. Can I see Jimmy now?'

Helen made to leave. 'I'll see what I can do. You'll need to wait back at the reception.'

\* \* \*

After leaving Lisa-Marie with an annoyed-looking Sergeant Keaton, Helen stopped in the corridor. There was no one else around for a change. She looked back down at the card. If Lisa-Marie was telling the truth, there was a possibility that someone gave her this card so that she would go with Osbourne to that jewellers. Maybe someone was making it look like he was involved in the robbery. She puffed out her cheeks. It was hard to believe anything that came out of either of their mouths.

\* \* \*

Helen sat in her favourite spot in the canteen, offering her views of the grassy fields nearby, and far enough away from the other tables that she could hear herself think without having to listen to chatter about football or who could chug the most pints. Or whatever the daily gossip was; the station was worse than a high school sometimes. Her eyes and head felt heavy after speaking with Lisa-Marie Malone. She took a sip of coffee and shuddered, tasting mostly hot milk. She had skipped dinner last night and it had finally caught up with her. Feeling famished, she had grabbed herself a tuna roll and some crisps. She peeled the cling film off her sandwich, thinking it looked like leftovers from yesterday's lunch.

'The food in this place is getting worse.' McKinley plonked himself down in the seat opposite. 'We could go back to the café round the corner. The egg and chips are good.'

'I've got too much to do.'

'Sorry.' He took a sip of his coffee, and she could tell from his face that he had put too much sugar in it. He did it to hers often enough.

'Coffee all right?' She smiled.

He shrugged and pushed the cup to the side. 'You don't mind me joining you, do you?'

'No, I'm just trying to clear my head after speaking to Lisa-Marie Malone.'

'Didn't go well then?'

'She said they were ring shopping two days before the robbery.'

'You believe her?'

Helen considered this for a moment. 'I think I do.'

'Still doesn't mean that he wasn't planning to rob the place.'

'No. No, it doesn't.'

'Where are you going after this?'

'I'm going to visit the Quicky Save supermarket again.' McKinley checked the time on his watch.

'There's a lot to get through.' Helen looked down at the food on her tray, suddenly losing her ravenous appetite and thinking about the poor boy in hospital. She forced herself to take a mouthful of sandwich — she would need the energy later.

'I've still had no luck finding out more about Dennis's family either. I spoke to the school, but there's been an influx of new teachers since he left.'

She sucked in air through her teeth. 'None of this is good. Osbourne has an alibi and we have nothing to charge him with.'

'Unless Randall comes up with something. That's the hardest part of the job, I think.' McKinley frowned. 'Not all the grisly stuff but actually having to let someone go who you know is guilty.'

'Not the grisly stuff? You forget I was there the first time you were at the scene of a murder — your face went the same colour as the Hulk.'

'You don't forget anything, do you?'

She couldn't blame him for that though. Some of the things she saw still went around in her mind at night as clear as the day they happened.

'There must be something we can do.'

'When I was talking to Ian about the case, I mentioned wanting to track down the person who took the picture of Osbourne outside the jewellers, but he didn't seem keen. I got the feeling he was hiding something.'

'Are you thinking he orchestrated the picture being taken?' McKinley asked.

'I don't know. I have no proof. This needs stay between us.' Helen's stomach twitched and she looked away, remembering her earlier conversations with Craven about someone in the department talking to the press.

She scooped up the rest of her sandwich. 'Right, I better get going. So much to do, so little time.'

'Helen?'

'What?'

'I hope you're taking time for yourself.'

'You don't need to worry about me.'

'Don't let the job consume you. Life is sometimes like — blink and you miss it.'

She sat back down. 'Where has this come from?'

He rubbed his forehead. 'My mum's just not doing well.'

'What's wrong?'

McKinley shook his head. 'She's away for some tests today.'

Helen knew he was close to his mum and his younger siblings and had spent a lot of time looking after them.

'Let me know how it goes?'

He nodded.

'Sometimes, I think I spend all the time seeing the horrible in the world but not the good. I don't want it to change me.'

'We can't have that.'

'No.' A smile twitched on his lips. 'I'll try.'

'You need to do something to take your mind off it.'

'Maybe.'

'I'm talking from experience.'

'What about ice skating?'

He arched a brow. 'You think I should start skating again?'

'Aye.'

'It's been years though.'

'You'll feel better for it.'

'I don't know.'

'I've never been skating before.' Helen gave a small shrug.

'What, never?'

'Just never got around to it.' She rose from her chair. 'I have to go, but one evening this week you're teaching me how to skate, right?'

'I guess I could.' McKinley chuckled.

'I have no coordination, mind, and take no responsibility for injuring us both.' She gave his shoulders a squeeze.

'Fine. It's not like I have anything else to do.'

Helen's stomach ached as she climbed the stairs back up to CID. She didn't really fancy ice skating after a long shift and with ribs that still niggled, but she remembered how hard it was when her dad was ill and what she would have given just to not to think about it for a while.

# CHAPTER 27

Dennis's home was a room in a sprawling Victorian manse on Ferry Road that from first glance looked like it had been subdivided into flats. Helen could already see that the house next door was a B & B, as well as the one directly opposite. The front garden had been paved to make a car park and weeds sprouted from the cracks in the stones. A Ford Escort was parked next to the gate, and the only parking space left was barely big enough for the Mini due to boxes of rubbish and what looked like bits of scrap metal that were stacked at the side of the fence.

The front door opened and Helen squeezed out of the car, taking a deep breath of icy air to steady herself as the pain in her ribs niggled from the exertion.

A woman in her late fifties, with half-pinned, shoulder-length grey hair and an oversized, olive-coloured knitted cardigan, stood on the front porch. She gave a slight nod as Helen approached then shoved out her hand. 'My name's Arlene. I think we spoke on the phone.'

'We did.' The hand felt cold and clammy. 'I'm DS Carter and this is DC Loughton.'

'Hello.' Arlene gave a nod to Loughton. 'Dennis's room is the one up on the top floor. Feel free to have a look around.'

Helen glanced up towards a converted attic extension where a small window protruded. Nets hung limply against the window, and Helen could see what looked like a stack of books against the circular glass window. A thin layer of moss covered the tiles above.

'Thanks, how many people live here?' Loughton asked.

'I have two other men here.' She pointed to the middle window.

'And are the other residents at home at the moment?' Helen asked.

'I don't know, I don't keep that close an eye on their comings and goings.' She directed her answer to Loughton as she fished in her pockets and produced a bundle of keys. She unclipped a brass one from the ring and handed it to Helen. 'That's for his room.'

'Thanks.'

The doorway was narrow, and Arlene pressed herself against the wall to allow them to pass. The inside of the building was deceptively wider, with oak-panelled doors leading off in both directions. Helen followed a hall that smelled of chip fat and was surrounded on both sides by mould-mottled peeling wallpaper. The staircase narrowed after the second floor and Helen's shoulders brushed against both sides of the walls as she took the creaking stairs. She grabbed the handrail for support, but even that felt loose. The smell of Loughton's aftershave tickled her nostrils, making her want to sneeze.

She shivered and slotted the key into the lock. The room was larger than she has anticipated, with a single bed under the window and a teal desk with a mirror on top in the corner. Piles of clothes had been folded neatly in piles around the room. Helen stepped inside feeling a rush of cold air from the single glazed window.

'Not bad this, for a doss house.' Loughton made a show of looking around the room. 'Certainly looks like he spends a lot of money on clothes.' He bent down and felt one of the shirts. 'These are good quality. Labels are still on them too.'

'I didn't know you were into fashion.'

'I'm not, I just know quality when I see it.' He shrugged. 'Maybe they are stolen?'

'Could be, I'll go to the car and make some enquiries.'

Helen manoeuvred past him and over to the desk. Some pencils and a blank notebook that looked like it had pages pulled out of it were resting on top. There was a small waste-paper basket to the left, but that was empty too.

Helen yanked the drawer open. It was rammed full with paper, most of it ink stained, a collection of comic books and other odd bits like batteries, screws, small tools and a screwdriver with its various different attachments. Her eye caught a small box on the shelf. She lifted it down — empty, apart from a couple of dog-eared, ancient-looking family photographs. One caught Helen's attention: a dark-haired young woman clutching a baby in an ancient-looking hospital room. Helen turned the picture over. No date mark. She pulled out an evidence bag from her pocket and slipped the pictures inside. The older woman appeared in the doorway with arms crossed and an unlit cigarette dangling from her lips. 'Have you got everything you need?'

The woman moved aside for Loughton to pass.

'I think so,' Helen answered. 'How long has he been living here?'

'Past few months, never gives me any trouble and pays on time. Unlike some. I felt sorry for him — one of the reasons I let him have a room here.'

'But he was paying rent?'

'Oh, aye. Well, I'm not running a charity,' Arlene stated.

'Why did you feel sorry for him?' Helen asked.

She looked like she was considering this. 'He seemed like a good boy. He looked lost. Alone.'

Helen nodded. 'Did he tell you much about his past?'

'No, he was shy. Barely told me more than his name.'

'Did he have any female visitors?' Helen slipped the evidence bag into her pocket.

'No, I've only seen his wee pal, Robbie. I think that's his name.'

'When was he last here?'

Arlene puffed out her cheeks. 'I saw him a week ago, but he could easily have come in without me knowing.'

'What about Dennis, when did you last see him?'

'A few days ago — maybe three or four, I'm not sure. He left early in the morning.'

'Did he often leave at that time?'

'Aye.'

'Do you remember what he was wearing?'

'No, I don't. But I remember he had a gift for someone. It had a little bow on top.'

'What about a girlfriend?' Helen tried again.

'No. No one. Mind you, I'm not in all the time. ]I don't watch anyone's comings and goings.'

'I understand.' Helen shrugged.

'Do you know if he's going to be coming back?' Arlene gave a tired smile. 'I hate to ask but . . .'

'Coming back?'

'Aye.' She motioned to the room. 'Should I keep the room for him?'

Helen gave her a look. 'He's not dead yet.'

'Aye, of course. I shouldnae have asked, it's just the house costs a lot of money in upkeep.'

Helen glanced around the dilapidated interior from the peeling wallpaper to the threadbare carpet. The woman certainly wasn't spending the money on the upkeep of the property.

'Just one more question. What about his sister, does she ever visit?'

'I don't think he has a sister.' Arlene arched an eyebrow. 'He never mentioned one.'

'That's very helpful. I'm just going to see if any of your other tenants can answer some questions.'

'If you must.'

* * *

Helen braced herself then knocked on the door directly underneath Dennis's room. She could hear the faint murmur

157

of a radio set but couldn't pick out the song. The door opened a crack, pulling the security chain taught. A bald man in his late fifties peered through the gap. He eyed her warily. Helen put on her best friendly smile and held out her warrant card for inspection.

'I'm DS Carter, I'd like to ask you a few questions.'

The man nodded slowly.

'Do you know the man who lives upstairs?'

'No. I can't help you.'

'Can't or won't?'

'Take your pick, darling. I know nothing about him. Seen nothing. Heard nothing.'

Before Helen could respond, the door slammed shut in her face.

\* \* \*

Outside, Helen breathed in the fresh air. Loughton gave a small nod as she approached.

'That was strange,' Helen muttered.

'What was?'

'I tried to speak to one of the tenants underneath Dennis's room, but he looked scared to speak to me and slammed the door in my face.'

Loughton frowned.

'And Arlene also doesn't think he has a sister. We need to find out who's telling the truth and who the woman was that visited Dennis.'

## CHAPTER 28

Helen and Loughton waited outside the supermarket. It was a small, single-storied, flat-roofed building, showing signs of age, with yellow paint peeling off to reveal exposed brick and rusted shutters left half up. Helen could feel the impatience building in Loughton as he bobbed on the spot for warmth. She gave him a sideways glance as she shoved her hands in her pockets.

'What's taking him so long?' Loughton muttered.

'He's trying.' Helen motioned to the manager, who was fumbling with a stack of keys on a hoop — he was now on his fifth go. Helen took a step back and surveyed the car park. Staring at the man was only making things worse.

Loughton pulled his coat around him as they waited for the automatic doors to slide open.

The manager on the other side looked flustered and dropped the bundle of keys to the ground. He looked no more than a teenager, with greasy slicked-back hair. His shirt collar was draped awkwardly around his scrawny neck.

Loughton sighed. Helen gave him a look. In the daylight she could see the heavy bags under his eyes, and the whites had a tinge of yellow to them. He returned her look with a forced-looking smile.

'Finally,' Loughton muttered again, as the door opened with a squeal. Helen ducked under the shutters first, and she noticed Loughton wince when it was his turn to do so. A blast of hot air hit Helen in the face.

'Sorry about that.' The manager gave a nervous smile and motioned for them to follow him up the frozen food aisle, navigating around palettes and boxes that were waiting to be emptied. 'I'm normally not like this.'

'Take your time,' Helen replied. 'I can understand what a shock you must have had.'

His faded name badge said 'Ed' with 'Assistant Manager' emblazoned underneath. 'The shop's shut again today, after what happened. That's why the door was locked.'

He ushered them into the staff room, barely big enough for a few chairs. The walls were bare brick, except for a couple of faded posters about staff productivity and an empty employee of the month frame. The floor was covered in dust and boot prints. 'I thought it would be best to talk in here. Can I get you a tea or coffee?'

'No, that's okay.' Helen smiled. She motioned to one of the hard plastic chairs. 'Why don't you take a seat?'

The manager nodded and plonked himself down. Helen remained standing but Loughton sat, still favouring his thigh, Helen noticed.

'Why don't you take us through what happened?' Helen continued.

'Well, it was how I already explained on the phone.' He sighed heavily. 'And to DC Randall.'

'I understand, but we need you to go through it again for us.' Helen stepped forward. The smell of damp and mothballs tickled her nostrils.

'I'm not sleeping well at night. It was horrible. All that blood . . . I can't get it out of my head. I didn't sleep a wink last night.'

She caught Loughton rolling his eyes.

'How can someone do that to another human being?' Ed asked her.

She couldn't answer that. It wasn't a sight she was going to forget in a hurry either. The amount of murder cases where someone was murdered for something trivial was inconceivable sometimes. One of the first cases that she had worked on was a woman who was strangled because she wouldn't loan her neighbour a pound. Life is cheap, that's what her dad used to say.

'So, you were the one that found him and called the police?'

'That's right. He was just lying outside in the alley,' he explained as he bobbed his head towards two rusted-looking double doors at the other side of the room.

'What time was this?'

'Just after seven. The shop was getting ready to open, and I was just doing my bit to tidy in here. It all needs to be empty from the evening deliveries.'

'I understand. Did you see a disturbance or hear anything out of the ordinary before that?'

He made a clicking sound. 'There was something, but at the time I thought it was probably nothing . . .'

'We'd like to decide that,' Loughton added.

'Of course.' He tore at a nail. He gazed up at Helen, blinking back tears. 'This is just really hard to go through again.'

'Any little thing might just give us the clue we need to find out what happened,' Helen prompted. 'I know it's hard.'

'Well, I heard a thud against the door at quarter to seven or so, but I just assumed that some of the rubbish bags had fallen against the door, that happens a lot. It was quite loud and gave me a fright at the time.'

'Could it have been someone trying to get in?'

'Possibly, but I didn't think much about it at the time, like I said. I've never seen anyone in the alley before.'

'Okay and what happened when you went outside?'

'It was raining and dark, so I couldn't see much at all. I hate going out there, so I try and get it over with quickly. I was about to chuck the bag on the pile when I felt something against my foot.' He swallowed. 'I looked down and that's when I saw him lying there with all that blood.'

'Did you touch the victim or try and perform any first aid?'

'No, no way! He looked dead to me and I am not good with blood. I ran back inside and called the police.'

'Did you see anyone else in the alley?'

'It was too dark to see but . . .'

'Go on.'

'I thought I saw a shape, a figure—'

'Male or female?'

'I think it was male from the shape of the shoulders.' He motioned to his own. 'But I might have imagined it. I was panicking.'

'What happened to the shape?'

'I looked down at the boy and back up again and it was gone.'

'Did you hear any strange sounds?'

The manager slumped down in one of the chairs and placed his head in his hands.

'I know this is hard. Please take your time.'

'If it was a person, they would have seen me, they were looking straight at me. Do you think I'm in danger?' He looked at her wide-eyed. 'They would know I was a witness!'

'We have nothing to suggest anything like that now.' Helen tried to give him her best 'everything is fine' smile. 'And as you say, it was very dark.'

'I can't believe this is happening. You don't expect this, do you, working in a shop?'

'No, I guess not.'

'I only work here part-time to pay for university. I even tried to get today off because I couldn't face it, but the boss wouldn't let me. He wants the shop tidied before he reopens.' He sniffed and rubbed his nose with his sleeve.

Helen paused for a moment. 'Did you see the victim in the shop the previous evening?'

He shook his head.

'What about anyone acting suspiciously?'

'No, sorry.'

Loughton fished in his pockets for his cigarettes and offered one to the manager, who took it and shakily placed it to his lips.

'Thanks, my nerves are shot.' He took a long hard drag and exhaled the smoke slowly through his nostrils, holding the cigarette close to his chest, as if someone was going to snatch it away from him.

'Did you see anyone outside acting suspiciously?' Loughton asked.

He shook his head and took another drag, the air in the dingy concrete room thickening with tobacco smoke.

'Are these the only doors to the alley?'

'Yes.'

'Do you have a list of employees for the shop?'

'Aye, but the laddie didn't work here. I've never seen him before in my life but I'll never forget his face.'

'That's very helpful, thank you.' Helen stepped past him. 'That's everything that we need right now.'

He looked relieved.

'Just one other thing though.' She pointed to his scraped knuckles. 'How did you get those?'

He looked down at them and flexed his fingers. 'It's from unloading the crates.'

'Thank you. We're just going to have a look outside, is that okay?'

'Aye, whatever you need to do.'

Helen pushed open the metal door, a blast of cold air hit her, and she shivered.

* * *

Loughton arched an eyebrow. 'What are you thinking?'

'I don't know yet.' She knelt beside the door. There were two bolts securing the door at the top and bottom, both apparently undamaged.

'Are you thinking he ran down here with a plan to get into the shop?' Loughton prodded.

'I'm not sure yet.' Helen moved around to the other side. It was scratched and warped and the paint was peeling from it. 'It's dented here.' She looked up towards the top of the alley. 'Dennis is local, presumably knows the area, so why would he run down a dead end?'

After the briefest hesitation, Helen walked past the remnants of the police cordon and through to the alley where Dennis was found. Bags had been stacked high against the left-hand side of the graffiti-stained wall. A faded chocolate bar wrapper fluttered at their feet.

The alleyway was smaller than she had remembered from her last visit. The smell of rotten food and vomit covered them like a blanket. Loughton cleared his throat behind her; she could feel his hot breath on the back of her neck. She glanced back at him.

'Sorry,' he muttered and took a sideways step, leaving a small distance between them.

'Are you all right?' she asked. 'I noticed you weren't looking too good back there.'

'My head's pounding. Think I'm coming down with that Russian flu or something.'

'Well, don't get too close to me then,' Helen countered and offered him a small smile. 'I've got too much work to do.'

She looked around. Blocks of grey concrete flats dotted the landscape. It was hard to believe that no one had seen anything.

Helen was glad to be heading back to the car, which sat alone outside the supermarket. Hopefully, the forensic reports would be waiting for her on her desk and she could make some actual progress with this case. She fumbled in her pockets for her keys.

'I could do with a drink after that.' Loughton rubbed his temples. 'I've got a splitting headache.' He stopped and nodded towards the pub across the street.

'At this time?' Helen wiped her boot on the grass. 'Too much to drink last night?'

'Not enough to drink, more like.' Loughton frowned.

'That bad?'

'You don't know the half of it.'

'Do you want to talk about it then?'

Her comment had caught him off guard, and he pursed his lips.

'I mean, a problem shared is a problem halved and all that.' She slipped her keys back into her pocket but kept them in her hand.

'I might take you up on that.' He gave her a half-smile. Helen instinctively looked down at his thigh. He winced as they stepped over a pile of rubbish.

'It's fine, it just hurts all the time,' he explained.

'That must be hard.'

'You get used to it.' He gave her a thin smile. 'Alcohol helps too.' He nodded towards the pub across the road.

An elderly man with a folded newspaper under his arm headed inside. Helen's stomach grumbled.

'It has been a while since lunch, so I suppose we could stop for a snack.'

'Great.'

'And an orange juice,' she warned him.

'Orange juice will do me just fine, although I've heard they do a good Irish coffee.'

After they were settled with their drinks, Helen caught the faint whiff of whisky. He looked up and offered a thin smile. 'This place looked nicer from outside.'

Helen nodded. The pub looked pre-war and hadn't had a lick of paint since. Helen sipped her warm orange juice. The glass felt greasy in her hand. He rubbed his thigh and looked like was trying to hide that he was in pain.

'Does it really hurt all the time?'

Loughton looked like he was taken aback by the question and nodded.

'That must be hard.'

'You'd be surprised what you can get used to.'

Helen looked down at his gold wedding band. 'Did you meet your wife before you joined?'

He nodded. 'I really wanted the promotion to get us a new house. We were going to have . . . It doesn't matter now.'

'A family?' Helen asked.

Loughton nodded again.

'I'm sorry.'

'It's fine, a long time ago now. After Leonard died and I was left like this . . . things just weren't the same. I changed. She couldn't love me anymore. She died not long after . . . The only thing that I'm living for now is getting justice for Leonard and his wife.'

'Aye.' Helen gulped her drink, feeling Loughton's eyes on her.

'What did Osbourne's ex-wife have to say for herself?'

'She gave an alibi for him.'

'No surprise there.' The words dripped with venom. 'Of course, we can't believe a word she says. He's guilty.'

Helen thought better of mentioning the receipt for the jewellers until she was able to make more enquiries.

* * *

Helen draped her jacket on the back of her chair. A couple of files had been added to the stack on her desk. She sighed and skimmed through them. Blood-splatter analysis — it told her nothing that she didn't already know. Dennis was shot at close range and staggered back a few steps to where they found him. The only blood found in the alley was the same blood type as his. She turned the page — no fingerprints either. The rain would have washed them away even if the perpetrator wasn't wearing gloves.

She dropped the folder back onto the pile and retrieved the photographs from her pocket. Terry McKinley was trying to find out everything possible about Dennis's history.

Hopefully he would have something for her soon. It was hard to believe he had no family. She lifted the receiver to dial the number for the ward. It rung out. She'd try again shortly.

* * *

Loughton sparked up a cigarette as he waited for a Morris Minor to trundle down the lane. He crossed the road towards the condemned grey tenements, most of them with boarded windows and soot-stained brickwork. There was a playpark on the other side of the courtyard, darkened by the shadow of the looming crane that stretched towards the mottled sky. A solitary swing groaned as it swayed in the wind. The door to the stairwell was off its hinges and he had to shove it aside to gain access. Loughton made his way up the winding staircase to the flat and drew sharp breaths as icy pain stretched around his thigh, clamping down on the muscle. He took a long drag on his fag to take his mind off the pain.

He rattled on the door and took a step back. He flicked his butt end off the bannister as the door opened slowly and an elderly woman with cropped, wispy grey hair peered at him through thick-rimmed glasses. Recognition dawned on her creased features.

'You're—'

He nodded and held out his warrant card. 'Do you mind if I come in?'

She gave a small shrug and turned on her heels. He followed her through to a mould-speckled lounge with foggy windows and a solitary wicker sofa.

'It's a bit different to when you were last here.'

'I can see that,' Loughton muttered.

'They're meant to move me on to Wester Hailes, but this is where I was born and where I intend to . . .'

'There can't be many people left around here.'

'There isn't.' A sigh heaved from her body as she sat down. 'What can I do for you?'

Loughton hesitated before speaking. 'I wanted to speak to you about Gina Osbourne.'

'What about her?'

'Have you seen her?'

'No . . . No, I haven't.'

Loughton could hear the hesitation in her voice. 'If you haven't seen her recently then when was the last time?'

'I can't remember.'

Loughton clenched his jaw in frustration. 'Jimmy Osbourne is back from Spain. Did you know that?'

She shook her head.

'But you were close with Gina. You told me that you thought of her as a daughter.'

'I did.'

'So, you expect me to believe she hasn't been in touch?'

'What do you want with Gina?'

'She might be able to help me regarding a serious incident involving Jimmy. I know she's had her issues with Osbourne in the past. She'd be glad to see him back behind bars.'

'She can't.'

'You've spoken with her?'

'No . . . not for a while.'

'When?'

There was a long pause.

'When?' Loughton repeated.

'Eight . . . nine years ago.'

'Nothing since?'

She shook her head. 'She had kept in a touch — letters and things — but they stopped. Haven't heard a peep since. It wasn't like her.'

'Do you still have the letters?'

'Sorry.'

'Do you know where she was living?'

'It was so long ago.'

\* \* \*

Loughton swallowed a couple of pain killers as he headed back to the car. *What a waste of time*, he thought, and he was still no closer to finding Gina.

## CHAPTER 29

DCI Murphy slapped a hand down on McKinley's desk, knocking one of the files McKinley had been going through to the floor, the pages spreading out in all directions. Murphy pretended not to notice, but his smile gave him away.

Helen glared at Murphy knowing it would do no good, but she couldn't help herself. She rose from her seat and scooped up the papers. Feeling Murphy's eyes on her as she bundled them up, she could see from the corner of her eye that he'd tilted his head to get a better look as she bent over. These were the types of situation that made her glad she didn't have to wear a skirt anymore.

'Where is he?' Murphy asked her, as he motioned to Craven's office.

'Who?' Helen asked, knowing exactly who he meant. The blinds in the inspector's office were drawn, and Helen hadn't seen him all morning. Not that she would tell him that.

Murphy's eyes narrowed. 'Who do you think? The Pope? Or that Oliver Reid all you woman seem to like?'

DC Randall snorted and shifted in his seat. Murphy gave him a wink.

'He was here not long ago. I know he was out on a job.' Helen shrugged. 'Don't feel that you need to wait here though,

I can let him know you're looking for him.' Helen dropped the folder back on the desk and onto Murphy's hand.

He flinched and pulled back. 'That's a shame. We seem to be like ships in the night.'

'Is that so?' Helen muttered.

'Well, every time I come down these stairs, I've always just missed him. Anyone would think he was avoiding me.'

Helen nodded towards the case board. 'We've all been exceptionally busy.'

With a sigh DCI Murphy loosened his tie and perched on the edge of McKinley's desk. He was still smiling at Helen. 'I had told him that I wanted him at the briefing this morning.'

'I normally attend those.'

'Not anymore.' Murphy shrugged.

Helen's stomach tightened. 'Can I ask why?'

Murphy frowned at her. 'Because I asked Detective Inspector Craven to attend them.'

McKinley exchanged a look with Helen as he handed Murphy a mug of coffee. Murphy grabbed it without acknowledgement and took an uncommonly loud sip. Helen expected he did it more to be annoying than anything else.

'There is another matter I want to discuss.' He pointed a finger towards the board behind Helen's head. 'The papers are having a field day with this story — gunman loose around Edinburgh, no motive, no clues.'

Randall coughed. 'I've interviewed all the staff from the supermarket. No one recognised the victim.'

'I'm going to the hospital later,' Helen added. 'We're still doing door-to door enquiries, but nothing's turned up yet.'

'I have a press conference this afternoon.' Murphy looked expectantly at her.

Helen nodded and went back to her own desk. She fumbled through the notes on her desk until she found the right page. 'I have a preliminary report from the hospital. There was some charring on the skin around the wound.'

'What does that mean?' Murphy replied, looking unimpressed.

'It looks like the victim was shot at point blank range. I have some photos too; the wound resembles a kind of star pattern.' She held out the report for him.

'Aye, I can see that.' He looked down at the report.

'That comes from the gases being released from the gun at close contact, and it means the barrel of the gun was touching him when he was shot—'

The phone rang, pulling Helen from the conversation. She snatched it up.

'Helen Carter.'

'I have a lad down here that wants to speak to you.'

'Who?'

'He won't give his name.' There was silence on the end of the line. 'Wee fella about eighteen with short brown hair.'

'I'll be right down.'

## CHAPTER 30

'Robbie.' Helen waved as she walked towards him.

He gave a small nod. He had his hands in his pockets and bobbed on the spot, as though he was ready to run out the door at any minute. He had a purple welt on his left cheek.

'How did you do that?'

'Oh . . .' He touched his finger to it. 'I . . . when I was playing football.'

'Shall we have a little chat?'

He gave a half-shrug. 'Will you tell my dad that I was here? He wouldn't be happy.'

'No, we can keep this between me and you.'

'Good.' A sigh heaved from his body and his shoulders slumped forward. 'I don't want to make my dad angry.'

'Does he get angry a lot?'

'Sometimes, but he only wants what's best for me . . . He doesn't really like the police either.'

'Do you know why?'

'Do you think Dennis will be okay?' He was wearing an oversized jumper and tugged at the sleeves.

'I'm not a doctor, but he has suffered a serious injury.'

'I want to go and see him, but I don't like hospitals.'

'Why did you come to see me?' She led him down to the canteen. It was just after the lunch rush, so apart from a couple of typists from the floor below, the place was deserted.

He took a seat in the middle aisle and kept his head down until she arrived back with two teas and some chocolate biscuits. He looked like he was going to take one then thought better of it.

'Help yourself.' Helen slid the tray towards him.

He sniffed and dabbed at his nose with his sleeve, and as he lent forward she caught a whiff of oil.

'Are you a mechanic?'

'No.'

'I just thought, since we saw you working on your bike . . .'

He shook his head again.

'Do you know anything that might help us find out what happened to Dennis?'

'I don't want to get him in trouble.'

'He can't really get in more trouble than he already is.'

'I don't want anyone else to get hurt.'

'Then let me help.'

'Okay.' He took a breath to steady himself. 'Dennis was worried this would happen.'

'Did he say why?'

'Someone was after him. I think he got himself involved in something dodgy. He suddenly had money in his pockets, and he seemed different.'

'Different how?'

'Started off as him being more confident, and he got himself a girlfriend.'

'Do you know her name or where she lives?'

'I never met her, and he wouldn't say much about her.'

'What did he say though?'

'Only that I wouldn't know her. I saw a photo though. She has blonde hair and looked a little bit older than us.' Robbie glanced around the canteen. 'He wanted me to drive him.'

'Drive him?'

'The morning, he . . .' His voice quivered. 'I feel so guilty.'

'You weren't to know what would happen to Dennis.'

'He was so angry at me that I didn't, but my dad had grounded me.'

'Where did he want you to drive him to?'

'Do you think it matters?'

'Yes, anything might help us find out who did this and why.'

'It was to a warehouse out of town.'

'Which one?'

'He never said.' He rubbed his bruised cheek and clambered to his feet. 'I can't help anymore. I'm sorry. I shouldn't even be here.'

'Okay.' Helen relented. 'But you know where to find me.'

Robbie nodded and kept his head down as he left the canteen. Helen clambered to her feet and downed the last of her drink. Robbie hadn't given her much to go on, but she had a few things to check.

* * *

A couple of hours later, Helen had trawled through the incident and intelligence reports for anything that fitted what Robbie had mentioned and found nothing useful. She also had her map book open — there was one warehouse close to Edinburgh but that had shut down a few months back. Her shoulders ached from being hunched over and she could feel the brewing of a headache behind her eyes.

With a sigh McKinley hung up his telephone.

She looked up and met his eyes. It was just the two of them in the office this afternoon.

'What is it?' Helen asked.

'It took me a long time, but I have details of the car crash that killed Dennis's mother.'

'Good work.'

His mouth tightened as though he was thinking about how to word something.

'Just come out with it, Terry.' Helen stood and stretched out her shoulders.

McKinley nodded. 'You're not going to like this.'

'What?' Helen demanded.

'Dennis does . . . did have a sister.'

'Did?' Helen's heart thudded. 'What do you mean, *did*?'

'She died in the car crash and he has no other siblings.'

'Who was that we spoke to in the hospital?'

McKinley shrugged. 'That's what we need to find out.'

Helen grabbed her jacket from the back of the chair. 'She gave us an address, so let's go.'

## CHAPTER 31

Loughton meandered through traffic towards the station. Pain dulled the anger that settled in the pit of his stomach. His mind wandered back to the last meeting with Leonard's widow. She hadn't wanted to see him, and it was only when he had told her about Osbourne's involvement in her husband's death that she had eventually agreed. That was when he had promised to make Osbourne pay one way or the other. Loughton wouldn't forget the faces of his two boys in a hurry — they were growing up without a dad, their poor shell of a mother struggling to cope. He'd go back to the station and try and track down Paula — that would take his mind off it.

\* \* \*

Helen made a clicking sound as they pulled up outside the dilapidated, fire-wrecked shell of a building on the outskirts of Leith. Soot stained the crumbling brickwork, all of the windows were smashed and the gardens at the front were overgrown and piled high with rubble. A sign said the site had been acquired and new work was to begin soon on luxury flats.

'Safe to say she's not living here,' Helen muttered.

'I'll see if I can find out who used to live here in case that gives us any clues.'

Helen nodded and turned the key in the engine. 'See what you can find and quick.'

* * *

When she got back to her flat that evening Helen slumped down on the sofa, having lost her appetite. The builders had stopped work for the day, so that was a small mercy. She struggled to get comfortable on the sofa. The cushions had started to sag, and she made a mental note to go sofa shopping at the weekend. She glanced around the room; she would have to decide soon if she was going to sell this place — if not, she might as well redecorate. The oak panelling that was in most of the rooms looked stained and mottled. The lime-coloured curtains that were draped over the window looked saggy and let in the light.

The kettle squealed, and she sighed, clambering to her feet.

A few minutes later, she returned to the living room with a cup of tea and a plate of digestives and set them down on the table. Her mind returned to the hospital as her eyes drifted towards the kitchen door, and she noticed her box of art supplies that she had been using as a door wedge.

She rummaged through the box — her heart constricted when her fingers hit the paint box that had been inscribed by Ted in ornate gold writing. She traced the words with her fingers: 'To Helen — with all my love, Ted.' She smiled. That had been a good day, spent perusing the art galleries. She'd never used the paints, maybe because she didn't want to ruin them. She retrieved her pencils and notepad and began sketching the woman she had met in the hospital.

# CHAPTER 32

Loughton had got himself to the station an hour before his shift was due to start the next morning. He retrieved a couple of aspirins from his desk drawer and washed them down with the dregs of his cold coffee.

Randall burped under his breath and crushed the greasy wrapper that had contained his bacon roll into the bin.

'Where did you get that from?' Loughton asked. His stomach grumbled — he could never eat first thing in the morning but wouldn't turn down a bacon roll now.

'There's a wee greasy spoon around the corner, better than the canteen.' He picked a bit from his teeth. 'The woman there does it the way I like, nice and crispy.'

Loughton pushed away from his desk. He had spent the last couple of hours of his previous shift going through the lists of known criminals, looking to see if his lovely date, Paula, was in the file. If she was, he would have her address. He could feel Randall watching him and tossed the paperwork aside.

'Is the inspector due in?' Loughton asked, rising to his feet.

'I think he's up in Murphy's office for their morning meeting.'

'Do you think he'll mind if I use his phone?'

'There's a phone on your desk.'

'This is private.'

'It's your funeral.'

'I'll take my chances.' He smiled. 'And I'll be quick.'

Randall grunted. 'I wouldn't let him catch you.'

The smell of stale alcohol and tobacco hit him as he pushed open the door then flicked on the light. Randall was watching his every move. He picked up the receiver and dialled the number; it was picked up on the first couple of rings.

'It's Ian here.' Randall was still staring at him, and he turned away to face the window.

'All right, mate? How's things?'

'Not good.'

'Oh.'

'That bird you set me up with, Paula?'

'Go well did it?'

'She emptied my wallet.'

There was silence on the other end of the line. 'Are you sure? That doesn't sound like her.'

'Of course I'm sure.'

'I'm sorry but—'

He kept his voice calm and level. 'No buts, I want it back. I want to speak to her.'

'I don't know where she is.'

'You know how to contact her though.'

'Aye, the wife does.'

'I couldn't find anything under her name, so she must be using an alias.'

'She goes by the name Paula, but her name is Pavla. Her mum's foreign or something. Is it worth all this effort?'

'Aye, it bloody is. You normally see her down the club?'

'Sometimes, normally on a Friday night. I thought you'd be a good fit. She worked with Tina in the factory until a few months ago. She's a lovely lassie.'

'Where does she live?'

'I don't know the exact address, but it's somewhere up Junction Street.'

'I've got to go, but if she turns up, tell her I'm looking for her.'

'Tina's going to be gutted. This was her idea to set you up.'

Loughton turned around as Helen entered the office, looking windswept and exhausted. He gave a wave, which she didn't bother to return. She was searching her desk and looked annoyed.

As Loughton exited Craven's office, Helen remarked, 'The DCI won't like you using his office.'

'Oh, I wasn't using it . . . I just needed to make a phone call.' He crossed over to the tea station and began spooning coffee into a mug.

'Even so.'

Loughton rubbed his face. 'He doesn't need to know though, does he?'

Before Helen could answer, a flustered McKinley appeared in the doorway. Loughton went back to stirring his coffee.

'I've done some digging.'

'Sounds ominous,' Helen replied. She shoved her chair aside to make space for him, and he dropped a folder onto the desk.

'Some interesting facts about Robbie's dad.'

\* \* \*

Helen skim-read the file. Three arrests for assault. She flicked the page — those were over ten years ago though. 'Maybe explains his reluctance with the police.'

Loughton came over and peered over her shoulder, supping his coffee loudly. Helen grimaced, a shiver trailing her spine.

'Sorry,' he muttered.

The trill sound of the telephone echoed throughout the office. Randall snatched it up. 'We're needed in the incident room now,' he explained.

* * *

The clock was ticking. Detective Inspector Craven paced the cramped incident room as Helen got him up to speed with all the latest reports. It hadn't taken long. Randall scribbled notes on the giant sheet of paper that had been tacked to the wall. It was something he did to help him think, although Helen struggled to read his handwriting. The rest of the officers had their pens poised in one hand and cigarettes in the other. Helen looked up at the small window at the top of the room to see if it had stopped raining, but the glass had misted up. She sighed, struggling to get comfortable in the chair.

'Do you want to say something?' Randall turned to face her, a look of annoyance etched on his face. He always did this whenever he was in a mood — tried to take it out on her.

'I didn't say anything.' Helen slid her cold mug of coffee away. 'But what we do know is he was shot sometime early in the morning. His landlady saw him leave the property around half six. He left carrying a gift box.' She flicked to the next page in her notebook. 'Nothing like that was found at the scene.'

Craven dragged a hand through his hair. 'There's going to be a press conference this afternoon. A shooting in Edinburgh city centre will attract a lot of public attention.'

Papers rustled and Loughton muttered something to McKinley which Helen couldn't hear. She looked down at her own notebook. There wasn't much that she could add at this point.

'All the bins in the area have been examined and nothing was found.' Loughton shook his head. 'Door-to-door enquiries have been useless too, no one has seen or heard anything.'

'They're scared, more like,' Randall muttered.

'The victim was also missing his jacket,' Helen added. 'I think there's some significance in that.'

'How so?' Craven asked.

'Well, maybe there was something about it that would identify the attacker? We also know that he may have had a girlfriend. Perhaps she made the jacket for him or customised it.'

'That's good.'

'The woman we met at the hospital visiting him is possibly our mysterious girlfriend, based on the description given to us by Robbie Fields. We now know his sister is dead.'

'What about him?' Craven asked.

'Robbie's father has given him an alibi for the time of the shooting. I think there's a chance he knows more than he's letting on, but I don't think he's involved.'

'What about the father?' Craven questioned.

'Well, William Fields, Robbie's father, doesn't like Dennis very much — he also has previous charges for assault. He just seems like an overprotective father at this stage, who knows? I wasn't convinced by their alibi, but Robbie seemed genuinely shocked. Robbie also has bruises on him that I think his father is behind.'

'I've had a look at buses from Dennis's address to the supermarket where he was found. There are three, fifteen minutes apart, that he could have taken.'

Craven spoke to McKinley. 'Find out about those. Maybe the bus drivers might remember something suspicious.'

McKinley nodded.

'I think the key is finding out who the woman was that visited Dennis in hospital. She may know who put him there.'

'She didn't look much older than Dennis, so I think it's worth trying the local college.'

Helen pulled out a sheet of paper from her notebook. 'I met her in the hospital, so I've done a sketch of her.' She slid the charcoal-and-chalk-coloured drawing across the desk.

'That's the woman from the hospital?' Loughton queried, taking the picture. 'How did you get this? I've never seen a composite drawing like this.'

'It's from memory, so I wouldn't say it's entirely accurate.'

Loughton took a close look at the drawing and made a clicking noise. 'You did this?' he asked.

Helen nodded. 'It helps me clear my mind.'

'How?' He kept his gazed fixed on the image. 'It's so lifelike.'

'I . . . I used to sketch portraits.' Helen shrugged. 'A long time ago.'

'I didn't know you were an artist.' Loughton smoothed out the dog-eared corner.

'I'm not.'

'You are.'

Helen felt heat rush to her cheeks and took a sip of coffee to steel herself.

'Great, we'll get that circulated in the newspapers,' Craven interjected.

'There's also a few cafés and places nearby that I think would be worth checking.'

'Agreed. Terry, you can do that.'

McKinley nodded. 'I'll get right on it.'

* * *

Helen found McKinley in the records room. He looked like he had been there for hours. His orange shirt was creased at the shoulders and elbows, and stubble peppered his chin. With no windows, the room was stiflingly hot all through the year. Some of the records were in the process of being computerised, and the bulky machines took up so much room that they added to the claustrophobic feeling. Helen knew it wouldn't be long until these machines were on every desk. There was a small fan on the desk, but all it seemed to do was shift the hot air about.

'How are you getting on?' she asked.

He flicked his dishevelled mop of hair out of his face. He had a mound of papers in front of him with a telephone on top and a slip of paper covered in writing that Helen couldn't decipher. Helen stepped further into the room and dust tickled her sinuses. She closed the door and edged closer to the desk. He slid the folders across so she could see and she caught a whiff of his stale coffee breath.

'I'm still trying to find out more about Dennis's family, but it's been really difficult. So far all I can still tell you is what we already know, that his sister was Barbara Levitt, but she died in 1965 along with their mother. She was a year older than Dennis, but Dennis had already been given up for adoption at six weeks old, so he grew up in children's homes and moved around a lot.'

Helen looked down at the notes. A car accident. She shook her head. 'Keep looking.'

## CHAPTER 33

As Helen was about to make her way back up to the CID office, the desk sergeant Robert Keaton called after her. She stopped in her tracks and held her breath. She could always carry on and pretend that she hadn't heard, but he'd probably just chase after her.

'Sergeant! Sergeant Carter,' he called out again more forcefully, and she could see from the corner of her eye that he had stepped out from behind the counter.

She could also see that he didn't look happy about something. She turned towards him and gave him a nod. The station was buzzing with life this evening. She manoeuvred passed a drunk being booked in; he had practically fallen asleep and was being held up by two exhausted-looking officers.

'I've been trying to speak to you all afternoon.' He gestured towards his office. She followed him in and waited for him to close the door.

A pit of nausea opened up in her stomach. She had a gut feeling that this was a conversation she wanted to avoid.

He looked like he was thinking how to word what he had to say.

'This is about Jimmy Osbourne, isn't it?'

Keaton nodded. 'We had to let him go a couple of hours ago.'

'You should have spoken to me before you released him.' Helen stepped forward, digging her nails into her palm, surprising herself at her own anger.

Keaton frowned. 'I stalled as long as possible, but we had nothing to charge him with.'

'There's the photograph of him leaving the jewellers after the robbery.'

'That photograph was too grainy to say for certain that it was Osbourne, and you know it. He also has an alibi.'

'You could have given us more time.'

Keaton smirked and slid his paperwork aside. 'What else did you expect me to do?'

'You could have spoken to me first.'

'I tried, all afternoon.'

'Okay.' Helen rubbed her forehead.

'My hands were tied. I did what I could, and you can't say you didn't know the score either. That's why you've been avoiding me all afternoon.'

'He's guilty.'

'I need more than your say-so on that.' He looked back down at his papers. 'Now if you don't mind, I have to get back to this.'

She stood in the doorway and sighed. He was right, and she would have done the same thing, not that she liked to admit it. She headed back up the stairs, a headache niggling behind the back of her eyes. She had her own paperwork to get through too now, and there was no point in going home just to sit there frustrated.

## CHAPTER 34

Nurses' sandals slapped against the floor, and the wheels on the trolley they were pushing squealed in protest. Helen stepped aside as they brushed past, not appearing to notice her as they slid their patient into the lift. From where she stood, Helen took in the artwork that adorned the walls. A small golden plaque told her that they were created by children from the local primary, supposedly to cheer the place up. She stopped in front of a chalk forest scene. It had been a long time since she'd done any real art of her own, apart from the police sketches. In the past, hardly a day went by when she wasn't sketching or painting. She lowered her gaze, her mother's disappointment filling the silence. 'Why join the police when you could go to art school? You're so talented, why waste that?'

She swallowed hard and pushed open the double doors to the ward. The nurse she had spoken to previously was at the nurse's station in the centre of the room. When she spotted Helen, she gave a weary-looking nod. She looked pale and her face was blotched with red. Helen surveyed the ward. Beds with yellow curtains lined both sides of the room. A lump formed in her throat when she noticed Dennis's bed was now being stripped clean. The smell of cleaning fluid hung heavily in the air. They would have telephoned the station if anything had happened, but then again, the message might not have got through to her.

She blinked and she was back there again in the alley, smelling the blood, hearing the rats scramble for scraps and their claws scratching in the puddles. She pushed the thought from her mind and breathed deeply to steady herself. She heard the words that her mother had said to her before she started at the policing college: 'You're going to see some horrendous things, why put yourself through it?'

'He's still with us.' The nurse closed a patient file. 'He's been moved into isolation. He had a hard night.'

'I am glad to hear that — that he's still with us, I mean.' Helen stepped aside to let a harassed-looking doctor past. He snatched up the file without a word.

'I'll get an update from the doctor shortly.'

'Has he had any more visitors?' Helen asked.

'There hasn't been anyone since you were last here.'

Helen nodded. 'I wanted to ask you about the woman who visited him.'

'I'll try my best.'

'Did she tell you anything about herself?'

The nurse grimaced. Then after a brief hesitation shook her head.

'We have reason to believe that she is not Dennis's sister.'

She shifted her weight. 'I didn't have any reason to believe that she wasn't. I mean, she seemed genuine.'

The nurse looked like she was trying to remember more details as she stepped around from the counter.

'Do you remember how she came to visit Dennis? Did she know he was here?'

'We didn't know who he was at the time, but she came in and said she had been phoning around the hospitals and it sounded like the unknown boy might be her brother. She seemed distraught.'

'Do you remember how long she stayed?'

'No, I can't say for certain.'

She bobbed her head towards the room he had been moved to. 'She looked heartbroken, bless her. She was crying, I remember that.'

'Did she say if she would be back?' Helen asked.

'I'm sorry . . . I can't honestly remember, but I think she said she would.'

'Thanks.'

'I think she asked about visiting times, but I see so many patients . . .'

'No, I understand. Has she telephoned to check his progress?'

'Not as far as I am aware.'

'I don't suppose he's going to wake up soon?'

'He's still critical, but he is a fighter.' She gave a small shrug. 'Hopefully he'll surprise us.'

'If she does visit again, can you let us know?'

'Of course.'

## CHAPTER 35

Helen stepped into the private room off the ward. It was big enough for two beds, but today Dennis was the sole occupant. The steady beep of machines next to his head echoed in the silence. He was surrounded by a web of wires and machines with dials that Helen couldn't even begin to understand. She stepped forward — his hands were swollen, his eyes screwed shut and the dim light made him look nothing more than a child. Helen blew out a sigh and slumped down into one of the chairs. Her ribs were throbbing, and she had a horrible taste in her mouth that she tried to swallow away.

'Should I come back another time?' the soft voice asked from behind. She recognised it.

'No, Robbie, it's okay.' She clambered up from the seat.

He nodded but made no move to cross the threshold. 'I should have come sooner but—' He fixed his gaze on Dennis.

'You're here now though, that's what matters.'

'Do you think?'

'Of course.' Helen gave a small smile.

'I can't imagine he really knows what's going on around him. I've heard you can speak to someone in a coma and they can hear you, but . . .'

'There's no harm in giving it a go.' Helen gestured to the seat.

'I don't know.' Robbie's hands started to shake.

'Having his friend here might do him some good.'

'My dad says I'm wasting my time.' He blinked and brushed away a tear that rolled down his cheek.

'I have heard that hearing a friendly voice can help.'

'Do you think he'll get better?' Robbie asked. He shifted in the chair, and looked like he was struggling to get comfortable.

'I don't know, I'm not a doctor, but he is strong and young.' Helen blinked away the image of finding him bleeding out on the rain-soaked ground.

'My mum came in for an operation. It was just a routine thing, nothing to worry about, they said.'

Helen drew a breath and stuck her hands tightly in her pocket.

'She never came out again. She died on the operating table.' Robbie shuddered.

'I'm sorry,' Helen answered.

There was a long pause.

'Dad's scared of losing me too. I don't think he would cope without me.'

'It must be hard with your dad not liking Dennis?' Helen asked.

'Sometimes, but my dad thinks everything is a bad influence. He doesn't like anyone.'

'My dad could be tough too sometimes,' Helen said.

'He hasn't always been like this. It's been five years since my mum died, and Dennis helped me through it. I don't know what I would have done without him.'

'He sounds like a good friend.'

'He is, one of the best. He's had it tough all his life, but he just gets on with it and makes the best of things.' He looked up at her, tears welling in his eyes. 'I don't think I can cope losing him too.'

'He's in the best place and getting good treatment. Things advance so quickly . . .' Helen struggled — the last thing she wanted to do was give him false hope, but the lad in the bed had surprised her so far with his will to live.

'Do you think you'll catch who did this?' His jaw tightened. 'Dennis doesn't deserve this, whatever he's done. No one deserves this.'

'We're doing everything we can.'

She drew in a breath. She would need to tread carefully. 'Did Dennis have any other friends he would spend time with?'

Robbie glanced away. 'There was this one time. Maybe three or four months ago. When I was visiting Dennis. This man turned up and I don't think Dennis was expecting him or wanted to see him. He was wanting Dennis to do something.'

'Do you remember his name or what he looked like?'

Robbie shook his head. 'I left as soon as he arrived. I didn't get a good look at him.'

'Was he about your age?'

Robbie frowned. 'No. He was older than us. It's hard because he was wearing big aviator glasses and a black woolly hat.'

'Was he thin, tall? Overweight?' Helen didn't like to prompt in case she put words in his mouth, but she needed more information.

'Just . . . I don't know . . . average.'

'Did he say anything?'

'Not a word.'

'Did Dennis say anything about him after?'

He swallowed hard. 'No, and when I asked him about it he told me he couldn't talk about it.'

'Did you ever see Dennis with a gun?'

Robbie stiffened in his seat. 'He used to have a BB gun, or I think it was one, I'm not sure.' A machine next to Robbie's head gave a loud beep and he flinched.

Helen let out the breath she was holding once the machine went back to making its usual noise.

'I haven't seen it since the man visited . . . I don't think Dennis had it anymore,' Robbie whispered.

She said her goodbyes and left him with his friend. She'd got all she was going to out of him.

Walking back to the car Helen dragged a hand through her hair. Robbie hadn't given her much to go on in regard to this mysterious man, but Helen couldn't shake the suspicion that he might have something to do with why Dennis was shot.

* * *

After the hospital Helen took a detour back to her flat for a much-needed snack and a rest. She found an unopened jar of fish paste that she couldn't remember buying, but it smelled all right, so she spread that on a couple of slices of toast, then cut and cored a Granny Smith. She needed a chance to unwind for a while — she was missing something on this case, and she needed to work out what. She also needed to speak to Dennis's landlady again and see if she had seen this mystery man.

She bit into her toast and brushed the crumbs off her lap, dropping the empty plate on the coffee table. She lifted out her pencil case and pad. It would be impossible to draw an accurate sketch, but she did a light drawing. It helped her clear her mind and think anyway.

## CHAPTER 36

The CID room was deserted by the time Helen made her way up the stairs, although the lingering fag smoke that drifted through the air told her that the room had not been vacated for long. The trill of a telephone cut through the silence but stopped before she could retrieve a handset from one of the stained desks that were piled high with papers, folders, ashtrays and half-empty coffee cups.

She slumped down into her broken chair and wiggled, trying to get comfy. Giving up she leaned forward, cracked her knuckles and began to leaf through the incident and witness statements that were in the tray next to her.

The door opened and DC McKinley entered carrying a pile of folders under one arm and a bundle of keys in the other. He was humming a tune, cheerful but not one Helen recognised. He didn't seem to notice her as he dropped the folders onto his desk, a plume of dust escaping them. She watched as he brushed the dust from his fingers onto his flares, then sparked a fag.

'Thought you'd given up,' Helen said, pulling out her sketch book from her satchel.

'Bloody hell!' He swung around, wide-eyed. 'And I thought I was alone.'

'I know you did.' Helen felt herself smiling then remembered why she had come back up the stairs. 'I got stopped by Robert Keaton on the way out the station, he's only gone and released Jimmy Osbourne a few hours ago.'

'Well, it was to be expected.'

Helen shrugged. 'I know, but it doesn't make it any easier.'

'No, it doesn't.'

'I think I need a drink.'

'Well, I have something that might help you feel better.'

'It better not be a box of Milk Tray.' She gave him a look.

'No, definitely not.' He lifted the slip of paper.

'We've had quite a few phone calls about your drawing in the paper, and there's one name that's cropped up twice.'

'What's the name?'

'Marnie, Marnie Harper. She's twenty. I have her address here, and place of employment. She was charged a few years ago with petty theft. Her work is less than half a mile from where the shooting took place.'

'Great, that's promising — let's go and pay her a little visit,' Helen replied, taking the slip of paper.

McKinley grabbed his coat as she led the way out of the room. She'd have to get to those reports later.

\* \* \*

Marnie worked at the Fish on the Shore, a modern fish and chicken bar. Helen could see from the window that it was big inside, with three rows of red Formica tables and chairs. A red-and-blue neon smiling fish flashed above the door. McKinley motioned to the giant poster of a battered fish on top of chunky chips that had been taped to the window. Helen nodded, and they both agreed the smell was making their mouths water. It was after teatime and the place was fairly quiet, with only one young couple sitting beside the window sharing a fish supper. They looked deep in conversation.

'I haven't been in here before,' McKinley muttered.

'I haven't either.' Helen pulled on the door.

'That's surprising.'

Helen glared at him.

He held up his hands in mock surrender. 'I just know how much you like your chips.'

'Not that much. I've not been to every chippie in Edinburgh.'

'I didn't mean it like that, I—'

Helen gave him a nudge on the shoulder when she noticed the girl step out from the staff room in the process of tying her pink apron.

'That's her, isn't it?' She looked different at the hospital and Helen couldn't be sure.

McKinley nodded. 'Yes, it is.'

Warmth from the fryers hit them as they headed to the counter. The girl looked up as they approached, but it was only when Helen retrieved her warrant card from her pocket that realisation dawned on her face.

'Hello, Barbara, or should I say Marnie?' Helen smiled.

The girl's emerald eyes darted between the Helen and McKinley. Helen could see she was thinking of making a run for it. 'We just want to ask you some questions.' She looked younger than she had at the hospital; she wasn't wearing any makeup and her blonde hair was tied up into a tight bun and covered in a hair net. She stepped sideways and looked at the door.

'Don't even think about it,' Helen warned. 'You'll only make things worse for yourself and you're in trouble with us already.'

'We went to the address you gave us, but it was just an abandoned block of flats,' McKinley added. 'You could be charged with wasting police time, among other things.'

The girl's shoulders sagged, and she swallowed loudly.

'We just want to talk to you, and it's important we get some answers. I shouldn't have to remind you that we're investigating a very serious crime.' Helen directed her to the table closest to the counter.

'I didn't hurt Dennis, all right?'

'Do you know who did then?'

'No.'

'Then why did you pretend to be his sister at the hospital?'

'I panicked.'

'Strange behaviour that,' McKinley scoffed.

'I was scared,' Marnie snapped back.

'Why?' Helen asked.

'I was worried that you would blame me.'

'Where were you the morning he was shot?'

'This is exactly what I mean. I was here.'

'Any witnesses?'

'The manager was here. You can ask him.'

'We will. How do you know Dennis?'

'He's . . . I guess he's my boyfriend.'

'Guess?' Helen shifted in her seat. 'Surely you should know?'

'We haven't been seeing each other that long, only a few months.'

'Did you see him the morning he was shot?'

Marnie looked down at the counter then back up at them. 'No, but he was on his way to meet me. It was my birthday.' Her mouth tightened. 'I was really looking forward to it.'

'How did you know he was hurt and in hospital?' McKinley asked.

'I just had a feeling.' She paused, as if she was remembering something. 'Last week, he was really edgy.'

'What do you mean?'

Marnie shook her head.

'We need to know everything, any little detail might help us find who did this to Dennis,' Helen reminded her.

'He was scared that someone was out to hurt him, and when he didn't turn up, I went to his place. He wasn't there, and then I heard someone talking in here about a shooting up the road and I just put two and two together. I knew it was Dennis.'

Helen didn't say anything in response, waiting for the girl to continue.

'I phoned around all the hospitals to see if someone fitting his description was brought in. He told me if anything ever happened to him that I wasn't to visit him, it would be too dangerous — but I needed to see if he was all right.'

'Did he say why it was dangerous?'

'I think he borrowed money from someone he shouldn't have, and he couldn't pay it back. I don't know for certain, but that was the impression I got.'

'What gave you that impression?'

'He seemed to suddenly have a lot of money.'

'Do you have any idea who this person is?'

'No.'

'Do you know if Dennis had access to a gun?' Helen looked up from her notebook.

Marnie's brows lifted. 'I know he had some kind of replica one — it meant a lot to him. I think he was working on it to try and get it to fire real bullets, but I don't know if he managed to do it. I know sometimes he gave it to his friend, Robbie.'

'Robert Fields?'

She nodded.

'Have you met Robbie before?' Helen asked.

'A couple of times.' She wiped a tear away from her eye with the back of her hand. 'I don't know him very well.'

'Do you know where the gun might be now?'

'I haven't seen it.'

'Do you know anyone else, besides this person he owed money to, that might want to hurt Dennis?'

'No, he only has the one friend, Robbie, or did have.' She shrugged.

'What do you mean "did have"?'

'They had a bad falling out, I am not sure what about. I do know that Robbie's dad doesn't like Dennis, so it might have had something to do with that. Dennis wasn't allowed to go to Robbie's house.'

'When did they have this falling out?' Helen asked.

The girl frowned in concentration. 'It's hard to remember exactly — a couple of days before he got shot? Dennis didn't always tell me everything.'

'What do you mean?'

'He's just private, I guess.'

Helen nodded. 'When we found Dennis, he wasn't wearing a jacket and it was a cold morning.'

'That's strange. He normally wore a black leather one. He'd customised it with different badges that he'd sown on.' She motioned to her own arms along the sleeves. 'He was very proud of it.'

'Okay, well thank you for talking to us. If you remember or hear anything else, call me on this number.' Helen handed her a card. 'We know where to find you if we have any further questions.'

\* \* \*

Robbie Fields sat opposite Helen in Interview Room 1. His father sat next to him, wearing an expensive-looking charcoal suit with a lime-green shirt. He had his head down and was twisting his gold wedding band. Helen was scanning the information in front of her. They were waiting for McKinley to return with a cup of water for Robbie. Robbie sat up in his chair as the door opened.

Once McKinley was seated, they began. Robbie gulped the water and stopped when his dad gave him a look.

'Okay, Robbie, we've been talking to Marnie Harper this afternoon. Do you know her?'

He nodded.

'She says that she's Dennis's girlfriend. Is that correct?'

Robbie shrugged. 'If she says so . . .'

Helen leaned forward. 'Robbie, you're not in trouble, but we need to know everything so that we can find out who hurt Dennis and stop them hurting someone else.'

Robbie looked at his dad, who nodded.

'I'll try and help any way I can,' he murmured.

'Marnie said that you and Dennis had an argument.'

'I . . . we didn't. That's not true.'

'Maybe it was a disagreement?'

'We . . . just . . .'

'What was it about?'

With shaky hands, Robbie reached for his cup but made no move to drink from it.

'Did you often fall out?'

'Sometimes . . . I didn't really think much about it at the time. We would disagree on stuff, but we were still friends.'

'What did you disagree on?'

Robbie considered this. 'Football, stuff like that.'

'Marnie?'

'No, I don't even know her that much.'

Robbie's father directed a warning look at Helen. 'I don't think it was anything — you know what boys are like, officer.'

'Of course.' Helen forced a smile. She had to tread carefully so that his dad wouldn't take him from the interview room.

'What about Dennis's gun?'

Robbie's blond brows rose. 'What about it?'

'Marnie mentioned that you sometimes look after it?'

Robbie shook his head and looked down at the table. 'No, it's too precious to Dennis.'

'Do you have any idea where it might be?'

'I haven't seen it in a long time.'

'I haven't seen it either. Ever,' his father added. 'Will that be everything now?'

'Almost.'

'I feel Robbie has been extremely helpful.' He placed his hand over his son's. 'And he is obviously very upset by all this.'

'I understand, but just one last question. Are you able to describe the gun?'

'It was just small. Silver and faded.' He squeezed his eyes shut. 'Maybe Dennis gave it to the man.'

Helen exchanged a look with McKinley.

'In the newspaper this morning, there was a man. That's the man I saw in Dennis's room. He knew about the gun.'

Helen's stomach lurched. 'What man?'

'Jimmy Osbourne.'

'Are you sure?'

'Yes, I'd never forget his face.'

'Thank you both for coming in. I'll be in touch.' Helen stood up from the table.

* * *

Helen stood out in the car park, leaning back against the cool brick wall. If Jimmy Osbourne had visited Dennis, it wouldn't have been for anything good, and it fitted with what Marnie had said earlier about Dennis being in trouble with money. She gave a small nod as McKinley joined her.

'That was an interesting development.' He squinted against the low sun.

'It gives us a motive as to why someone would want to hurt Dennis if he was involved with Jimmy.'

McKinley nodded. 'Or Jimmy Osbourne was involved in it.'

'That's something we need to find out.'

He bobbed on the spot for warmth. 'I'm going back inside. I'm expecting more documents regarding Dennis's time in the children's home. They might help.'

'Let me know as soon as you have something.'

'Are you not going to come back inside?'

'I will in a minute.' Helen looked up at the gritty sky. 'At least we have another excuse to bring Jimmy Osbourne in again.'

CHAPTER 37

Alfie MacMillan was comfy in the works van, a half-eaten bacon butty on his lap. He supped on the dregs of his tea, then wiped his greasy fingers on his overalls. The building works were now a month behind schedule and already today he had noticed that two of the lads had not turned up. He made a clicking sound. That was four this month that had quit, according to the schedule.

The weather was due to take a turn too, that would slow progress further. Any more delays and the council contract would be in jeopardy. With the Right to Buy scheme in full swing, the councils wanted the new flats up yesterday. He clambered from the van as the lights from the first lorry appeared on the tracks and the sound of churned-up gravel filled the silence.

It was just before seven when they wrenched open the gate and the lorry backed into the site with glaring lights and sirens, followed by two more.

Needing to keep himself busy, Alfie directed the concrete mixer in. The foundations had been dug up and were now ready, and he wanted them in before the rain that was forecast for the afternoon. The cigarette in his hand glowed in the dawn light. Around him, builders with yellow hard hats negotiated planks of wood into one of the shells of a building, making idle chat about the football, fags dangling precariously from their lips.

He grabbed the last of his morning roll and watched as the crane swung into position with a creak. The sun had now risen higher into the sky. Progress at last.

'Boss.' The unknown voice came from behind him. 'Boss!'

He slipped a glance over his shoulder.

A young lad of about eighteen wearing a hard hat that looked at least two sizes too big was waving and jogging towards him.

'Aye?'

'Boss . . .' His breath was haggard. 'There's something you need to see.'

Alfie sighed, trying not to let his annoyance show. 'What is it?' If they had damaged one of the lorries again, he was going to lose it.

'It's horrible, I've no' seen nothing like it in my life.'

'Not seen what?'

'We're going to have to call the police.' The lad put a hand to his mouth and looked like he was going to spew his guts.

'Dinnae tell me someone's been in to steal the copper?'

'No.'

This bloody generation was soft. 'What is it? Old Murphy sawn off his thumb again?'

The boy shook his head and his hat landed on the ground with a thump. 'It's a dead body.'

'Show me,' Alfie commanded.

The lad doubled over and grabbed his stomach and spewed up his breakfast into a puddle.

* * *

Alfie's heartbeat accelerated as he approached the scaffolding. His mind raced at what he was going to find and how much this was going to cost him.

'It's just up here,' the lad muttered and pointed with a shaky hand. 'I don't want to see it again.'

Alfie looked around for any indication that he was walking into a joke. The lad stopped in his tracks. Alfie carried on down the path.

Three of the workmen were huddled around what looked like a bundled-up carpet. Hopefully, it was just one of their stupid attempts at a joke. Their shoulders were hunched, and they were muttering something he couldn't hear. They parted as he approached. He took a deep breath and unclicked his torch from his tool belt. Petrol vapours hung in the air and even the ground looked burnt. Whatever they were looking at was down in one of the foundations. Nothing else around him looked out of place.

'It's probably a dog or something,' he remarked. 'Have one of you checked it out?'

'Aye, I have,' one of the workmen retorted. 'I've never seen a dog that looks like this.'

'Do you know how far behind schedule we are?' Alfie waved his torch over the hole. There was something down there all right. A knot formed in the pit of his stomach.

'The schedule's out the window,' one of the others scoffed. 'There's no way we can carry on now.'

'Has anyone phoned the police?' the third one asked.

'Just hold your horses, we need to think about this.'

'What's to think about?'

'All our jobs for a start.' His torch illuminated a pair of black boots, melted with the steel toe cap exposed, sticking out of a bundled piece of carpet that was black from soot and badly burnt. 'Nah, I know what this is. Someone's just trying to get rid of some rubbish or started a bonfire for heat or something.' None of the others looked convinced.

'Naw.' The young man he had spoken to earlier was shaking his head wildly and pointing his gloved hand towards the gap. 'I climbed down there. I've seen it.'

'What did you see?' Alfie knelt forward, his knees creaking in protest. He held his torch down as far as it could go.

He forced his gaze further up and saw a tuft of brown hair peeking out.

# CHAPTER 38

Helen brushed a stray strand of hair from her face that the wind whipped back and forth. She was looking forward to getting home later, running a hot bath and having a glass of wine or two. The cigarette smoke from the CID room hung in the back of her throat and her mouth felt dry. She felt sorry for Dennis. She hadn't realised how lucky she was growing up. Her parents hadn't been around much. Mum needed her hobbies after her brother had died, and Helen couldn't really blame her. Dad was always working or drinking, but she'd had a nice home to come back to after school and all of the material things that she could have wanted. Not that she appreciated it much at the time.

'There you are.'

Helen looked over to the where the voice had come from and noticed Loughton waving at her.

Her stomach tightened as she noticed the serious expression etched on his face. Hopefully, it wasn't Dennis. She was starting to build hope now he had survived this long. The images of him lying in the alley filled her mind. She blinked them back. She took a deep breath to prepare herself.

'Everything okay?' she asked.

'It never rains but it pours,' he remarked, as he pulled his car keys from his pocket.

'What is it? Dennis?'

He shook his head. 'There's been a report of a body on a building site. We've been asked to attend. The site manager's kicking up a bit of a fuss apparently, so we'd better get there sooner rather than later.'

'You're kidding me?' Helen replied, sticking her hands in her pockets for warmth. She started to walk with him to the car. 'I was just talking to Robbie Fields, Dennis's friend.'

'Aye?'

'Apparently, Robbie was paid a visit by Jimmy Osbourne.'

'Interesting.'

'I'd have thought you'd have more to say than that.'

Loughton shook his head again. 'The body was called in over forty-five minutes ago.'

'Where is it?'

'Some construction site near the docks. MacMillan and Sons.'

Helen had driven past the site a couple of times. They were building blocks of high-rise flats at extortionate prices, if she remembered rightly.

'Shall I drive?' He motioned towards the maroon Granada parked in the bay opposite.

'No, I will,' she said, pulling the driver's side door open.

'Don't trust my driving then?'

'I like to drive . . . It's a long story.'

'I'd like to hear it sometime.'

'Maybe,' she muttered, turning the key in the ignition.

# CHAPTER 39

Less than twenty minutes later, the Mini churned up gravel as they took a left-hand turn onto a narrow road that looked more like a dirt cycle path. Helen glanced through the window — a rain-soaked, desolate wasteland as far as she could see in the dim morning light. The earlier forecast had said it was going to be a bright but grim morning, and heavy rain was forecast for the afternoon. She kept a tight grip on the steering wheel, the tyres feeling like they were going to rip away from the car at any second. She squeezed on the brake.

'Take this road.' Loughton pointed to some lights in the distance on the right-hand side.

'That's a road?' Helen muttered, winding her window down a crack to try and stop the condensation that was creeping up the windscreen. Helen hadn't expected to be going off-road. The car skidded and Loughton lunged forward, managing to put a hand on the dash to catch himself in his seat.

'You do have a driving licence, don't you?' he asked, with a half-smile.

The engine revved, spraying up puddle water around the sides of the car.

'Okay, it's up here, I believe.' Loughton motioned towards some scaffolding erected behind thin-looking fences that swayed with the wind. Signs tied to them were promising redevelopment and new houses — apart from the construction vehicles, Helen saw little progress. A police van was blocking most of the scene and a group of builders in yellow hard hats smoking fags were talking to a uniformed officer, looking freezing and bored.

As she unfastened her seatbelt Helen could see Alex Winston, the pathologist, trudging towards the scene, the ankles of his cord trousers caked in mud. He gave her a glum-looking nod. She returned his gesture with a wave. He was close to retirement age, with wispy grey hair that stuck out in tufts. He always seemed to wear expensive-looking suits that were either too short in the sleeves or a size smaller than he needed.

'Who's that? Loughton asked.

'That's our friendly local pathologist,' Helen said, wrenching up the handbrake.

Loughton peered over at the scene. 'So, apparently the body was found when they were about to pour the concrete in.'

'Right then, let's see what we've got.' Helen shrugged. 'Sounds like we're lucky they found it.' Mud squelched under Helen's boots as she trudged towards the scene. She grimaced as a load of puddle water soaked through her socks. This was going to be the beginning of a long day. She looked down at Loughton's shiny black brogues.

'I bought these new for the job.' He shook his head. The words escaped his mouth in a plume of frosty vapour. She turned up the collar of her coat against the wind, though it made little difference. Her toes were already beginning to go numb.

'I've never really got used to this.'

'Got used to what?' She coughed to try and clear her throat.

'The weather. Always cold. Always bloody raining.' He looked around the bleak landscape — from here they could see out to the choppy grey sea.

'We do get a summer one or two days a year.' She smiled.
'I'll look forward to that.'

'Is it always this busy in Edinburgh CID?' he asked. 'I was expecting to be able to focus on Osbourne more.'

'What will you do when that case is closed?'

'If it ever is closed,' he corrected her. 'When this is over, who knows? Maybe I'll go on holiday or something.'

'To the coast of Spain?'

He gave her a look. 'Those weren't holidays.'

Helen arched an eyebrow. 'Just making conversation.' She thought about asking him about the photographer who had taken the image of Osbourne outside the jewellers, but stopped when she noticed a couple of uniformed officers cordoning off the area with rope. Helen held out her warrant card for inspection. After close scrutiny of her pass, one of the officers lifted up the rope for them.

'Thanks. Where have we to go?'

'It's just around the corner, around the back of the crane.'

'Cheers.' Helen carefully stepped over bits of rubble, rocks, half-bricks and what looked like a rusted ladder that was embedded into the dirt. The path was a riot of boot prints and tyre marks and was the consistency of clay. There were a couple of moments when Helen thought she was in danger of losing her shoe.

Loughton swore under his breath as his shoe connected with a rock. He stumbled but managed to catch himself. Helen stifled a smile.

'It's just no' my day, is it?' He lifted his leg to show Helen the white scrapes around his shoe.

'Ach, I'm sure they'll be fine with a bit of polish.'

'Not bloody likely.'

Helen noticed that he was holding his thigh as he walked, but he withdrew his hand as soon as he noticed her looking.

The scene was easy to find. Winston was kneeling next to the corpse. It was covered from the elements by rickety scaffolding that was swaying and creaking too much for

Helen's liking. As she got closer, she could see that the corpse was in a trench.

Winston's face looked red from the exertion of kneeling. 'Glad you could make it. This one is definitely dead this time.' He spoke with an air of impatience.

Before Helen could respond a crime scene photographer slotted between them to capture the corpse at different angles. Not a job she envied. She waited for the photographer to move on before speaking.

'So what have we got here then?'

'Where to start?' Loughton peered into the gap.

The body was wrapped in a red Persian rug. It was frayed, burnt and stained yellow, and it stank of petrol but had survived largely intact. Muddy boot prints surrounded it and the ground looked shiny from accelerant. She made a mental note to ask the site manager if anything like that was kept here overnight.

'I'm not able to confirm the cause of death yet.' Winston puffed out his cheeks. Four spotlights had been set up around them blasting out white light.

'Isn't it obvious?' Loughton stepped forward to get a look.

'Fire can hide a multitude of sins,' Winston reminded him.

'I can see that,' Loughton replied.

'There's not much blistering on the body, it looks like the body was burnt after death. The body itself looks relatively intact,' Winston concluded.

'How can you tell?' Loughton knelt forward.

'If the victim is still alive when burned I would expect to see more blistering.' He pointed to the victim's bare arm.

'You call that intact?' Loughton asked, exchanging a look with Helen.

'What I mean is the body is not damaged apart from—'

'What about the position of the body?' Helen interjected and peered down the hole. She could feel Loughton's gaze on her. The smell of petrol and charred flesh and fat made the bile rise in her throat. She swallowed hard, trying to hide her disgust. The victim's shoulders looked broad and tall.

'I thought a burnt corpse would end up in a foetal position. Something to do with—'

Winston nodded. 'Contraction of the muscles and dehydration? Yes, that would be common.'

'Any reason why this one isn't?' she asked. Helen thought she caught the faint whiff of whisky on his breath. It was still early morning, so she supposed it could have been from the night before.

'The body was wrapped tightly in the rug. I think that sealed the body in. Still, I'll be able to give you more answers once I get this gentleman in for a post-mortem.' Winston grunted as he lifted himself back up to a standing position. He looked a couple of fry-ups away from a heart attack and was struggling to get a good breath in.

'Will you be able to tell us if it was the fire that killed him?' Loughton asked.

'I'll be able to see if there's any soot in the airways and lungs.' He straightened out his crumpled jacket and brushed the dirt from his trousers. 'If I don't find any then it wasn't the fire that killed him.'

'Not a good way to go though.' Helen knelt forward and placed her hands on her knees. She wanted to get a good look at the corpse now that Winston was out of the way. The jaw was parted slightly, showing a bottom set of crooked brown teeth and a missing front tooth. The hairs on the back of her neck bristled and her shoulders tightened as she clambered forward, but she couldn't get a closer look without the risk of falling in.

'Excuse me, Sergeant?' Helen turned to see one of the constables who had set up the cordon walking towards them clutching a plastic evidence bag. He was looking directly at Loughton as he approached.

'What is it?' Helen replied and held out her hand for the bag.

'We've found a wallet . . .' A look of confusion knitted the constable's brow as he tried to hand the evidence bag to Loughton, who made no move to accept it.

Helen spoke through gritted teeth. 'I'm the sergeant. Now, you say you've found a wallet.'

'And none of the builders have claimed knowledge of it.'

'Let me have a look, and make sure none of the builders leave the site until we get statements.'

Nodding, he handed Helen the bag. It contained a scuffed, dark-brown wallet. The evidence bag was big enough for her to be able to thumb the wallet open.

'Where exactly was this found?' she asked.

'In one of the rubbish bins by the entrance.'

'Well, well, well.' She held up the wallet for Loughton to see.

He took it from her and stared at the photo open-mouthed. 'I don't believe it.'

'I don't know if I do either.'

She looked back down at the charred corpse. The build looked the right size and so did the height and what little was left of the hair. Helen tried to remember what he was wearing the night they brought him in. She was certain he was wearing a lilac shirt. A shirt similar to this one. 'I want all the forensic information on this as soon as you have it.'

'Of course,' Winston replied.

She stepped back and exchanged a look with Loughton. 'Let's go find the site manager.' She wanted to get a look around the site for herself.

'Were you first on the scene?' she asked the officer.

He nodded glumly.

'Have you got a list of employees for the site? I also want to know the names and address of any previous workers and I want to know if anyone hasn't turned up this morning.'

* * *

'I can't really tell you much,' the site manager who introduced himself as Alfie explained. They walked up towards his van as they spoke. Helen was glad of the chance to get some fresh air.

'Do you keep any accelerants on site?'

'No, we've had problems with thieves in the past so . . .'

'What about keys to the site?'

Alfie shrugged. 'I have a set, so does the foreman.' He pulled open the van door and handed Helen a grease-stained clipboard from the passenger side. 'That's a list of all my employees.' Helen flicked through the pages — there was around twenty or so names to check.

He scratched his head. 'Wait a minute though.' He moved around to the other side of the van and began raking through the footwell. 'I did have a spare set of keys . . .'

*That was secure*, Helen thought.

He made a clicking sound then slammed the door shut. 'There was a spare set in here I kept for emergencies.'

'When was the last time you definitely saw them?'

'It would have been a few weeks ago, I think.'

Helen sighed. 'What about all your employees, are they all accounted for?'

'No. Thing is, I'll hire a bunch, and they'll just not show up the next day.' He shook his head. 'Even with all this unemployment. I had one guy in for a few weeks, and he just didn't bother showing up one day.'

'Might any of these men have access to the keys? Or to this van?'

'Aye, the last one did, he'd do a lot of the driving.'

'Right, I'm going to need his name and address.'

'I hope you don't mind me asking, love, but how long is this going to take? We've got a lot of work to get through.'

'It will take as long as it takes,' she replied, biting her tongue to avoid adding a 'love' herself. 'This is the scene of a murder. The building work is going to have to wait.'

\* \* \*

Helen found Loughton at the back of the police van talking to the officer that had called it in.

He gave her a wave as she approached.

213

'Any luck?' he asked.

'I have the name and address of a former employee who had access to some missing keys.'

'Interesting.'

'They also don't keep any petrol on site.'

'Aye, that's what I heard.'

'So, this is premeditated.' Helen scanned their surroundings — she could see the outline of a few houses in the distance. She motioned to Loughton. 'They might have seen something, maybe noticed a vehicle coming into the site late at night. It might give us a timeline?'

'Worth a try.'

'I'm finished here for now. Shall we go and check them out?'

It had started to rain again by the time they got back to the car. Helen peeled off her damp jacket and threw it onto the back seat then shoved the key into the ignition. Her stomach grumbled and she couldn't remember the last time she had eaten, or had a coffee for that matter.

They parked in front of a row of three terraced cottages. The first two showed no signs of life, the inhabitants probably out for work for the day. Helen looked at her watch. It had just gone eight thirty. Candlelight flickered in the front room of the last one — the brickwork looked like it had been painted red a long time ago but had now faded to pink in places.

Loughton opened the gate. The small front garden was immaculately lawned with a narrow, pebbled path leading to the royal-blue front door that was lined with various potted plants. Helen recognised daisies and roses among some she had no clue about.

A woman in her late seventies opened the door. She was wearing a floral dress and a lilac apron with flour stains.

'Can I help you?' She eyed them both suspiciously. 'I don't like cold callers.'

'That's a good policy to have.' Helen retrieved her warrant card for inspection. 'But we're police officers. I'm DS Carter, and this is DC Loughton.'

The woman slipped a thin pair of spectacles from her pocket — as soon as she put them on they slid right down her nose and she peered over them. 'What can I help you with, hen?'

Helen pointed to the building site. 'I don't want to alarm you, but a body was found at the building site this morning. We just need to ask you a few questions, if that's alright?'

'Oh dear, that's terrible. Why don't you both come in and have a cup of tea. I have a pot on. It's far too cold to be standing out on the step talking about things like that.'

Helen exchanged a look with Loughton. 'That would be lovely, thank you.'

The cottage looked a couple of hundred years old with most of its original features. Oak support beams lined the ceilings and a narrow hallway opened to a quaint front room. The earthy smell of the fireplace hung in the air. The crackling fire warmed Helen's cheeks and she suddenly became aware of how cold she was. She rubbed her sore knuckles and took a seat in an overstuffed floral armchair next to the fire. Loughton remained standing and was looking at the photographs on the mantelpiece. She followed his gaze. The pictures were of a male teenager with closely cropped blond hair. The pictures looked old, most likely her son.

A few minutes later, the woman returned with a tray with a teapot, cups and a plate of biscuits on it.

'I'm really sorry, I don't have any milk,' she replied, setting the tray down beside Helen. 'Can't stand the stuff, I only take it with lemon.'

'This is lovely, thanks.'

The woman handed her a delicate bone china teacup. The cup felt cool in her hand and the tea was disappointingly lukewarm.

Helen took a pink wafer and Loughton a custard cream. Helen took a sip of hers, it tasted weak, but it reminded her how thirsty she was. A gust of wind rattled the single-glazed window and for a brief second Helen thought it was in danger of blowing in. The heat from the fire was starting to feel stifling. Helen shifted in her seat.

'Did you see any lights on at the site last night?' Helen asked placing her cup back on the tray.

The old woman considered this for a moment and nodded. 'I did. Just after nine, it was. It looked like they were burning something. I just assumed they were getting rid of some rubbish. They don't normally work until that late, right enough.'

'How long did that last for?' Helen resisted taking another pink wafer. She was hungry, but all she seemed to eat recently was chocolate, biscuits and sandwiches, and it was starting to take a toll. She could feel the band on her trousers digging into her stomach and hips.

'I went to bed at ten and it was still burning then, but it wasn't burning when I got up this morning at around five. I have terrible arthritis in my hips, so I'm always up early,' she explained.

'Have you ever seen them burning things on the site before?'

'I don't think so.' The woman moved a shaky hand to her glasses.

'What about working at night?' Helen carried on.

'Oh no, they always seem to be away earlyish, definitely before five.'

'I think that's all we need to ask you for now. Thank you for your time,' Helen said as she stood up from the armchair.

'It gives me the creeps thinking of a dead body so close to my house.'

'Try not to worry. It's very unlikely they'll be coming back to the scene of the crime,' Loughton said as they left.

Helen appreciated him putting the old woman's mind at rest.

The woman gave a small smile. 'Let me show you the way out.'

Helen was glad to get back in the car. They drove towards the station, and from this direction Helen could see right out to sea. It was choppy this morning, with white-capped waves crashing against the shore. She wound her window down a crack, hoping to smell the sea, but she couldn't.

'Why don't you want anyone else to drive?' Loughton asked.

Helen's grip on the steering wheel tightened. 'It's silly, really.' She could feel Loughton staring at her.

'I want to hear it.'

'I crashed my car a while back, and since then I've had trouble giving control to others. I was the only one in the car, but I can't help thinking about what could have happened.'

She kept her eyes on the road but couldn't help but catch Loughton's stricken expression from the corner of her eye. Well, he did ask.

* * *

A soon as Helen got back to the station, she grabbed herself a strong cup of coffee and savoured the first sip. She didn't have long before the briefing and wanted to go through the statements from the other builders first. The autopsy was scheduled for tomorrow afternoon. That wasn't going to be pleasant, but at least she would hopefully have some answers. She couldn't imagine there would be many forensics to go on though, as the site had been well trampled through.

She looked through the photographs from when Jimmy was booked in. He was wearing the same shirt and shoes as their victim. She slumped back in her chair — there was something bothering her about this, something she felt she was overlooking, but she couldn't think what. She looked up and sniffed. The office stank of wet clothes. Helen noticed someone had draped their jacket over the radiator to dry and it was dripping onto the carpet.

Terry McKinley was still organising files, frowning as he did so. The rest of the team had headed into a briefing already, so it was just the two of them in the office. Helen was glad of the peace and quiet, even though it wasn't going to last long, and she was proved right when less than a minute later the phone rang. She snatched it up, trying not to let her annoyance show.

'DS Carter.'

'It's Randall here.' She never understood why he liked to be called by his last name. 'We've tried to track down Jimmy this morning on the off chance the body in the pit wasn't his.' Helen could hear the exasperation in his voice.

They both knew he was most likely lying down in the morgue. Helen stood up and gave her shoulder a stretch. 'What about Jimmy's ex-wife?'

'Jimmy's *fiancée*,' he corrected her.

'Sorry, fiancée.'

'Well, she thinks the body you've found is his.'

Helen sighed. She expected that.

'Do you believe her?'

'She was so upset we had to take her to hospital for shock.'

'Where is she now?'

'Finished up at the hospital and back at the station. Down in Interview Room 1.'

Helen grabbed her jacket and headed for the door.

\* \* \*

Lisa-Marie Malone was nursing a cup of tea in a polystyrene cup. She looked up at Helen with teary eyes. 'I can't believe that he's gone,' she wailed. 'He had everything in front of him.' Her mascara tracked down her cheeks. Randall was right, if she was acting, she was bloody good. Helen sat down opposite and leaned forward to get a good look at her. Lisa-Marie narrowed her eyes and gave Helen a hard stare. 'I've already spent hours talking to your colleague, what more—' She broke off into a sob.

'Are you sure the body that you saw this morning was that of Jimmy Osbourne?'

'Of course I am.' She slid her hand across the table, showing Helen an impressive-looking white diamond. 'I know my fiancé.'

'What made you sure that it was Jimmy?'

Lisa-Marie looked taken aback by the question.

'It's just . . .' Helen carried on. 'He . . . Jimmy was badly disfigured.'

'He was wearing Jimmy's clothes—' she began to count with her fingers — 'he was missing the same front tooth as Jimmy, he was the same size, same hair colour . . .'

Helen could have told her that herself. Time would tell if she was right.

## CHAPTER 40

Loughton's left thigh ached, and the muscle twitched all the way down to his knee, protesting with each step. He tried to shake it off when no one was around but it did little good. He was tempted to sit on the wall and take the weight off for a moment but he didn't want anyone in CID to see him. Anyway, once he was in the car it wouldn't take long to get home, then he could relax with a good whisky or two to dull the pain. Maybe get some fish and chips too, lathered in salt and sauce, pickled onions on the side. His mouth watered at the thought.

It had been another drawn-out day, and the headache that had plagued him for the past few days had shown no sign of easing. The sun was low in the sky, casting an orange shadow across the car park. He shielded his eyes from the sunlight — why had he decided to park at the far side of the car park this morning?

He nodded to a couple of uniformed officers. Most of the spaces were full compared to this morning and he struggled to remember where he had parked.

'Ian,' a voice called out, female, soft, shaky. It took him a moment to work out where it was coming from. 'Ian.'

As soon as he noticed her, acid rage rose in his stomach. He took a step towards her. His shoulders stiffened and fists clenched.

She stepped backwards and looked at him wide-eyed.

He stopped and took a deep breath to steady himself. He was taken aback by how terrified she looked. She was standing at the other side of the fence, and from the look of her she had been waiting there some time. She gave a small shrug of her shoulders.

'You told me you were going to be working here. I've been—'

'Looking for me, were you?' Ian muttered, trying his best to keep his voice low and level. He was aware of someone getting into a car behind him and could sense they were stalling to get a look at what was going on. The gossips in this station were unbelievable, and he could imagine how this would be twisted.

'I'm sorry, that's why I wanted to come here.' A tear trailed down her cheek and she rubbed it away with her cardigan sleeve and sniffed. She looked different from the night they had met. Her blonde hair was scraped back into a messy-looking ponytail. It looked like it had not been brushed in a while. Her face looked free of makeup and the cold and her tears made it look red and blotchy. He could have almost walked past her and not recognised her. Her shoulders were hunched. She held a cigarette close to her body, looked away and took a few sharp drags as if she was worried they would be her last.

He cast a glance over his shoulder at the man getting into his car. He didn't recognise him but gave him a friendly smile, which he returned warily.

'I wanted to explain,' she carried on. 'I want you to know why I did it.'

'Let's go and have a coffee, then we can talk.' He headed towards the gate.

'Are you sure? I . . .'

'There's a place around the corner I heard is good.'

'I . . . that would be great. I'm freezing.' She kept her distance and looked around the car park cautiously. She looked like a caged animal backed into a corner.

'I could do with a coffee anyway.'

'I know you've been looking for me.' She tugged at the arms of her cardigan. 'I thought it would be safer to come here than . . .'

'Why? What do you take me for?' He found himself softening.

She gave a small shrug and slipped a glance over her shoulder.

'Are you looking for someone?' he asked.

She shook her head slowly.

Loughton hunched his shoulders and felt her fall in behind him. He knew he shouldn't be doing this but he had to speak with her.

\* \* \*

'I can't believe I didn't manage to talk my way out of this,' Helen groaned as she slumped down onto the bench with a typically ungracious thud. Muscles that she never knew she had were already aching in protest.

'It was your idea,' McKinley reminded her.

'It seemed like a good idea at the time.'

'I thought you'd back out.' He was in the process of zipping up his jacket.

'Thanks for the vote of confidence.'

He chucked her a green woolly hat. 'Here, I brought one for you too.'

'Cheers.' Helen looked at the olive-coloured hat with the giant bobble on the top. 'I'm going to look great.' She looked down at the orange snow jacket she had found in the back of her cupboard. She was sure it had belonged to her mum.

He held out his hand and helped her to her feet. She took in a shaky breath and held out her arms for balance. 'Why did I suggest this?' She wobbled as her knees wanted to buckle under her. Maybe this wasn't such a good idea after all. She could imagine the laughs she would get at the station if she was forced to spend the night in A & E with a sprained ankle or worse.

He smiled and stepped out onto the ice, skating a couple of strides, weaving between a group of teenagers. The cold coloured his cheeks and his blond hair stuck out from under his hat. Helen gulped and stepped onto the rink, keeping a tight grip on the handrail.

If nothing else, it was good to get away from the office for a while and clear her mind. Maybe have a laugh in the process. She glanced around —McKinley was on the other side of the rink now, skating in circles.

'Bloody show off.' She let go of the handrail and was surprised to find that she was still standing. She hadn't skated yet, but she hadn't fallen on her arse yet either. A couple holding hands and gazing at each other with daft grins brushed past, and when she finally managed to manoeuvre herself around, McKinley was standing behind her, a slow grin spreading on his face.

'This is more fun that I remember.' He held out his arm. 'Come on, let me take you for a spin.'

* * *

Loughton carried a tray with two coffees towards their table in the local greasy spoon just around the corner from the station. Randall had recommended it, but he was hardly a connoisseur of fine dining. Luckily they were the only customers in this evening.

Paula had picked the table next to the window and directly in front of the door, no doubt for an easy escape. She kept her gaze fixed on something outside and was picking at the sleeve of her cardigan. She looked a lot smaller and thinner than he had remembered.

He placed the tray in front of her and shook his head. 'I can't believe I'm buying coffee for someone that stole from me.'

223

Paula's eyes narrowed. 'Sorry.' She made no move to take her mug from the tray and retreated further into her seat as he sat down. Her breath sounded shallow.

'Aye, you keep saying that.' He took his coffee — the mug felt slippery in his hands. He grimaced and wiped away what looked like a faint trace of lipstick from the rim with his thumb.

'This was a bad idea. I don't know what I'm doing here,' she muttered.

He looked at her not really knowing what to say. Part of him wanted to shake her, the other half wanted to help her. After a moment of silence, he asked her, 'Why did you do it then?' He glugged his coffee, wanting to get it over with quicker. It tasted better than he expected. The smell of chips bubbling away in the deep fat fryer made his stomach grumble.

'I didn't plan to do it. I did have a good evening . . . I just . . .' She shrugged and shifted uncomfortably in the seat.

'That's some way to show it. It couldn't have been that good an evening.'

She sighed. 'It was, it's just—'

'You wanted my money.'

'You don't mind if I smoke?' She slipped out a packet of Player's and placed one to her lips. Her hand trembled as she lit it. 'You spent a lot of the evening telling me how well off you were and how well you'd done for yourself. Don't you remember?'

He shook his head and closed his eyes. Most of the memories from that night were gone.

'I just saw all that money in your wallet.' She carried on. 'I didn't think you would miss it.'

'So you thought you'd help yourself?' He placed his mug down on the table. 'What's mine is yours, eh?' He followed her gaze to the traffic outside. It had started to rain again and the glass was slowly misting up.

'I acted on impulse, alright. I was desperate. It felt like it was a way out.'

'Way out of what?'

'It doesn't matter. It's not your problem.'

'You do know it's wrong to steal, don't you?'

'Of course, I do, I'm not some kleptomaniac.' She shrugged. 'You won't believe me, but I've never stolen anything before in my life.'

'You're right, I don't.'

'I've lost my job. I thought I'd pick another one up easily enough, but there's just none going right now. I can't seem to get anything, but I've still got to pay my bills every week.'

'That tugs at the heart strings, it really does.'

She glared at him. 'I don't need this. This was a mistake.' She swallowed hard and stubbed out her cigarette on the overfilled tin ashtray in the centre of the table. She brushed away some ash from the rubber tablecloth.

'I thought you were so drunk that you wouldn't have noticed. I knew you didn't know my last name or where I lived.'

'The money was a kick in the teeth, but I could have got over that. Cut my losses.'

'Really?'

'If the only thing that you took was money. But you took a picture of my wife. What is that about?' He rubbed his thigh — the pain was really building and there wasn't enough room at the table to stretch it.

'It got caught between the money, I didn't notice it until I got home.' She pulled it out from her handbag. 'I'm surprised it's important to you, considering.'

He snatched the picture from her hand. 'She's been dead for two years.'

'Has it been that long?'

He slipped the picture back in his wallet without looking at it.

She lit another cigarette and exhaled shakily. He hadn't remembered her smoking before. She closed her eyes, and he watched her hands flex and tremble.

'I don't suppose there's any money left?' He wasn't sure why he asked that. He didn't need it back. He wasn't rolling in it, but he certainly wasn't going to starve either.

'I've used most of it.' She took a raspy breath. 'Paid my bills.' She made a move to stand. 'I felt really guilty and I just wanted to give you a reason. I know it's too late now, and you won't believe this, but I did actually enjoy the date.'

Loughton rolled his eyes.

'I was really scared coming here. I wasn't sure if I was going to be arrested. I had nightmares about being chucked in a windowless cell, and you throwing away the key.'

He shook his head. He could only imagine what Helen Carter would say if he tried to pull a stunt like that.

'I can give you some of the money back now.' She rummaged in her handbag, pulling out a couple of pound notes in between some crumpled-up letters. 'I can give you the rest back next month. That's as soon as I can get it.'

'Just forget it. Keep it.' Loughton had heard enough, he should have been angry, but he was too sore, too tired and had more important things on his mind.

'No, I will pay you back. I promise.' She looked out the window again.

'Aye.' He drained his coffee. 'I just want to go home and have a drink.' He noticed her purse her lips to stop them trembling.

'You keep looking over your shoulder and you've barely dragged your eyes away from the window since we got here. Why don't you tell me what's really going on here.'

She shook her head and sniffed.

'I might be able to help.'

'You can't.'

'Try me. You've already stolen from me and I haven't hurt you.'

Paula nodded warily.

'Did someone set this up?'

Paula swallowed hard. 'I don't know if . . .'

'Look, if someone's watching you then they've already seen us together. They'll already suspect you told me, so you might as well actually do it.'

'Fine. It was a set-up.'

'In what way?'

'I was paid money to go out with you.'

'There's a confidence boost.'

'It wasn't just the money I took.'

Loughton held his breath.

'I was told to look for some files.'

'Who put you up to this?'

'I never got a name. She just approached me.'

'She?'

Paula nodded. 'It was after a night out with Tina. I didn't want to, but I'm not lying about needing the money.' A tear rolled down her cheek, she wiped it away with the back of her hand. 'I took Polaroids of the files in your bedroom when you passed out.'

The files from his private investigation into Jimmy Osbourne.

She offered a thin smile. 'I am sorry.'

Loughton turned away and looked out the window. The street was empty. He bobbed his head towards the door. 'I'll take you home and make sure you get there safely. If you hear from her again, you need to let me know.'

'I will.'

'How did you give her the photos? Did you meet her somewhere?'

'She was waiting outside your flat.'

Loughton's stomach flipped. 'What did she look like?'

'It was dark . . .'

'You need to give me something.'

'She was wearing a heavy red jacket. It looked too big for her and she had straight brown hair, but it might have been a wig.'

227

'Might have?'

She gave a small shrug. 'I didn't get a good look at her face. That's really all I know.'

\* \* \*

Helen hit the ice with a thud. 'I feel like an old woman,' she groaned as McKinley skated towards her with all the grace of the American figure skater Tim Wood. She pulled herself off the ice with the help of the handrail. 'How many times did I fall there?'

'I wasn't counting.' McKinley had his arm around her waist and was carrying a lot of her weight. 'But I think that was enough anyway.'

'It must've been five or six times.'

'More like ten.'

She made a face. 'I thought you said you weren't counting?' Helen plonked herself down on the bench. She gave her toes a wiggle, or at least she thought she did, but they had been numb for the past hour.

'Why did you give up skating?'

He shrugged. 'My dad left. Anyway, I was good but not good enough.' He gave her shoulder a squeeze. 'I'll be back in a minute.'

Helen closed her eyes and took a long deep breath. Her right knee throbbed and so did her tailbone. She was getting far too old for this kind of stuff. Not that she was even sporty in the first place. The teenagers that were on the ice early had thinned out, leaving only one of them and the loved-up couple. They were gazing into each other's eyes and swaying to the sound of Rod Stewart's 'Hot Legs'.

'I thought you needed this.' McKinley handed her a foam cup. 'It's tea.'

He sat down on the bench opposite her.

She cradled the cup and smiled. Despite the pain she was in, it had been fun. She had decided when she had broken off her engagement to Ted that she was going to live a little more and learn to relax.

McKinley leaned forward and dragged a hand through his dishevelled hair. 'I had fun tonight. It was a good distraction.'

'How's your mum?' Helen took a sip of tea and grimaced as it burned the back of her throat.

'We're not sure yet,' he answered after a brief hesitation. 'I just don't have a good feeling about it.'

## CHAPTER 41

The next morning, Helen had barely got back to her desk when the phone rang. She snatched it up.

'DC Carter.' She noticed Terry McKinley's desk was empty. She wanted to speak to him about Dennis's case and see if he was any further forward in tracking down his family.

'I have an Alfie. He says he's the building site manager? He's down here at reception. He said you wanted to speak to him.'

'That's right, I'll be straight down.' He was half an hour early. Helen hung up the phone then raked through her desk for the right folder, typically on the bottom of the pile.

Alfie was down in the reception area — he had his hands in his pockets and was peering up at the posters on the wall. He forced a smile as she approached.

'I haven't been able to start work at the site yet.'

'We're still doing forensics there, but we're working as quickly as possible.' He looked very different to the previous day at the site, wearing an expensive-looking shirt — the top couple of buttons were open, and she caught a strong whiff of aftershave.

'If I don't start soon, I am going to have to cut down on my crew — that means people will lose their jobs,' Alfie explained.

Helen gave a small sigh. 'I'm sorry, I'll try and see if I can find out how long it's going to take.'

'I would appreciate that,' he said, and Helen could tell he was trying to hide the impatience in his voice.

Helen directed him over to the reception area and opened the folder out on the desk.

'I wanted to ask if this man ever worked at your site.' She handed him a colour photograph.

He took it and narrowed his eyes. 'Aye,' he eventually answered. 'A few weeks ago, but he just didn't turn up one day.'

'How long did he work for you?'

He cleared his throat. 'It wasn't long, a couple of days maybe.'

'Thank you.' Helen took back the photograph of Jimmy Osbourne and slid it back into the folder.

* * *

Loughton gave her a confused look. 'What was Jimmy doing at the building site?'

'Just general labouring and any other odd jobs that needed doing.' Helen shrugged. 'He only lasted a couple of days, apparently.'

'What was on that site before the building work started?'

'It's just been empty land for years.'

Loughton made a face. 'This doesn't smell right to me. When's the post-mortem?'

'This afternoon.'

'Good,' Loughton replied pushing away from his desk. 'I'm just going to check something.'

'What?' Her desk phone rang, pulling her from her train of thought. 'I better get this.'

Loughton nodded.

'Helen Carter.'

'It's Randall . . . Just wanted to let you know that forensics have finished at the building site.'

Loughton stepped forward, angling his head, so he could hear.

'They found a bracelet in the pit inscribed with the name Jimmy Osbourne.'

Helen let out a sigh. 'Thanks for letting me know.'

# CHAPTER 42

Helen was scanning the information on the board, trying to make sense of it all. Her shoulders felt tense and the frustration was building within her —getting anyone to tell her what happened was like pulling teeth, like she was the enemy. They had pinned a new picture up on the board of Dennis, one that they had got from Robbie, next to her sketch of Marnie. He was smiling broadly at the camera.

'Why?' she muttered. 'Who did you piss off?' She stared hard at the photograph, not that it would do any good. 'How did you know Jimmy Osbourne?'

McKinley sipped his tea loudly behind her.

She gave him a look over her shoulder, and his face reddened.

'Sorry,' he muttered and took a step back.

'I'm just tired. I feel like we're not getting anywhere.'

'I know.' McKinley looked around the room. It was empty apart from the two of them.

'This is probably not a good time, but I really enjoyed the skating last night.'

Helen smiled. 'That's because you can actually skate.'

'And the company.'

'I'm still sore. I don't know why I thought it was a good idea.'

She saw his expression change.

'What is it?'

He shrugged. 'I've just come back from seeing my mum.'

'Oh.'

He took in a shaky breath.

'Is it bad?' It looked like he was trying to keep himself composed. 'Is there anything they can do? I mean there's medical advancements all the time.'

She reached out for his hand, it felt warm in hers. He gave her hand a squeeze and forced a small smile on his face. 'Maybe . . . I don't know.'

'I'm really sorry.'

'Thanks,' he muttered and released her hand.

'What are you doing tonight?'

'I don't know.'

'Are you going to see your mum?'

'She's going to my aunt's.'

'I don't think you should be alone.'

'I'll be fine.'

'Come to my house.'

'Are you sure?'

She nodded. 'I can cook.'

He arched an eyebrow.

'I will try to cook,' she corrected herself.

'I don't know, I might eat in the canteen.'

She knocked his arm with her elbow. 'This is a one-time deal. I'll do something from my Delia cookbook. Ted got it for me when he wanted me to get into hosting dinner parties for his friends.'

'I remember that.' He smiled. 'I'll come to your flat around seven?'

The office door opened. McKinley took a step back like he'd been electrocuted. Loughton stopped in his tracks. 'I'm not interrupting something, am I?'

'Of course not,' Helen replied.

McKinley kept his gaze down as he sat back at his desk and began sorting the stack of papers on it. His cheeks burned red.

'How did you get on?' Helen asked Loughton.

'Jimmy Osbourne's flat is still being watched, but no one's been back to it.' He shook off his jacket and draped it on the back of his chair.

Helen nodded and went to sit at her own desk, trying not to think about how walking into the office and seeing her and McKinley jump apart like that must have looked.

## CHAPTER 43

Helen had just got back to her desk when she spotted a note asking her to call the pathologist. She dialled the number.

'Hello,' Winston said in a singsong tone.

'Hello, Alex, it's Helen. How are you?' She moved around her desk and sat down, rifling through the papers for her pen in case she needed it, and cursing under her breath as it rolled under her desk.

She heard him sigh. 'Not bad, just counting the days until retirement.'

She checked her watch — Winston would be finishing for the day and so should she shortly. 'What is it I can do for you?'

'It's more about what I can do for you,' he chuckled. He was clearly in a better mood this evening than when she saw him at the building site.

'You've got me intrigued.'

'I have some post-mortem results for you. So, because of the damage to the corpse, we weren't able to do any fingerprints.'

That didn't surprise her.

'What I can tell you though, is the victim was dead prior to the fire. He wasn't breathing when it was lit.'

Helen sat back in her chair; she pretty much knew that anyway.

'However, it does get more interesting.'

'Go on?'

'When was the last time that Jimmy Osbourne was alive?'

'He left this station just over forty-eight hours ago.'

'And this corpse was found around thirty-six hours ago? Correct?'

She looked down at her notes. 'That's correct,' she confirmed.

'I believe this body has been dead longer than that.'

Helen's heart raced. 'How can you tell?'

'The body was fairly far through the putrefaction process. It's not an exact science, but I believe this man has been dead a week or maybe more.'

'But he was wearing the exact clothes that Jimmy Osbourne had on at the station. He was missing the same tooth as Jimmy. Even his so-called fiancée identified him.'

'Someone wanted us to think it was Jimmy, but there are some suitable differences. I was able to tell this man's original cause of death. His heart was severely enlarged, and he died of a heart attack.'

'What about dental records?'

'I couldn't get any for Osbourne to do a comparison, I'm afraid.'

'Right . . .'

'All I can say is this man had a few chipped and misaligned teeth, so it may make it easier to identify him.'

'I'll see if there's anyone reported missing that matches this. Thank you, Alex, that was incredibly helpful.'

They would have to find Jimmy Osbourne and quick.

* * *

'I bloody knew it,' Loughton muttered through gritted teeth after Helen had given him the update from the pathologist.

Helen stood up from her desk and glanced down at the pictures from the building site she had spread out in front of her. 'We need to find out where Osbourne is and why he wanted us to think he was dead.'

'I know why he wants that.' Loughton said, clambering to his feet. 'He gets free reign then. No more looking over his shoulder for a police car.'

'He's smart,' McKinley interjected.

'Not smart enough if he thought he would get away with this.' Loughton slammed his fist down on the desk. 'I should have known but I wanted to believe he was dead. He's got more lives than a cat.'

'We have to move fast. Maybe he's just trying to buy himself some time.' Helen lifted her bag. 'You better get a move on.'

Loughton nodded. 'I'm coming.'

Helen had just got to her car and was in the process of unlocking it when McKinley caught up with them.

'Helen, wait!'

The wind whipped around them and blew Helen's hair into her mouth.

'What is it?'

'I know the connection between Dennis Levitt and Jimmy Osbourne.' He smiled.

Helen heard Loughton take in a sharp intake of breath.

'Osbourne is Dennis's paternal uncle. It took me a long time as Jimmy's brother, Martin, was not on Dennis's birth certificate.'

'How did you find out?' Loughton demanded.

McKinley raised a blond brow. 'Dennis needed an operation on his eyes at three months old, and the medical notes list Martin Osbourne as the father.'

'Where is Martin now?' Helen asked.

'He died not long after Dennis was born.'

'If Dennis was involved with Jimmy in some monkey-making scam and made him angry, I wouldn't be surprised if Jimmy shot him.' Loughton dragged a hand across his stubble. 'He's quick-tempered and incredibly violent when it comes to money . . .'

'Aye,' Helen agreed. 'We know Dennis was involved in something that was paying him well.' She pulled open the driver-side door and gave a nod to McKinley. 'Thanks for letting me know.'

# CHAPTER 44

Lisa-Marie Malone's address was in the Gorgie area; Helen
had thought it would be a fifteen-minute drive, but it took
more than thirty minutes to snake their way along Princes
Street, and it was start-stop the rest of the way. Helen looked
at her dash — she was low on petrol but would have enough
to make this trip. Loughton drummed impatiently on the
passenger-side door and puffed out his cheeks. She gave him
a look and could see the worry clouding his eyes when they
met with hers. If Osbourne had got away, she didn't want
to think what it would do to him. Loughton fumbled with
the radio, settling on a static-laden channel — a pile up, the
presenter explained, was behind the delays they were seeing. It wasn't too far from her own flat near Fountainbridge.
Loughton had his window down and the car filled with the
smell of the nearby brewery.

'I just hope we're not too late.' Loughton shook his head.

'I know.' Helen slowed as a car pulled out in front. 'Do
you think Jimmy is capable of hurting his own family?'

'He'd hurt anyone if it made him some money — or
saved him some.'

Helen ran her tongue over her teeth. The sooner they
found Osbourne the better.

'I think it's this block up here,' Loughton said, his voice a weary rasp as he turned off the radio.

Helen slowed and flicked on the indicator before pulling into a gap behind a delivery van. She looked up at the sky. It looked like one giant, angry bruise. Soulless tenements lined both sides of the street, and in the distance a pair of tower blocks jutted into the sky. Nearby, a couple of boys in school uniform were sitting on the edge of the pavement, counting out marbles. Malone's tenement flat was directly above a greengrocer that had closed for the evening. The stairwell door had been wedged open with a thick piece of cardboard. Inside there was an antique-looking pram that was filled with sticks. The door they wanted was on the first floor. It was blue and had a rusted nameplate that said 'Malone'. Helen paused a moment to listen for any life inside. There weren't any lights on, but she could hear the faint sound of a television or a radio. She rattled on the letterbox and took a step back. No answer. Loughton pounded on the door with the side of his fist. The television noise stopped.

'Lisa-Marie Malone, it's the police and we're not going anywhere.' Loughton peered through the letterbox.

'Anything?'

He shook his head.

As Helen was about to give up, Lisa-Marie opened the door just enough for her to look out. Helen could see her head was wrapped in a towel and she was wearing a matching pink dressing gown. 'What do you want?'

'We want to speak to you about Jimmy Osbourne.'

She let out a dramatic sigh then pushed the door open for them to enter. She started to back up the hallway, leaving Helen to catch the door before it slammed in her face.

Lisa-Marie made a move to close the bedroom door, but not before Helen caught sight of a suitcase open on the bed and a mountain of clothes next to it.

'Going somewhere nice, are you?' Helen asked.

'No.' She folded her arms. 'What do you want?'

Loughton opened the bedroom door and peered inside.

241

'Here, you can't do that.' Lisa-Marie looked at Helen, slack-jawed.

Loughton ignored her and disappeared into the room. Helen took a quick scan of her surroundings in case Jimmy was inside the flat. It looked like there was just the one bedroom, an open-plan kitchen and the bathroom. Helen checked them and all were empty.

'What are you doing?' Lisa-Marie asked.

'Where's Jimmy?'

Lisa-Marie arched an eyebrow and looked at Helen like it was the most stupid question she had ever heard. 'Eh? I'm guessing Jimmy's down in the morgue, where you last had him.'

Loughton appeared from the bedroom with a slip of card in his hand.

'What is it?' Helen asked.

'Plane tickets.' Loughton held them out for inspection. 'Two one-way tickets to Brazil.'

'Brazil, and here was you saying you weren't going anywhere nice.' Helen smiled.

'They're not mine, you planted them.'

'They have your name on them.' Loughton shrugged. 'Leaving at seven this evening. Very nice, I'm jealous.'

'Anyway, there's no crime in going on holiday. I'm a grieving widow; I need a break.'

'Grieving *fiancée*,' Helen corrected her.

'And you're not going anywhere except down to the station. I don't think you'll be seeing the inside of an airport for a very long time.'

'How do you work that out?'

'The man you identified is not Jimmy Osbourne.'

'Aye, it is. I thought it was . . .' She gave a small shrug. 'Jimmy is dead.'

'Someone went through a lot of trouble to make us think that Jimmy was dead.' Helen moved around the room. She could hear a car idling outside. Helen moved towards the window and slipped the curtain aside. A black taxi had pulled up behind the Mini. 'There's a taxi outside. Is that yours?'

Lisa-Marie nodded. 'Obviously he was very badly burned, and he was wearing the clothes I last saw Jimmy in. What else was I to think?'

'Where's Jimmy?' Helen asked.

'I don't know.'

Loughton chuckled.

'What's so funny?' Lisa-Marie sneered.

'I should have seen it before.'

Lisa-Marie directed the question to Helen. 'Is he on something?'

'You're the one who set Paula on me, aren't you? Had her drug me or something. Trying to knock me off Osbourne's scent.'

'How did you work that one out?' Lisa-Marie looked stunned.

Loughton sneered. 'It's not Osbourne's style.'

'You'll have a hard job proving it.' Lisa-Marie recovered herself quickly. 'This Paula doesn't even know who I am.'

'What were you hoping to find, eh?' Loughton stepped forward.

'Haven't you guessed yet?' Lisa-Marie lifted an eyebrow. 'Jimmy told me all about you.'

'Then you'll know I won't let this go.'

Lisa-Marie shrugged uneasily. 'You've been trying to get him back for years.'

'You're the only one who seems to care enough to find out how much I had on him. I admire your dedication to a man that couldn't give a crap about you.'

Lisa-Marie looked to Helen for support, but Loughton carried on.

'How long had Jimmy been in Spain for?'

'I don't know . . . Six, eight years.'

'And have you ever been to see him?' Loughton asked.

She shook her head.

'Why not? It's not that far.'

'Jimmy has you lot on his back all the time. He knew if I went to Spain you lot would know where he was living.'

'But we already knew where he was.' Loughton raised his eyebrows, interested in her response. 'I have been out to Spain on the taxpayer's money,' Loughton continued. 'He was living in a beautiful pink villa off the coast. Stunning view right out to the sea. He had a stunning girlfriend out there too. You are all right, but I mean she was something else.'

'You're lying.'

'You really think Jimmy would stay faithful to you after all this time? Come off it, even you're not that stupid.'

Lisa-Marie slumped down on the sofa and pulled off the towel from around her head.

'Think about it, Lisa-Marie. You know what he's like.'

'I don't need to.'

'You're so dedicated to him that you would even risk murder.' Loughton made a tutting sound.

'Murder? What are you talking about?'

'The man you told us was Jimmy.'

'Hang on a minute, I didn't murder him.' She looked up at Helen, her blue eyes looked damp from tears.

'Do yourself a favour and start talking.'

'Jimmy would kill me.'

'We'll protect you.'

Her top lip curled into a sneer.

'It's up to you. You can spend the rest of your life in prison and Jimmy can sun it up with his new fiancée in Spain until we catch him for something else.'

She looked down at the ring on her finger. 'The man wasn't murdered.'

'Who is he?'

She put her head in her hands. 'We took him from my uncle's funeral parlour.'

'Took him?'

'Yes, I work there.' She looked up and glared at Helen. 'His family buried a load of rocks. I didn't murder him, he died of a heart attack.'

'Why did you do that?'

'Jimmy needed you lot off his back long enough for . . .'

Helen exchanged a look with Loughton.

'He needs to pick up the money from his last job.' Lisa-Marie relented.

'Where?' Loughton stepped forward.

'Lisa-Marie, if you want us to protect you, you need to tell us everything you know.'

'I don't know exactly where it is. There's a man named Steele that knows all about it. I know it's in a safe deposit box.' She shook her head. 'Jimmy's going to meet me at the airport in two hours, so I think he was going to meet Steele first. His plan was to have all the money at the airport.'

Loughton disappeared back into the bedroom, appearing a few minutes later with a bundle of clothes. He chucked them on Lisa-Marie's lap.

'Get yourself dressed — you're coming to the airport with us.'

'I can't.'

'Jimmy's expecting to meet you at the airport and that's what's going to happen.'

\* \* \*

Back at the station Helen didn't have long to get ready to intercept Osbourne at the airport, and DC Bell was already in the car that she would go in. Randall and Loughton were with Lisa-Marie in the other. Helen applied a thick coating of mascara, then scraped her brown hair up into a tight topknot. Her disguise sat in a pile on the bench in front of her — a thick-looking blonde wig and a summer dress with ruffles. It came out at the waist and hid her radio set perfectly. She slipped the dress over her shoulders, surprised at how flattering it looked when she caught sight of herself in the mirror. She grabbed the wig. She'd put that on in the car. She was out of time. Craven looked up from the steering wheel, a smile tugging at his lips when he noticed her.

Helen gave a twirl then tugged open the car door.

'You should dress like that all the time,' Craven chuckled ruefully. 'You actually look presentable.'

Bell looked amused and gave an approving nod.

'Oh, thanks,' Helen muttered, not hiding the sarcasm in her voice. She reached for her seatbelt. 'Hopefully it will be enough to fool Osbourne too.' She slipped the wig onto her head.

'Aye, it will.' Craven turned the ignition and reversed the car out of the car park.

Helen fastened her belt, dreading what she was about to do. This would normally be the job of an undercover officer, but staff shortages and secondments had made that difficult. On the other hand, if this worked, she would have the satisfaction of making the arrest.

## CHAPTER 45

Craven weaved the car in and out between the traffic, showing no regard for the vehicles in the lanes around them. Helen remembered the last time that she'd been at the airport. Ted had planned to whisk her away, but in the end, she couldn't go through with it and pretend to be the person that he wanted — the perfect housewife who would be waiting for him to come home every night with a cooked meal on the table.

The Granada pulled out noisily and overtook a meandering taxi. Helen was shoved back into the passenger seat as Craven swore under his breath and pressed the accelerator down as far as it would go. She could hear groans coming from DC Bell in the backseat. Chatter from the radio filled the car. DC Loughton and Randall were five minutes away, as well as a second undercover car.

Helen caught sight of herself in the passenger-side mirror; it was amazing how different she looked. The peroxide-blonde hair emphasised her tan and her brown eyes, but the thick coating of makeup made her face feel dry and itchy. She wiped away the mascara that had already started to collect under her eyes. As they passed the first sign for the airport, the butterflies in the pit of her stomach grew. Craven seemed to pick up the pace even more as the groans of the engine competed with the static from the radio. Helen's mind raced. Would Osbourne take one look at her and notice her instantly? Randall would love that, she thought, then it would be all her fault if Osbourne got away. Another reason for her not to be the permanent sergeant within the department.

Her heart thumped as she saw the outline of the airport in the distance with its brand-new terminal building, where hundreds of passengers would be waiting.

The car pulled up outside the terminal and she stepped out, catching sight of Lisa-Marie Malone entering the building ahead as planned.

A wave of warm, diesel-tinged air met Helen as she made her way through the double doors, carrying a battered suitcase. Most of the seating area was occupied. She looked up at the departure television set — Jimmy Osbourne's plan was to catch the 7 p.m. flight to London, then it would be off to Rio De Janeiro. The flight was showing as 'On Time'. She weaved her way through the herd of passengers, keeping Lisa-Marie in her line of vision all the way. From the corner of her eye, she could make out another undercover officer, who was wearing a Canadian jumper and had a large camera draped around his neck, doing the same. There was no sign of Jimmy anywhere yet.

Lisa-Marie Malone took a seat in the middle of an empty row of chairs, near to the check-in desk.

Helen stood next to a couple of other passengers who were excitedly chatting about their first trip to London. Her heart continued to hammer in her chest and her mouth felt dry. If Jimmy was going to catch this flight, he'd need to get here soon. Helen turned to get a look at the rest of the room. Maybe she'd be able to see him approach, but it was no good, there was too much movement around her. She'd also lost track of the other officer.

Lisa-Marie drummed her fingers on the top of her suitcase, her eyes darting everywhere. Less than ten minutes to go, or they would miss the flight.

Then it happened. Lisa-Marie got to her feet. Jimmy Osbourne was next to her, clutching a small holdall strapped over his shoulder. Jimmy started to take Lisa-Marie's hand and lead her to check-in. Lisa-Marie exchanged a look with Helen, which Jimmy noticed. He glanced over his shoulder a couple of times, then shoved Lisa-Marie into a group who were walking towards them. Lisa-Marie crumpled down onto the floor with a sickening thud.

Helen dropped her suitcase. Jimmy ran, shoving and elbowing anyone who got in his way. Helen pounded after him, her thighs burning. She managed to get her radio out and was shouting for backup.

Helen thought he was heading for the exit, but he must have known it was surrounded. He skidded to a stop and dived up the stairs, sending an elderly woman tumbling down them. Helen pushed on, grabbing the handrail for support. Her dress kept catching under her feet and she nearly tripped over it a couple of times but thankfully managed to keep her footing. She stopped at the top of the stairs to catch her breath, and Jimmy Osbourne was nowhere to be seen. She heard a woman scream, followed by angry shouts — it was a male voice, but she couldn't make out what it was saying. It was coming from the corridor to the left. She ran into another waiting area and stopped. Jimmy was up on a ledge — he had got one of the windows open and it billowed in the breeze. He had managed to get his body half out when Helen caught up with him. Icy air whipped around them. He stepped out further and the crowd around them gasped.

'Jimmy! Stop!' Helen called out. She had to shout as the wind whistled around him. 'You won't survive a fall from this height.'

Jimmy looked down, considering this. 'I'm not going back to prison.'

'Why did you hurt Dennis? He's lucky to be alive and will probably be left with lasting damage.'

'Hurt Dennis? What are you talking about, you stupid cow!' His eyes were wide and wild. Concern creased his forehead. 'I never hurt Dennis.'

Helen swallowed hard. 'He's lying in the Royal Infirmary in intensive care.'

'I don't believe you.'

She took a step forward. 'He was shot . . . What was he involved in?'

'Nothing. I gave him money whenever I could, so he wouldn't be involved in anything.'

'Come down and we can talk. You can see Dennis.'

'You'll never let me do that.' He looked at her, but it was like he was looking through her. All the bravado of their earlier encounters had washed away.

'I just wanted to start again and get you lot off my back,' he muttered, 'but that was never going to happen. Loughton was never going to let that happen. He tried to set me up.'

'Come down and tell me about it.'

'As if that will do any good.'

Helen turned to see Craven and Loughton approaching. Loughton was limping.

'Get down, there's no way out from this,' Loughton called out.

Jimmy's lips curled into a smile. 'My biggest regret is not making sure that you were dead that night — but at least you were left a cripple.'

'Just get down, Jimmy. What are you planning to do? Freeze us all to death?'

'Right, show's over.' Helen had seen enough. She and Craven began moving the onlookers away to give them some privacy.

'Loughton tried to set me up. He won't get away with that.'

'Jimmy, there's only us now. You've had your five minutes of fame. Jimmy—!'

Helen froze as Jimmy vanished out of the window. It felt like the world around her stopped. She swallowed hard.

Loughton clambered up to the window frame and grimaced.

Helen didn't move. She didn't want that image in her mind. Those were the kind of things that you could never forget.

Sirens wailed in the distance.

## CHAPTER 46

Helen blotted her face with damp tissue paper, scrubbing away with the cold water until she had removed all traces of makeup. The top of her cheeks and forehead nipped. She sighed as she slipped back into her regular clothes. She had found out on the way back to the station that Jimmy Osbourne had survived the fall, breaking both legs in the process. When she got back to the desk, Randall informed her that McKinley needed to meet her down in the canteen.

'I am glad to see this.' Helen sat down at her favourite chair. 'Please tell me that this is mine.'

'It is.' He smiled as he slid the tray towards her. Pie, mash, peas and lashings of thick gravy. She scooped up a mouthful of mash. It was still warm. She closed her eyes and savoured the flavour. The tiredness of the past few days had caught up with her.

McKinley was looking at her. She noticed that he had a box of files on the seat next to him.

'What's in there?'

'That's what I wanted to talk to you about.'

'Okay.' Helen nodded and scooped up a pile of mash. She was hungrier than she thought.

'I think Jimmy Osbourne was telling the truth. I managed to get a look at Dennis Levitt's bank account, and Osbourne's been paying him a regular stipend for as far back as the records show.'

'And how long is that?'

'Over ten years, monthly payments of twenty pounds a month, regular as clockwork.'

Helen nodded again. 'I believed Jimmy when he said he hadn't hurt Dennis.' That would explain how Dennis had money despite the confusion on what he was doing for a job.

'So maybe someone hurt Dennis to get revenge on Jimmy.' McKinley shrugged.

'That's possible — a man like Osbourne will have a lot of enemies.' Helen pushed away her plate, losing her appetite. They were still no closer to finding out who had hurt Dennis. 'I feel like I need to do something.'

'You need to get some sleep, your shift finished ages ago.'

Helen stifled a yawn. 'Maybe you're right.'

\* \* \*

Back at her flat Helen slung her satchel down and drew an unsteady breath as she bolted the door. Her DIY nut of a downstairs neighbour sounded like he was drilling into a wall. She thought about going down there and telling him to pack it in, but after today she couldn't face speaking to anyone, even if it was just to tell them to shut up.

She groped for the light switch as her foot connected with something hard. A small box wrapped in brown paper. She recognised the ornate handwriting and felt herself smiling as she tore open a corner of the package. She moved through to the lounge with it and sank down on the sofa.

Inside was a velvet box containing a pair of expensive-looking pearl earrings and a card. She turned it over. *Saw these and thought they would suit. Love Mum and Steve.* It felt strange seeing another name next to her mum's. A pang of guilt settled in the pit of her stomach. Mum seemed finally happy, and all she could think was the worst. Maybe that came from her years in the police, constantly seeing the worst that people were capable of. She dropped the box on the coffee table and made a mental note to call her mum tomorrow.

## CHAPTER 47

The following morning, Helen got into the station later than usual after the previous evening's exhausting events. She arrived at her desk to see a note asking her to urgently call the hospital. She lifted up the slip of paper — it looked like it had been scribbled by Randall. There was no time like the present, and if it was bad news, there was no point in putting it off. She dialled the number and drummed her fingers on the desk as she waited for someone to answer, growing more impatient with each ring. As she was about to hang up, a woman answered. She sounded breathless like she had just run up a flight of stairs.

'Sorry to bother you, but my name is DS Helen Carter and I was asked to give this number a call. It will be about a patient called Dennis Levitt.'

'Hang on.'

There was a long pause before the nurse that Helen had met in the hospital came on the line.

'DS Carter, I wanted to let you know that Dennis is awake.'

'Is—?'

The nurse knew what she was going to ask.

'He's not ready to speak with anyone just yet, but it's looking likely that he'll be able to do so shortly.'

'Thank you.'

Helen waved McKinley over to her desk. She cupped her hand over the speaker. 'Dennis is waking up.'

McKinley arched an eyebrow.

Helen returned to the call. 'When do you think we can speak to him?'

'Hopefully over the course of the next three, maybe four hours.'

Helen hung up the phone, and McKinley retrieved a sheet from his in tray.

'I've just been going over all the statements for this case,' McKinley explained. 'The shopkeeper from the newsagents never came in to have a look at the criminal record book.'

Helen stood up eagerly. 'Let's go and see him while we're waiting for Dennis to wake up.'

* * *

'Ach, I've just been too busy,' the shopkeeper muttered. He was in the process of stacking a box of magazines onto the top shelf.

'Busy?' Helen looked around the deserted store. It was only the three of them and Helen could smell the dust in the air.

'Aye, don't let the lack of customers fool you, there's still plenty of work to do in here and I didn't see the point. The lad didn't get anything and no one got hurt.'

'No one got hurt here, but it could happen somewhere else and it might not be such a happy ending then.'

'Fair enough.' He sighed as he slipped the last magazine into its slot.

Helen pulled out a plastic evidence folder protecting the photograph of Robbie and Dennis from her satchel. 'Do you recognise these young men?'

He took the bag then went back to the counter and slipped on a pair of ancient-looking spectacles. He held the photograph up to the light.

'Actually, I do. Aye, that's him. That's the one who came in here with the gun.' He tapped the face with his finger. 'I'm sure of it.'

Helen looked down at the photograph. He was pointing at the smiling Robbie Fields.

'Are you sure?'

'Without a doubt, officer.'

\* \* \*

'Do you think we should speak to Marnie again?' McKinley asked Helen as they walked back to the car. 'Maybe she knows more than she's letting on.'

'She did say that Dennis and Robbie had an argument.' Helen turned up the collar of her jacket against the wind. 'I should have pushed it more with Robbie.'

'I don't know, Robbie seemed convincing to me.' He looked back at the shop. 'The old man in there might be confused. I read through the previous report and it was conflicting.'

'He seemed certain there,' Helen countered. 'I see no reason to doubt him.'

'Still doesn't mean that Robbie shot Dennis.'

'No, it doesn't, but he has lied about the gun.'

\* \* \*

Loughton stood outside the ward window with his fists bunched. Osbourne was sparked out after surgery. There was a bored-looking constable sitting guard next to the bed, flicking through a paper without looking up. The nurse informed him that Osbourne had smashed his left ankle from the fall and had broken the other leg in two places. There was a strong chance that he might not be able to walk again. Loughton had waited for this moment for all those long years, but it did nothing to ease the pain. Leonard was still dead, and the guilt still wormed its way through his stomach. That was maybe something he would just have to live with.

# CHAPTER 48

'Hopefully they've finished the roadworks up here,' McKinley muttered.

Helen didn't bother answering.

The radio crackled to life as McKinley slipped the Granada into fourth gear along Telford Road. Rain coated the windscreen and battered the roof. Helen squinted to see out of the windscreen at the passenger's side, the wipers squealed but were doing a poor job of clearing the downpour. She could see McKinley squinting and leaning forward in his chair. The whites of his knuckles were showing as he gripped the steering wheel. Helen took a deep breath to steady herself. Why did she pick today to not drive? The radio crackled as the words of the dispatch filtered into the car: 'Gunshot . . . Corstorphine . . . Clement Road . . . Are you packing?' Before she could answer and ask for clarification, the radio died. She smacked the handset with the palm of her hand. Dead as a dodo. Helen looked out the passenger's side windows as a bolt of lightning tore up the sky — that would be the reason.

They both recognised the street Dispatch had mentioned — that was where Robbie Fields lived. No way was that a coincidence. McKinley slowed the car. He exchanged a look with Helen, who nodded.

'I think Dispatch were asking if we had guns,' McKinley said, after a beat.

'The line was so bad — we can't be certain,' Helen muttered, but she knew what she had heard. 'Why don't we just check it out?'

'It's your call.'

'Let's do it.'

She heard McKinley sigh but there was no way she was going to leave this. Horns blared around them. McKinley did a U-turn on the two-lane road. He floored it from there, the engine squealing in protest. Helen screwed her eyes shut as the car wobbled then skidded left to right, right to left. Helen bit down hard on the inside of her mouth until she tasted blood. She opened her eyes as the car careered down Clermiston Road, churning up puddles all the way.

A couple of minutes later, they were pulling up behind a marked police car a few doors down from Robbie's house. A uniformed officer in his thirties with thinning ginger hair approached them with a look of annoyance knitting his brow together. His face was red, and he looked as if he had just stepped out the shower — water dripped from his hair onto his shoulders. Helen retrieved her warrant card as he approached. He took it from her then gave a small shrug.

'I wasn't expecting you here this quickly.'

'What have you got?' Helen replied, taking her card from his hand and shoving it back into her pocket.

'Next-door neighbour called it in,' the officer confirmed.

'Which house?' Helen asked.

'The call's about number 7. Neighbours at number 5.'

Helen gritted her teeth. That was Robbie Fields's house. She would have been surprised if it wasn't.

Helen slung her jacket over her head and jogged over to the neighbour's house. A man in his fifties was standing in the entrance. He moved aside to let Helen and McKinley inside and out of the rain. The aroma of fresh coffee wafted towards them, but there would be no time for that.

'I heard a lot of shouting and banging coming from next door.'

'When was this?'

'About half an hour ago. It's been silence ever since but it sounded like someone was throwing furniture.'

'Right.' Helen pulled out her notebook and flicked to a blank page.

'I was out in my conservatory when I heard it. So, it seemed to be coming from the back of their house, where the kitchen is. I went out into my garden and had a look over the fence, and that's when I saw him with a gun.'

'Who did you see with a gun?'

'Young Robbie. He was waving it about like a mad man.'

'Can we go through to the conservatory?' Helen asked.

He looked down at their damp shoes. Helen's boots had left a muddy puddle on the floor tiles. 'Fine,' he grimaced. 'It's through here.'

'Do you have a phone?' McKinley asked. 'I should phone the station and get backup,' McKinley told Helen.

Helen stepped out into the conservatory. She strained to hear any noise from next door, but it was silent. The double doors were open and she stepped straight out into the paved garden. Robbie's house was over to the right. She moved over to the fence. Backup would be here shortly.

*Bang.*

The noise rattled her eardrums. Helen braced herself and scaled the fence. She jumped down awkwardly, and her ankle twisted as she hit the grass. She grimaced and bit down on her lip so she wouldn't make a noise, then limped towards the back of the building so that she would be out of sight. She could see a frosted glass window, and two French doors to the left of that, one of which was ajar by a couple of inches. She kept her head down and moved under the window. Then she stopped for a moment to gather her senses. Not hearing any sound inside, she scurried forward and pulled the patio door open, just wide enough for her to get through. She stood motionless in the kitchen. She swallowed — her mouth was dry and her lips began to tingle. She forced herself to take long, deep breaths to put off the panic attack she could feel coming on. An archway led out to the front room. That was empty too. Nothing looked out of place. Helen peered down the hall, nothing out of the ordinary there either. A creak came from upstairs.

Uneasily she glanced up the stairs and placed a shaky hand on the banisters. As she slowly edged her way further upstairs, she could hear noises from a room to the right and the sound of footsteps as if someone was pacing up and down. She got to the top of the landing and that's when she saw them.

## CHAPTER 49

Craven's phone rang. He took another gulp of black coffee. He had been staring at reports for the past hour and was getting nowhere. The phone stopped as abruptly as it started. When it rang again, he snatched it up.

'Inspector Craven, there's a man down at the reception desk asking to speak to you.'

Craven rose from his desk. 'Who?'

'It's Milton Nairn, sir.'

'You've got be joking.'

'No, I've double-checked. I told him you're too busy, but he's insisting.'

'Fine, I'll be down in a minute.'

Milton was standing outside the station with his hands shoved deep in the pockets of his oversized tweed jacket. He plastered on a big smile as Craven approached.

'What do you want?' Craven asked, trying to swallow down the rage that was in danger of burning up.

'I'd like to talk.'

Craven looked him up and down. Nairn's hair was normally dyed charcoal black, but Craven could see grey wisps at his temples and heavy bags under his rat eyes. It served him right.

'I wouldn't normally bother you, Jack, but I'm desperate.'

'Mad, more like.'

Craven thought he would argue back but instead he looked deflated and dipped his head. 'I need to fix things.'

'Fat chance.'

Nairn shook his head. 'There's got to be a way. With your help, I hope.'

'Aye, right.' Craven narrowed his eyes. 'Why would I do anything for you?'

'I made a mistake, Jack. A big mistake, yes, but I've looked after Liz and the twins.'

'I wouldn't call what you did a mistake.'

'I tried to help a friend.'

'Your "friend" was implicated in a murder.'

'I know . . .'

'You're lucky you're even out wandering the streets.'

'True.' Nairn looked him straight in the eye. 'If I could take it back I would. I've lost everything.'

Craven looked around. 'Why don't you just go and talk to her?'

'I've tried.'

'She won't see me. I need you to talk to her for me.' He retrieved a small jewellery box from his pocket. 'Can you give her this?'

Craven drew a breath. Liz wouldn't be bought so easily. He knew from experience.

'You know I looked after her,' Nairn continued. 'We were happy.'

'Couldn't have been that happy.'

'That's not fair.' He took a step forward. 'I have been there for her.'

'She's been drinking. That's how much you looked after her.'

Milton looked like he was going to say something, then stopped.

'What?' Craven demanded.

'She was drinking before this. I've been trying to keep it under control.'

'How long?'

Milton dragged a hand across his stubble. 'Months, it wasn't too bad at first, then it gradually got worse. I started to find empty bottles that I didn't remember buying in the bin and under the cupboard by the sink, then she started getting up later, going to bed later and missing her aerobics classes. She would be really annoyed at me telling you this.'

'You should have told me sooner.'

'It wasn't my place. I had it under control. I was helping her.'

'My children live in that house.'

'I'm a doctor. I know what I'm doing.'

Craven slipped a glance over his shoulder to make sure that no one was listening.

'I helped her stop drinking for a long time and I can do it again,' Nairn carried on.

'I'll speak to Liz and see what she wants to do.'

Craven felt like he might be sick as he made his way back up the stairs to the CID office. He was going to need to sort this out with Liz. The image of her lying comatose on the sofa with the cigarette in her hand filled his mind.

* * *

McKinley hung up the phone. Backup was on the way. He listened for any noise from next door, any indication that she was in trouble. A shout and thud filled the silence. He needed to get in next door and make sure she Helen was all right. His chest tightened as he sprang towards the door. He was the one that should have gone in there, and if anything happened to her, he would never forgive himself.

## CHAPTER 50

Helen pushed the door to the bedroom open a crack, so she could get a look inside. Robbie was standing with his back to her. His right arm was outstretched and she could see the gun in his hand. His shoulders and arms were shaking. 'Don't move,' he was saying. 'Don't do anything.'

Helen could not see who he was saying this to, but it was most likely his dad. The muscles in her back tightened and her pulse raced. She froze but forced herself to breath. Robbie started to pace, waving the gun around. 'I'm going to do it, I'll do it,' he said. 'I've got no choice.'

'No, I'm sorry.' That was his father's voice. 'Come on, son . . . Son, don't do anything daft.'

'Shut up! Shut up!' Robbie screamed. 'I can't think, stop talking, just stop talking.'

'It's going to be okay. We can sort this out.'

'This is your fault.'

'Put the gun away.'

'I'm going to do it. I'm just going to do it.'

Helen swallowed hard. Her hand tightened around the doorknob as she pushed it open. 'Robbie? It's DS Carter here.'

'No, no!' He turned to face her. His blue eyes flashed as bright as a flame. Tears shined on his cheeks.

He lifted the gun towards her, and Helen raised her arms and shook her head.

'Please, Robbie, whatever it is you think you need to do, you don't.'

'I don't know what to do.'

Helen tried to force a smile. 'Why don't we sit down, and we can talk and work things out.'

'It's too late.'

The barrel of the gun was raised level with her face. Bile rose in Helen's throat. 'It's not, but it will be if that gun goes off.'

'Robbie, don't be stupid.' His dad stepped forward and held out his hand for Robbie to hand him the gun. 'Give me the gun now!'

'Robbie, do as your dad says. You don't want to hurt anyone.' She forced herself to keep looking at him.

'It's too late for that.'

'No, it's not.' Helen kept her voice soft.

'Dennis is going to die.'

Helen shook her head. 'I got a call.' She looked down at her watch. 'Nearly an hour ago. He's waking up.'

'You're lying.'

'Why would I do that? I would never tell you that your friend was going to be okay if that wasn't true.'

The anger and fright drained from his body and his shoulders heaved. The gun dropped to the floor with a thud in front of Helen. She snatched it up from the carpet and slipped it into her pocket.

'It's my fault. I caused all this.'

'Don't tell her anything.' His dad grabbed Robbie by the shoulder, but he shrugged free.

'Why did you hurt Dennis?' Helen questioned.

Robbie shook his head.

'That's good, son. I'll sort this. Keep quiet'

'No!' Robbie snapped at his dad. 'This is your fault.'

'Mine?' Robbie's dad snarled.

'You had an argument?' Helen carried on. 'Was it about Marnie?'

'No, I didn't mean to — he was going to rob the supermarket, but I didn't want to.'

'That dirty little thief,' Robbie's dad chimed in.

'I know you attempted to rob a newsagent.'

'I . . .'

'The owner identified you.' Helen added.

Robbie's dad bunched his fists. 'You stupid boy.'

'That's why I knew we couldn't do this one. Dennis and I . . . We had a fight for the gun and . . . it went off.' A sob burst from his chest. 'I never wanted anyone to get hurt, least of all Dennis. There was just this bang and Dennis collapsed on the ground. I tried to get him up, but he told me to leave him.'

'And you did?'

'I ran to a payphone to call an ambulance. I didn't want him to die. I didn't know the gun was loaded.'

Helen nodded.

'Is he really going to be okay?'

'I hope so. I should be able to speak to him in the next couple of hours.'

Helen swallowed hard. 'Why did you take his jacket?'

A raspy sigh escaped from Robbie. 'I was scared, and I tried to make it look like someone robbed him.'

Helen shook her head and turned to see McKinley standing in the doorway, his eyes wide with concern. She gave him a nod and his lips curved.

'Are you all right?' he stepped forward and his hand brushed against hers. Before she could answer, two uniformed officers brushed past them and proceeded to detain Robbie. His dad looked like he was going to put up a fight then thought better of it.

Helen's stomach quivered and she let out a wobbly laugh, 'I think so.'

* * *

Helen's head pounded as she walked down the ward to Dennis's room. McKinley followed behind her. He hadn't said much since Robbie's arrest a couple of hours ago. She gave him a sideways glance and he offered a thin smile. She knew he thought she was reckless. Maybe she was. She pushed open the door to Dennis's room. He looked up wide-eyed.

'We're police officers,' Helen advised. 'You're lucky to be alive.'

Dennis frowned, then winced as he tried and failed to pull himself up into a seated position.

'Do you want me to get a nurse to help you?'

Dennis shook his head.

'Can you answer a few questions?' Helen stepped forward. His face looked drained of blood and his forehead was slick with sweat.

Dennis swallowed. 'Aye.'

'Do you remember what happened?'

Dennis shook his head.

'We have Robbie in custody.'

'It was an accident,' Dennis muttered. 'Nothing for you lot.'

'You do remember?'

'I just want to forget about it.'

'It's not as simple as that. You suffered a serious injury.'

Dennis's jaw tightened.

'He said you were going to rob the supermarket.'

'We needed money.'

'Didn't you get enough from your uncle?'

'Him. I only got that for doing stuff.'

'Like what?'

'Checking on his flat. Moving stuff.'

'Where did you get the gun from?'

'Jimmy. Gave it to me as a birthday present years ago.'

'Interesting gift.'

'Is Robbie alright?'

'He's in custody.'

'Will I be able to see him?'

'Why? He doesn't seem like a good friend,' McKinley interjected.

'I never said he was . . .' Dennis wouldn't meet his eye. 'But he's the only one I've got.'

## CHAPTER 51

Helen rummaged through one of the boxes in the kitchen, but she couldn't find the cookbook in any of them. She must have left it with Ted. She glanced up at the clock — there wasn't really time to cook anything fancy anyway. She closed the box and clambered to her feet. Perhaps they could go and eat out somewhere. There was an Edinburgh tour book belonging to Ted somewhere in this mess, that had some good restaurant recommendations in it. She brushed some dust from her trousers. The fire was burning on three bars, and for once the flat felt warm. She changed her mind: she couldn't be bothered traipsing back out in the cold. She had got in a shop a couple of days ago, so there was plenty of food and there was no point in letting it go to waste.

'What to make . . . what to make,' she muttered to herself as she pulled open the fridge door. She retrieved a carton of eggs from the top shelf and found some cheese at the back.

She cracked the eggs in a jug and was just about to start whisking them when there was a knock on the door.

'Oh, ye of little faith.' She looked down at the carrier bag in McKinley's hand.

'It's just a few bits and bats,' he explained as she took the bag and headed through to the kitchen with it.

A bottle of wine, a fancy-looking loaf of bread wrapped in paper and some French cheese. She weighed up the cheese in her hand. She would use that in the omelette.

She could see from the corner of her eye that McKinley was standing in the doorway.

'Make yourself comfortable,' she said, peeling the cheese and cubing it. 'You like eggs, aye?'

'Sounds nice.' He slipped off his jacket and draped it over the back of one of the kitchen chairs. Rain battered the single pain window above the sink, drowning out the noise of the frying pan. She poured the eggy mixture into the pan then retrieved two glasses for the wine.

'Just pour me a little bit,' she warned him.

A couple of minutes later, she sliced the omelette and divided it between two plates. It was a little charred around the edges, but she was happy with that.

McKinley cut two slices of bread and placed them on each plate.

Tiredness hit Helen as she chewed. The heat and the wine didn't help. She slid her glass to the side.

'Is it not good?' McKinley asked.

'I'm just tired. It's been a long couple of days.'

He tore off a hunk of bread and nodded. She looked down at her meal but could still feel him looking at her.

'What is it?' she asked.

He gave a small shrug. 'I appreciate this, you trying to take my mind off things.'

He smiled. It was helping her too, keeping her distracted from her thoughts. That was partially why she had suggested it.

She motioned to his untouched eggs. 'You don't need to eat them.'

'No, it's nice . . . chewy.'

He drained his glass of wine and poured himself a second. 'I'm not very hungry though,' he admitted. 'I've just got a lot on my mind.'

'I'm not surprised.'

'My gran died when she was the same age my mum is now.'

'I'm sorry.'

'No, don't be, I'm just not much fun to be around right now.'

'You're too hard on yourself.'

McKinley snorted.

He looked up at the watercolour painting of a fruit bowl that was hanging above the table.

'Did you paint that?' he asked.

She gave a small nod.

'It's lovely.'

'Thank you.'

'Why didn't you go to art school?'

'Honest answer?'

'Yes.'

'I just never thought I was good enough and I was worried that it would become something that I didn't enjoy.' Helen thought about this for a moment. 'I used art to help me get over the loss of my brother, or at least help me understand it.'

He looked like he was considering whether to ask her about this or not.

'I can talk about it now.' Helen swallowed a mouthful of wine.

'You don't have to if you don't want to.'

'This was meant to cheer you up.' Helen sighed.

'If you want to go depressing, I feel sorry for Robbie.' McKinley sighed. 'He seemed like a good kid that just wanted to get away from an abusive dad.'

'Robbing shops at gun point was never the way to go about it though,' Helen countered.

'Well, no. Obviously not. I just mean he was forced into it and now he'll do a stretch in prison. I hope it doesn't make things worse for him, you know?'

Helen shrugged then pushed away from the table. Maybe McKinley was right, but Helen knew Robbie needed to face up to what he did. Helen poured her wine down the sink. She didn't want to risk becoming tipsy; she had too much to do.

* * *

After McKinley left the flat Helen pulled back the curtain in the lounge and watched his car pull away. She looked around at the various cardboard boxes in the room. A box of her father's photographs sat in a container under the table. She knelt and tugged it open. Her stomach knotted; the first two photographs were baby pictures of her younger brother. He had died when they were both children and it never seemed to get any easier. She placed them onto the table. It had been hard finding out that her dad had built up another family and that she had a ten-year-old brother out there. She steadied her breathing and felt the familiar sting behind her eyes as she dug deeper into the box.

His life with her mum and her had been so unhappy that he had built himself a new one. She pulled out a picture of her dad in the Police College. She had only really joined the police because she wanted to please him, but nothing she could do would ever be good enough. She wiped her nose and taped up the box. She didn't need them. She would give them to her dad's mistress, and hopefully she would give them to her son when he was old enough. Helen rose to her feet, ready to tackle another box. In her only meeting with the woman, she had made it clear she wanted Helen to keep away.

* * *

'My cooking's not that bad then,' Craven said with a smile.

Liz looked down at the empty plate, then out to the twins playing in the garden. 'I was hungrier than I thought.'

Craven lifted the plate and moved towards the bin. It hadn't been much, just some sausage and mash.

She dabbed at the corner of her mouth with a napkin. 'The twins said they enjoyed being at your flat.'

'Aye.' He scraped away the last crumbs of potato. 'I've enjoyed looking after them.'

'I thought you'd have struggled with work.'

'I have but . . . we got through it.'

'I'm feeling better now too, now that I've had a chance to clear my head.'

Craven nodded. 'Want some ice cream?'

'No.' She gave a thin smile. 'I've been speaking with my mother.'

'Good.'

'She wants us to go and stay with her for a while.'

'Us?'

'The children and I . . . She has a stunning house right by Central Park.'

Craven bit his cheek. The house might be nice, but it was at least a fifteen-hour journey, with all the transfers. He set the plate down in the sink and turned to face her.

'I think it's a good idea.' She carried on. 'She'd be able to help me with childcare and I'd have a real chance at getting away from it all.'

'When?'

'She said she can get us flights whenever we want. This week even.'

'That soon?'

'I don't see why not.'

He slipped another glance at the children playing ball outside in the garden. His heart felt like it was being squeezed in a vice. He had missed so much of their childhood with work already, he couldn't face missing more.

He stepped towards Liz and reached out for her hand. 'You're not alone. I'm here.'

She let out a sigh.

'I can carry on helping. I can take the children when I'm not working.'

She shook her head.

'Liz, I can't face losing them.'

'You can still visit us.'

'It's not the same.'

'I need it.'

'What if I leave my job? Then I could help more.'

'You'd leave the police?'

He swallowed hard. 'I've done enough service for retirement.'

'I can't ask you to do that.'

'I can't face the alternative.'

'I don't know.'

'Will you promise to think about it?'

'Yes.' He noticed her lips tremble and let go of her hand. He wasn't happy with the way things were going in CID anyway. Maybe it was time for him to leave before it was too late.

## CHAPTER 52

The next morning, Helen drummed her fingers on the steering wheel as she waited for the lights to change en route to the station. In recent months Edinburgh had become one giant roadwork that was never finished. Still, she had left in plenty of time, so there was no chance of her being late. She hummed to the disco tune that crackled from the radio, as the cars began to snake around the corner. The arctic morning breeze had given way to the sunrise. Helen slipped off her jacket and tossed it on the passenger-side chair. She pressed on the brake as the car in front slowed for a striped workman's tent in the road. Her smile faded to a cold dread as she caught sight of the newspaper headline fluttering on the rack outside the newsagent. Her gut tightened. She slapped on the indicator and pulled into a space behind a milk float. Horns blared. She read the headline again. Her shoulders sagged and she gripped the steering wheel as hard as she could. She now knew exactly who the mole in the department was.

\* \* \*

Helen's heart hammered as she clenched her fists. She stood for a moment on the landing to catch her breath. A baby was crying in one of the flats, but she wasn't sure which one. Giving it enough time, she rattled the letterbox and stepped back.

The door opened and McKinley smiled. 'You're just in time for breakfast, I've just been shopping.'

'Why?' Helen bit down on her lip hard as she watched the smile drain from McKinley's face.

'Why what?' He opened the door wide and motioned for her to come in.

She held up the newspaper. 'How could you?

'No—'

'The George Stanley case too.'

'It wasn't like that. It was an accident.'

'That was you, this whole time? That's why you felt so guilty afterwards, taking me out for dinner, staying at my house.' Hot tears stung her eyes, and she blinked them back. There was no way he was going to see her cry. Not this time. 'I thought you helped me after that case because you cared for me?' She thought back to the first case they worked on together and how he had helped her to come back from what had happened.

'I did. I do.'

'We both started in CID at the same time.' Helen's lips trembled. 'I thought we had each other's back?'

'Come in and we can talk.'

He looked past her to see if anyone else was in the stairwell.

'You can relax, I came alone.'

She followed him through to the living room. He slumped down onto the sofa and placed his head in his hands.

'Why, Terry?'

'I don't . . .'

'I need to know.'

'How did you find out?' McKinley glared at her.

'I fed you false information, information that is on page four of this paper.'

'Why did you do that? Why would you do that to me?' He looked up, anger creasing his features.

'We needed to know who was giving out information to that slimy journalist Savoy, information that could jeopardise cases.' Helen shuddered at the thought of Savoy, a local journalist that would do anything to get a story.

'We?' McKinley snapped back. 'Nice to know how I'm thought of in the team.'

'Was it worth it?' Helen asked.

'No.' He shook his head slowly. 'Why did you suspect me?'

'I didn't until . . .'

'Until what?'

'It doesn't matter.' Helen gritted her teeth.

'It does.'

'I told you all about us not having enough to charge Osbourne, and you were the only one that knew I suspected Loughton might have tried to set Osbourne up with the jewellers. That was until a police setup was mentioned in the article.'

'You're so melodramatic, Helen. They were things Savoy would have found out anyway. You know what he's like.'

'That's not the point.'

He swallowed hard. 'I just wanted to get a bit of extra money. No, I needed it.'

'Why?'

'Because I didn't know how long I could keep turning up there every morning. It's okay for you Helen, you're strong.'

'I'm not.'

'You are. More than you know.'

Tears dripped from his eyes. 'I'm treated like an idiot day in, day out. It doesn't get better, it's never going to get better. I'm shouted at. Blamed for things I had no part in. Only yesterday, Randall hadn't filled out his statements, yet to Craven that's my fault. I should've reminded him. You know what it's been like.' He shook his head. 'I even turned a blind eye with the DCI and Sally. I mean, who does that? Everyone knew there was something going on with them. I'm such a coward that I pretended I was too stupid to notice. No wonder I'm thought of as the office clown.'

A sigh heaved from Helen's body. She looked away not knowing what to say.

'You're lucky,' he carried on, 'you inherited a house that you don't even know what to do with. You don't even need to work there. You can afford to walk away. That would be my dream, that. I can barely scrape by on the rent.'

'I didn't know things were this bad. Why didn't you speak to me?'

McKinley chided. 'I told you I was thinking of leaving, what else was I meant to say? I can tell you struggle to speak to me sometimes, that you want to keep your distance from me.'

There was a long silence.

'What are you going to do now?' McKinley dragged a hand through his hair.

'I don't know. You've put me in such a difficult position.'

'I didn't mean to. I didn't plan this. I just had too much to drink when Savoy approached me one night.'

'Terry . . .' Helen muttered.

'Just do what you need to do. I understand, it's not like I don't deserve it.'

Helen moved to the window and looked out. Terry's flat was in a tenement above a shop. She noticed a couple huddled in the bus stop across the street for warmth.

'I take it the DCI doesn't know.'

'What makes you think that?'

'He'd be here, knocking my block off. He threatened that of whoever was leaking to the press, remember?'

'Yes, I remember.' A single-decker bus pulled up and the couple huddled inside. Helen watched it pull away into traffic.

'I never meant to betray your trust, Helen. I never set out to do that. It's important to me that you know that.'

She couldn't look at him, and a painful lump rose in her throat. She knew what the others would do — she didn't

279

need to be reminded of that, it was the reason she had come alone. He must have known that too.

He rose from the chair with a sigh.

'Where are you going?'

'I need a drink. Do you want one?'

She shook her head.

He returned a moment later, swigging from a can of lager. He wiped foam from his top lip with the back of his hand.

'You sure I can't get you one?'

'I'm still on duty.'

He swigged again. 'I wanted to join the police since I was a young boy. I think it was all the Westerns I used to sneak into the pictures to see. I always fancied myself as the sheriff.' He smiled wryly. 'That didn't really work out for me, eh?' He drained the rest of the lager and set the tin down on the coffee table. 'And I thought I could make a difference. I'm just going to get myself pissed. I don't suppose you want to stick around for that?'

She could feel him staring at her.

'I do care about you, Helen, and I'm truly sorry that I hurt you.'

'I don't know what to do. How much did he pay you?'

'I'm not sure.'

'I want to know how much you sold us out for.'

'Fifty quid.'

He came cheap. Savoy had offered her far more than that.

'I won't hurt you again.'

'I need to get back to work. I can't do this.' Her voice shuddered and she swallowed back a sob.

'I didn't think I was harming anyone.' He stepped towards her. 'You can stay.'

Helen shook her head. 'Just because I won't say anything doesn't mean that all is forgiven. You need to be careful, Terry. The DCI is like a dog with a bone and he won't forget about this, you won't get away with it again.'

'I know.' McKinley shrugged. 'And that's if I decide to go back.'

Helen brushed past him and headed out of the flat. She blinked hard, pushing back the stinging tears that wanted to spill, but she wasn't going to let that happen. The sun hung low in the sky and she could feel the warmth of it on her cheeks. She crossed behind a bus and stopped in front of the travel agent, where rows of bright brochures promised 'new low prices' and 'winter sun'. A poster caught her eye — it was the inside of a Boeing 707 with a buffet table at the top of the aisle. She pulled open the door. It was time for her to think about herself.

## THE END

**ALSO BY JODIE LAWRANCE**

**DETECTIVE HELEN CARTER SERIES**
Book 1: THE UNIFORM
Book 2: THE EVIDENCE
Book 3: THE SUSPECTS

**Thank you for reading this book.**

If you enjoyed it please leave feedback on Amazon or Goodreads, and if there is anything we missed or you have a question about, then please get in touch. We appreciate you choosing our book.

Founded in 2014 in Shoreditch, London, we at Joffe Books pride ourselves on our history of innovative publishing. We were thrilled to be shortlisted for Independent Publisher of the Year at the British Book Awards.

www.joffebooks.com

We're very grateful to eagle-eyed readers who take the time to contact us. Please send any errors you find to corrections@joffebooks.com. We'll get them fixed ASAP.

Printed in Great Britain
by Amazon